The
HOUSE
GUEST

The HOUSE GUEST

NEW YORK TIMES BESTSELLING AUTHOR
PENELOPE WARD

First Edition
Copyright © 2025
By Penelope Ward

All rights reserved. No part of this publication may be reproduced, distributed, or transmitted in any form or by any means, including photocopying, recording, or other electronic or mechanical methods, without the prior written permission of the publisher, except in the case of brief quotations embodied in critical reviews and certain other noncommercial uses permitted by copyright law.

This book is a work of fiction. All names, characters, locations, and incidents are products of the author's imagination. Any resemblance to actual persons, things living or dead, locales, or events is entirely coincidental.

Editing: Jessica Royer Ocken
Proofreading and Formatting: Elaine York, Allusion Publishing,
www.allusionpublishing.com
Proofreading: Julia Griffis
Cover Design: Letitia Hasser, RBA Designs

CHAPTER 1

"Dorian is coming. I'd recommend clearing your paintings from the living room before he gets here."

"What?" My stomach sank. "When?"

"I'm not entirely sure, but it's likely to be soon."

"Crap." I looked around at my many large canvases. "Thanks for the heads up. This place has been like a ghost town for weeks. I guess I hoped the quiet would continue for a little while longer."

Patsy hung her head. "It was only a matter of time."

I clasped my hands together. "Do you think he's gonna kick me out?"

"I can't say." She shook her head. "Not sure if he's going to keep any of us around, or if he plans to live here or sell the place. We haven't been given much information."

I immediately felt foolish. Here I was, worried about whether I could continue to freeload off my poor dead aunt, and the staff here had to fear for their livelihoods.

"Well, let's hope he has a heart." I sighed. "You and Benjamin have been nothing but wonderful through all of this, and I would hate to see you out of a job."

"You've been a light in our lives, Primrose. If only this house was yours now, and we worked for you. Then I'd know we wouldn't have to worry."

Six short months ago, I'd moved in here after my aunt Christina had offered to let me stay with her and her billionaire husband, Remington Vanderbilt, while I enrolled in an art program. School was only a short drive from their wealthy community of Orion Coast, which was right on the Pacific Ocean in California. But I was still putting myself through school—I'd insisted on it despite my aunt's offer to help. Instead, I waited tables and lived off my savings.

But the opportunity to live in this mansion had been a dream. I had my own spacious bedroom and full use of the amenities. Christina and Remington had quite the social life, so I almost never saw them, making it easy some days to pretend the entire place was mine. My aunt would check in with me from time to time, but she gave me space. I greatly appreciated her providing me with a safe place to call home while I explored my passion: art. Christina knew I needed her support after my mother, her only sibling, had died a few years ago. My mother's death had left me alone, since from day one, my father had never been in the picture. And now with Aunt Christina gone, I felt more alone than ever.

Five months of stability here. That was all I'd had before the unthinkable happened.

Remington and Christina had taken their private jet to meet some friends in Hawaii. But they'd never made it home. There had been a carbon monoxide leak at the villa they'd rented. They simply went to bed one night and never woke up. The twisted part was, I'd learned the news from the Internet before hearing it from anyone else.

A month had passed since the incident now, and it was still a shock. Their home had become an eerie relic of what once was, everything still in its place, aside from the people it belonged to.

It felt like I'd been getting away with something as I continued to live here. Were it not for the handful of staff who kept things operational, I would've felt a lot like Kevin McCallister in *Home Alone*.

For now, I'd managed my grief by converting the main living area into an art workshop. It had the best lighting in the house, and I'd needed the space for my latest project. Since no one was living here but me, I didn't see the harm. The staff had encouraged it. But I'd always known it was only a matter of time until someone came in and took back this place. And it seemed that *someone* was Dorian Vanderbilt. Rightfully so.

Remington's only son had long been a mystery to me. I didn't know much about Dorian aside from the fact that he wasn't all that much older than me, maybe five or six years, which would make him twenty-eight or twenty-nine. From what Christina had told me, he was an only child and had moved to Boston several years ago. With Remington Vanderbilt's parents dead and no other siblings, Dorian was the last Vanderbilt left and the sole heir to his father's fortune. Remington's first wife, Dorian's mother, had died when Dorian was younger.

The housekeeper, Patsy, had started cleaning around me in the living room when I finally asked, "He gave you no clue at all as to when he's arriving?"

She shook her head. "I heard Benjamin talking to him on the phone. After he got off the call, I asked if he'd gotten details, and he said Dorian didn't give an exact time." She looked over at the grandfather clock. "It's late tonight. So my guess is sometime tomorrow or the next day. I prepared the bedrooms in any case. Not sure where he plans to sleep."

I swallowed. "Okay. Well…I'm gonna assume we're in the clear for now and put the final touches on my last painting before I clear them out in the morning."

"I'll miss looking at them." She grinned. "They make me smile."

"Maybe I'll gift you one, if I can't sell them." I winked.

Patsy finished her dusting and left me alone to handle my business.

I'd have to pull an all-nighter. I didn't have classes tomorrow, so I could catch up on sleep during the day. I looked around at my twelve paintings on various easels and sighed. Time to get to work. The clock was ticking.

A couple of hours later, it had to be close to midnight. The staff had gone, and I had paint all over me, my hair tied back in two pigtails.

When I heard footsteps on the marble floor behind me, I assumed it was Benjamin, the butler, who lived in a guest house just off the main property.

But then a gruff voice I didn't recognize jarred me.

"Who the hell are you?" he asked.

I turned to find a gorgeous man in a wool coat staring me up and down.

CHAPTER 2

My heart raced as I put down my brush. "Dorian?"

His brows drew in. "Who *are* you, and what are you doing in my father's house?"

"You don't understand. I'm not an intruder."

"You're *not* an intruder, but you've taken over this living room with paintings of..." He squinted. "What the hell are these? Monkeys?"

"Yes." I swallowed. "Twelve monkeys. It's part of an exhibition I'm doing for school."

"What the fuck am I even looking at?" He moved in closer to take a look at one of my paintings. "Why is this one wearing a suit?"

I straightened. "That's the point of the exhibit. It's called Primates in Power."

His shoulders shook in laughter.

Placing my hands on my hips, I frowned. "What's so funny?"

"If I have to explain it to you, I don't even know what to say." He ran a hand through his hair. "Christ. Am I dreaming?" He sighed. "How long have you been loitering here?"

"Loitering? I told you. I'm not an intruder. I live here."

"That's not possible."

"It is. I'm Christina's niece. She'd invited me to stay. I'd been living here for several months before they..." I paused.

"Went into the deepest sleep of their lives?"

"Well, I wouldn't have said it that way..."

"There's no clearer way to put it."

His eyes seared into mine. And suddenly a wave of reality came crashing down on me. This guy had lost everything. While his attitude certainly could've been better, he had every reason to question my intentions. He didn't know me from Adam.

I cleared my throat. "I'm very sorry for your loss. I can only imagine the shock of coming home after everything that happened and finding a stranger here."

"Don't forget the monkeys. I don't know them, either." His tone softened. "Actually, I...did forget. Benjamin mentioned to me some time ago that Christina's niece had been living here. I guess I just assumed you were gone by now." He paused. "I'm sorry for your loss as well."

"Thank you."

My moment of relief ended the second he spoke again. "But it's probably best if you leave."

What the hell? Nice to meet you, too. I straightened my shoulders. "That's fine. But I need a couple of days. Obviously, as you can see, I have a lot of stuff I need to transport. And I'll have to find another place to stay."

"I'll arrange to have movers come to the house tomorrow."

I wanted to cry. I'd expected to vacate the premises, but not *this* fast. He was basically kicking me to the curb. "How...nice of you. But I still need to find somewhere to live."

"I'll put you up in a hotel until you can find a permanent place."

"For how long?"

"For as long as you need."

"What are you going to do with the house?"

"I'm not sure what business that is of yours."

"Well, this was my aunt's house."

"Actually, no." He glared. "It was my *father's* house, and your aunt—God rest her soul—was a gold digger."

Heat filled my cheeks. "That's not true. They were in love."

At least I *wanted* to believe that.

Dorian laughed angrily. "My father never loved anyone but my mother. When she died, he buried his sorrows in beautiful women. Christina just played her cards better than most of the others."

"Well, it doesn't seem like you know my aunt very well, since you think she's a gold digger—she wasn't. So, we're going to have to agree to disagree." I crossed my arms. "Anyway, the reason I'm concerned about what you plan to do with this place is because I've grown to care about the people who work here—Patsy and Benjamin. I'm hoping you won't fire them. They need jobs. If there's a way you can keep them around—"

"What's your name?"

"Primrose Gallagher."

He nodded once. "Primrose, I literally just landed from Boston. I'm walking into the biggest shitshow you can imagine between having to take over the mess that was my father's company and the responsibility of this property. I was living a peaceful life before everything went to hell overnight. But I finally forced myself to come here and face it. After a long flight during which I could think about nothing but the mess waiting for me when I landed, I walk into this house expecting it to be empty—only to find it's been turned into a goddamn monkey museum." He gritted his teeth. "So, no. I don't know what the hell I'm doing in the next two minutes, let alone who's gonna get to keep working at a house that's basically haunted at this point. So while I appreciate your opinion, not sure I should be taking any advice from a stranger in pigtails wearing a *Kill Bill* crop top."

I looked down at myself then lifted my chin. "That was a good movie."

"It was," he muttered, rolling his eyes. "But that's beside the point."

"Well, at least you have taste." I flashed a smug smile.

"And *your* taste is..." He looked around. "Monkeys in suits?" He turned toward another one of the paintings. "And what the hell is this one? Is he wearing a bathrobe?"

"Playboy Monkey. Inspired by Hugh Hefner."

He broke out into laughter again.

"It's an assignment for a class. I'm an artist. I'm enrolled at Orion Art Institute."

When he finally stopped laughing, he turned to me. "Good for you."

"You don't mean that. You think you're better than me just because you have money. Money means shit to me."

"Clearly—if you aspire to be an artist. Although, you seem to be enjoying living in this lavish mansion. It's not paying for itself, you know."

I blew a frustrated breath up into my hair. "Yeah, well, I wasn't going to just abandon the place or the people who work here. Someone needed to look after things until you showed up."

"This is your idea of taking care of things? Infiltrating the main living area with primate paintings?" Another one of them caught his eye. "Fucking...George Washington Monkey?"

"Presidential Monkey," I muttered. "Not based on anyone in particular."

He walked over to another one. "Is this one supposed to be a singer?"

"*Hair*-y Styles."

Dorian rubbed his eyes and chuckled. "Look, I'm way too tired to continue this conversation tonight, and I can't be entirely sure I'm not hallucinating the entire thing. I'm gonna head to my room. Just make sure this living area is cleared out tomorrow. I'll have a truck arrive in the evening to help you move your things."

There goes catching up on sleep tomorrow.

"Thank you," I murmured, "I think."

His footsteps echoed against the floor as he walked away and started upstairs.

What now?

CHAPTER 3

The following afternoon, I'd cleared all of my paintings from the living room and packed most of my belongings into boxes. It had taken the entire day.

Thankfully, I hadn't run into Dorian. I would've been completely fine never seeing him again. I hadn't checked with Benjamin to see if a hotel had been booked for me. But either way, this absolutely sucked.

I had no idea how long Remington's son would be willing to foot that bill just to keep me away from this place. Finding an apartment as soon as possible would be prudent so I could cut all ties with him. I'd love to be able to refuse his offer to pay for the hotel, but I needed to save all I could if I was going to have to start paying rent. My waitressing job mainly covered my tuition, so it wasn't clear how I was going to afford rent now. There was a very real chance I'd need to drop out of school.

From my room, I heard dogs barking in the distance.

Patsy had taken them home overnight last night to groom them. She had an extra-large tub that made it easier to bathe them both in one shot. *Ah.* That's why they hadn't made a ruckus when Dorian came in. They would've been all over him otherwise and would've provided me some warning that he'd arrived.

I headed downstairs to see what was going on. The sight of the two Dobermans pinning Dorian against the wall gave me immeasurable pleasure. He was literally trapped. The best part? They were going straight for his balls. I couldn't have orchestrated it better myself.

Serves him right.

"Ladies!" I called out, snapping my fingers. "It's okay. Come here."

Tallulah and Tess backed off immediately and ran toward me, wagging their stumpy tails. When I knelt, they began licking my face.

Dorian ran a hand through his now-tousled dark hair. "What the hell is wrong with those dogs?" he griped. "I thought they were gonna bite my balls off."

"They most likely wouldn't have done that. But they're crotch sniffers."

"Crotch sniffers?"

"Yes. When they meet someone, they go straight between the legs. It's like an initiation."

"That's disturbing."

"Everyone has their thing." I narrowed my eyes. "I'm surprised they don't recognize you."

"I never met them. I haven't been home in two years."

I nodded. That made sense. Remington had said he'd acquired the two Dobermans about a year ago, not long before I moved in.

"Well, they're doing what they're meant to."

"Sniff my crotch?"

"No." I chuckled. "Protect the house from someone they assume is a stranger."

He rolled his eyes. "I suppose."

"They'll calm down once they get to know you." I petted them. "These dogs meant everything to your father. They were always by his side whenever he was home. And clearly, they thought you were an intruder. Just like you thought I was last night. The irony, right?"

Dorian cleared his throat. "Well, thank you for saving me from unwanted attention below the waist."

Something told me this guy was likely used to females trying to get a piece of him below the waist. I hated to admit it, but Dorian Vanderbilt was smoking hot.

"No problem." I flashed my teeth.

As I continued to pet the now pacified animals, silence filled the room.

Dorian finally spoke. "Actually…I'm glad you're here, Primrose. I was going to come find you."

"Oh?" I stood.

He pressed his fingertips together in a steeple formation. "I want to apologize about last night."

"You were going to apologize even before I saved you from T and T?"

His eyes fell to just below my crop top ever so briefly. If you blinked, you might've missed it. But I didn't. I couldn't tell if he was admiring me or judging me for my wardrobe choices. I'd bet on the latter. After all, he'd made a condescending comment about crop tops last night.

"This morning I spoke with Benjamin," he said. "He let me know that you've really helped keep things running around here since the accident, and that the dogs, in particular, like having you around. He mirrored what you said about the dogs meaning a lot to my father, which is why I can't bear to get rid of them, even if I don't need the complication of pets right now."

Nodding, I said, "Benjamin has told me nice things about the kind of person you were when you were younger, which is why your attitude last night surprised me."

He clenched his jaw. "Yeah, well, life has hardened me since then, I guess."

"I don't suppose losing your father helped. I truly am very sorry for your loss, if I didn't make that clear last night."

He paused for several seconds, looking down at the dogs before he met my gaze again. "I have a proposition for you, Primrose."

I straightened. "All right..."

"If you're willing to stay at the house, keep things copacetic with the dogs and staff, I'd be happy to fund your tuition for as long as you're living here."

One minute he wanted to kick me out. Now he wanted to let me stay *and* pay for my tuition? *Hello, Mr. Hyde.*

"I can't let you do that. I don't need a handout. As much as you might think I like freeloading, I won't accept that. My aunt never paid my tuition. But having a place to stay is much appreciated, because it's hard finding anything remotely close to school that I'd be able to afford. So, I will take you up on the offer to continue living here." I tilted my head. "What would you need me to do specifically, though?"

"Nothing much. Just be here...keep morale up with the staff, so I don't have to. Or maybe just keep a look out for anything that might need to be brought to my attention. Not saying you have to manage anything formally. But I'm going to be too busy to pay close attention to what's going on around here. And as long as there are people on the payroll, it would be helpful to have another set of eyes and ears."

Relief washed over me as I reveled in the fact that I no longer had to look for an apartment. "I can definitely do that."

"Good, then. Feel free to stay as long as you need."

"You're not selling the house anytime soon?"

"Not anytime in the near future, no. With having to take over operations at Vanderbilt Technologies, I need to be nearby, unfortunately."

"Why unfortunately?"

"Because I'd much rather be back in Boston."

"You don't like it here?"

"It'll always be home. But with that comes things I'd rather not remember."

"Do you know what you're doing, in terms of your father's business?"

I was embarrassed that I didn't exactly know *what* Vanderbilt Technologies produced. Now didn't seem like the right time to ask, though.

"He'd been training me to work alongside him for years. Even though I've been based on the East Coast, we'd been working together remotely. His plan was that if anything were to happen to him, I would move into his position. I just never thought I'd have to take the helm so soon. I still have a lot to learn."

"Well…" I exhaled. "I'll stay out of your hair unless I need to let you know anything pertinent. And I'll make sure my art stays out of the living room."

His tone softened. "What did you do with your monkeys?"

"They're currently in my bedroom. As you know, I was expecting to pack them into a moving truck with the rest of my stuff tonight before you so graciously got your head out of your ass. But I'll take them back to school. They have a storage room for student projects there. Hopefully they'll eventually be sold."

"I see."

I waited for him to mock my art again, but he didn't.

I looked down at the dogs. "Anyway, you should probably try to get to know the ladies, so they don't freak out around you again."

He shook his head. "I'm not crazy about dogs."

"Ohhh." I gave him a disappointed look.

He tilted his head. "What?"

"People who don't like dogs can't be trusted. Cats, too."

"And monkeys, I presume?"

"All animals, yes. It says something about you if you can't tolerate the kind of pure, unbiased love they have to offer. It's the purest form of love there is."

"I didn't say I couldn't tolerate them. Just not interested in getting my face licked."

"Face licked is better than balls nicked. The sooner you warm up to them, the better off you'll be and the less chance of that happening. They're yours now, whether you like it or not."

He grimaced. "Clearly they're not happy with me."

"They will be once they can sense the good in you. If what Benjamin says is true, I know it's in there somewhere." I grinned.

"What's Benjamin saying about me exactly?"

"Just that you're not all that bad."

He cracked a smile. I was now able to appreciate just how gorgeous Dorian Vanderbilt was, as the ugly personality that had masked his face faded a bit. Actually, *stunning* was probably the right word to describe him. A perfect, symmetrical nose to match his perfectly angular jaw. His eyes were a blue-gray color, like oxidized steel.

"Well, if you'll excuse me..." I cleared my throat. "Now that I don't have to move my crap out today, I'm gonna go make myself a late lunch."

He gestured toward Tallulah and Tess. "Feel free to take them with you."

I pointed to a chair in the corner of the room. "Go sit over there, Dorian."

His forehead wrinkled. "Why?"

"That's where your dad would sit at night and read or have a glass of scotch. Just humor me."

Dorian moved to the corner of the room and sat in the upholstered chair.

I led the dogs over to him. "Come on, ladies. It's okay. This is Dorian. Your brother."

Dorian rolled his eyes and chuckled. "Great."

"Tallulah likes to be rubbed between the ears. Tess, too. Don't be surprised if Tess rubs her asshole on your feet, though. That's just something she likes to do."

"Something to look forward to." He reluctantly rubbed between each dog's ears until they seemed completely unaffected by him. Slowly enamored, actually.

I giggled. "I'll leave you guys alone."

After I left the living room for the kitchen, I ran into Benjamin.

"Dorian is letting me stay," I announced.

He winked. "I knew he'd smarten up."

"Smarten up, huh?" I nudged him with my elbow. "Seems to me like *you* talked him into it."

"I might've put in a few good words for you." He shrugged. "I wasn't gonna let you go without a fight."

"I appreciate it, my friend."

"You deserve to stay here as long as you need to. Christina would've wanted that."

"No one *deserves* a place like this. It's a privilege. And the fact of the matter is, it's Dorian's decision now."

"Well, he made the right one." Benjamin smiled.

"You must've known deep down that Dorian had a heart if you even attempted to convince him to let me stay."

"Of course. I've known him since he was a kid—since before his father began setting expectations so high that it burned Dorian out. He left home to put some distance between them. Dorian is good people, but it might take you a while to see it."

"He's lucky to have someone like you around who knows the real him."

"Believe me, I still don't want to piss him off. But I don't lose sleep at night worrying about my job like Patsy." He chuckled. "I probably know too much for him to get rid of me."

I leaned in. "Like what?"

"Well, for one, it's kind of hard to fire someone who used to help change your sheets when you pissed the bed as a kid." He winked. "But you didn't hear that from me."

I covered my mouth in laughter. "Oh shit."

Patsy entered the kitchen and whispered, "Are we gossiping about Dorian?"

"Yeah." I nodded.

"Seems we're safe." She pretended to wipe sweat from her forehead.

"I'm so happy I don't have to say goodbye to you guys." I grinned.

I lingered in the kitchen for almost an hour, shooting the shit with them.

After I finally managed to stop chatting long enough to make a sandwich, I carried it upstairs. To get to my room at the far end of the hallway, I had to pass all the other bedrooms. It occurred to me that I had no idea where Dorian was sleeping. I assumed he wouldn't want to take his dad's room, as that might be a little strange, especially since the walk-in closet was still filled with Remington and Christina's clothing. Talk about haunting. But maybe he would want to claim it, since it was the best room in the house.

Halfway down the hall was a small window that overlooked the patio below. I peeked out and noticed something moving outside.

Dorian stood at the edge of the pool. His thick, black hair was wet and slicked back. His skin glistened with water droplets, every gorgeous ripple of muscle on display. *Well, damn.* I'd suspected the body probably matched the face, but here was my proof. I was practically drooling, and it wasn't anything to do with this sandwich. That was the body of someone who worked out religiously.

His gaze rose without warning to meet my stare. I nearly fell back from the shock of getting caught. Embarrassed, I did what my mother always taught me to do in awkward situations: lean into it. I smiled and awkwardly gave him a thumbs up.

His eyes slowly narrowed as he returned the gesture, probably officially regretting his decision to let me stay.

CHAPTER 4

After that, an entire week went by without further run-ins with Dorian. That seemed like a miracle considering we were living in the same house. But if this was the way it was going to be, I could definitely get used to it. It felt as quiet around here as it had before he came back.

Dorian left super early for the office each day. I knew that because the garage door would wake me in the wee hours of the morning, since my bedroom was right above the bay where he parked. After the garage door shut, I'd roll over and go right back to sleep.

I also heard him returning late most nights. I wasn't sure if he was working long hours, or if he'd been going out on the town. But if it weren't for the sound of that garage door, I might've doubted whether he was here at all.

On Friday night, I felt restless and wanted to spend some time outside my bedroom. I'd overdone the hiding thing and had started to feel cooped up. I checked the garage for Dorian's Porsche, which was still gone, so I assumed I could safely watch a movie in the home theater down in the basement. Aunt Christina and I had watched movies once in a while down there when she was alive, and it seemed just the thing this evening.

After popping some popcorn in the kitchen, I went downstairs to the theater. It was small compared to most of the other rooms in the house, but really nice, featuring three rows of purple velvet seats and recessed lighting that automatically dimmed when the screen was activated. There were also vintage movie posters hanging on the walls.

Benjamin had showed me how to work the sound system, which could be controlled from a laptop. After looking up the instructions I'd saved on my phone, I called up the movie I'd chosen for myself tonight, *Pulp Fiction*.

The Royale with Cheese scene had started when the theater door suddenly opened.

I straightened in my seat and reached for the remote to pause the movie.

Shit.

Dorian stood in the doorway. But that wasn't the worst part.

He was with a woman.

They must've wanted to watch a movie.

"Oh...hey." I waved awkwardly.

She was blonde and wearing a form-fitting dress. "Who is *she*?" his date asked.

"This is Primrose. She's..." He paused.

"I'm his...stepcousin." *Stepcousin? Really? I barely know the guy*. But technically, I guessed it was true.

Dorian narrowed his eyes. "Primrose is an artist staying here at the house, I was going to say. She also happens to be the niece of my deceased father's late wife."

Her eyes widened. "You *live* here?"

Apparently, she couldn't hear very well.

"Temporarily, yes," I told her. "My aunt invited me to stay here while I attend Orion Art Institute. Dorian was kind enough to allow me to continue the arrangement." Picking a stray piece of popcorn off my chest, I added, "I didn't realize you were home tonight, Dorian. I wouldn't have come down here if I'd known."

"We were just gonna watch a movie," the woman said.

I stood. "I'll get out of your way."

"No." Dorian held his palm out. "You were here first."

"You're both welcome to join me," I offered, sitting back down. "What were you hoping to watch?"

She batted her lashes. "I was in the mood for something romantic."

I inwardly gagged. "There's…romance in this." I shrugged. "If you're open to interpretation."

Dorian arched a brow. "When Vincent jabs a needle into Mia's heart?"

I tilted my head, impressed that he knew what I was watching from just the paused image. "One of my favorite parts." I grinned.

The woman looked between us with a horrified expression. "That sounds terrible."

He turned to her. "Have you ever seen a Tarantino movie?"

"Who?" She narrowed her eyes.

Dorian chuckled. "Okay, then."

I clutched my popcorn bowl and stood again. "Seriously. I'll leave so you guys can watch…*Titanic* or something."

"No." He shook his head. "We'll catch a movie another time. Enjoy your night."

Dorian led his date out the door before I could protest. I sat in silence for several seconds before pressing play, surprised at how respectful he'd been about the whole thing. This was his house, and he had every right to kick me out and entertain his guest, if he wanted.

Eventually, I was able to put Dorian out of my mind and continue my movie night for one. *Pulp Fiction* was almost finished when the theater door opened again.

I turned to find Dorian entering—alone.

"Is it over?" he asked.

My pulse raced as I paused the movie. "About ten minutes left."

Without further comment, he took the seat next to me, sinking into the chair and stretching his long legs. He closed his eyes and let out a long sigh. His delicious cologne wafted my way, sending unwanted arousal through me. I pressed play on the movie, hoping to move out of this hyper-aware state.

"Where's your date?" I asked after the movie finished and she still hadn't reappeared.

"She left."

"Is she a...girlfriend or...?"

"Definitely not," he said, staring at the screen.

"Someone you hook up with?" I pried.

He turned to me. "You always this nosy?"

"Well, we are stepcousins," I teased. "You can tell me anything."

"We go way back, don't we? So much I nearly kicked you out when I got here."

"Details…" I shrugged.

He chuckled. "She's someone I used to hook up with when I lived here years ago. Thought it might be interesting to reconnect with her, but I was grossly mistaken."

"Why? What was wrong with her?"

"Nothing *wrong* with her. I was just bored out of my wits. It's probably *me* that's changed more than anything. That happens when you leave home, I guess." He reached for some popcorn. "Anyway…found myself more in the mood to watch *Pulp Fiction* than I was to make pointless conversation with her."

"I can start it over, if you want to watch from the beginning."

"Nah." He shook his head. "But I'll watch another movie with you, if you're down."

Ohhhkay.

Hesitant excitement washed over me. I'd been pretty lonely lately if the idea of having someone to watch a movie with felt exhilarating. But at the same time, this was Dorian Vanderbilt—not exactly someone I could relax around yet. But I sure as hell wasn't going to say no.

I finally nodded. "That'd be cool."

"You choose."

"Well…" I took a moment to think on it. "If you were in the mood to watch *Pulp Fiction*, maybe another Tarantino?"

He scratched his chin. "Actually, have you ever seen *Snatch*?"

"Guy Ritchie, right?" I nodded. "I've heard of it but never watched it."

"His style reminds me of Tarantino. I think you'll enjoy it. Would you want to watch that?"

"Yeah." I nodded, impressed with his effort to think of a movie I would like.

Dorian went over to the laptop and pulled up the film, then returned to the seat next to me. He reclined his chair as I pressed play on the remote. He once again stretched out his long legs.

For the next couple of hours, we watched the movie intently, neither of us saying a word until it finished. That was exactly how I liked it. But he did look over to see my reaction at certain parts, which I *also* liked. Any nervousness I'd had dissipated as the movie went on. And I certainly couldn't complain about sitting close to him, since he smelled like heaven. I hadn't been out with a member of the opposite sex in what seemed like ages. Sitting this close to an attractive man made me miss dating, even if the man sitting next to me currently was out of my league.

When the credits came on the screen, he reached for the remote and lowered the volume. "What did you think?"

"It was awesome. I love movies where you don't know what to expect, and the power dynamic can change at the drop of a hat."

"Ah...sort of like how you suddenly had the power when I discovered you could control those dogs?"

"Maybe, yeah." My mouth curved into a smile.

"They actually like me now. But they did *not* like Savannah."

"Savannah was your date tonight?"

He nodded. "Yeah. Tess saved me, actually. She helped me get out of the rest of the date."

"What do you mean?"

"I wanted to end the night early and had been thinking up an excuse. Then Tess rubbed her asshole on Savannah's shoe as we were standing in the foyer. She decided right then and there she wanted to call it a night."

I cracked up. "Saved by the asshole."

"Exactly. It was perfect."

"Did you drive her home?"

"I called her a car."

"Well, I'm sorry again if I disrupted your evening."

"Trust me, I had more fun watching the movie with you than I would've sitting through whatever sappy film she picked." He sighed. "And…I'm sorry if she was rude to you. She was probably just intimidated."

"Intimidated? Why?"

He glared. "Really? You're gonna make me say it?"

"Sure." I smirked.

"Because you're attractive…" His eyes fell to my abs. "And you seem to have no other wardrobe besides crop tops."

I sat for a moment with the knowledge that Dorian thought I was attractive. I wasn't about to return the compliment, even if all I could think about was how handsome he was. How long his lashes were. How sexy his hands were as they wrapped around the armrest. He had a dark and mysterious look to him, which was right up my alley.

"How's school going?" he asked, snapping me out of my thoughts.

"I have to sketch someone nude," I blurted.

His eyes widened. "Really…"

"Yes. In the next week or so."

"Male or female?"

"I actually don't know. It'll be a surprise."

"Which do you prefer to draw?"

"There's something very beautiful about the female body, but I think drawing a man would be more challenging because it might make me more uncomfortable."

"So, we're hoping for low-hanging balls?"

I cackled. "I've never been one to turn down a challenge, no."

"So that's a yes on the balls?"

"I'll take whatever the universe blesses me with in that regard."

"Well, I have no doubt you can handle it, if you created those monkeys from scratch."

"Thanks for the confidence."

He looked at me a few moments. "You're definitely interesting, Primrose. I'll give you that."

"And you're still a bit of a mystery to me, Dorian."

"How so?"

"That first night, I thought you were a pompous prick. But then you softened. And now, I come to find out you have impeccable movie taste. So you can't be all bad."

"I'm glad you no longer think I'm a prick. I'm really not. I have dickish moments, but overall, I like to think I'm a good person."

"Still lots to figure out when it comes to you, though."

"Like what?" He crossed his arms and leaned back.

I hesitated, unsure whether to continue. "You never came to visit your dad, for one. You were always spoken of almost in whispers. I just don't know what to make of you. Not really much of an opportunity to get to know you, either, since you're never home. If you hadn't walked in here tonight, I might've doubted whether you were still living here."

He nodded. "I've been spending a lot of time trying to figure out the mess my father left behind. It's easier to do that at his office. But I'd be lying if I didn't say this house unnerves me. Too many memories here." Dorian turned toward me. "I'm trying to keep busy outside the mansion so it never actually registers. I'm not sure if my father being gone has even truly hit me yet. Living in denial and throwing myself into work is pretty much how I'm handling things."

He looked up at the recessed lighting. "Dad and I had our issues. But there was so much more I needed to learn from him, things I wish I could say, but I'll never have a chance to. A lot was left unresolved. I feel like I'm still in shock." He sighed. "Despite our differences, he was all I had."

The room was so quiet you could hear a pin drop. My chest felt heavy with emotion as I absorbed his words. "I can relate to that feeling," I said softly.

He brushed his thumb along the velvet of the armrest. "Your aunt, you mean?"

I shook my head. "No. My mother. I lost her a few years ago. She was all *I* had. And my father was never in the picture. That's why I moved in with Christina and your dad. Christina was my mom's only sibling."

"So, Christina was the closest relative you had left?"

I nodded. "Growing up, Christina and I weren't that close. She was always traveling. She was my mom's younger, wilder sister—the dreamer. I always wished to know her better. But she was never in one place. When my mother died, Christina made an effort for the first time to be a part of my life. And I appreciated that."

He frowned. "I'm sorry. I know I minimalized her when we first met. I don't know if she was a gold digger. I never tried to get to know her. It was easier to believe my father was being used than to consider that he had a genuine, loving relationship with someone who wasn't my mother."

"I get that." I nodded. "And look..." I chuckled. "She might've been a gold digger. I don't know, either. Like you, I believe what's easiest to digest."

He looked away. "I guess we'll never know now, will we?"

I thought we might need a new subject. "What is it that your father's company does? I've been afraid to ask because I feel like I should know."

"It's okay." Dorian smiled. "Dad started out as a physicist. He developed many products over the years. I can't talk about anything currently in development because of intellectual property issues. But in the past, he created solar-powered orbital devices and synapse glass that responds to brainwave sequences. He sold his inventions to huge corporations over the years. And there are many more still in the process of being sold."

"Wow." I nodded. "What did you study in school?"

"Well, I wasn't given much of a choice. My father essentially told me that if I didn't follow in his footsteps, I would lose my inheritance. He insisted that I study physics for undergrad and get my master's in business. So that's what I did. The plan was always for me to take over."

"That wasn't what you wanted?"

"If I'd had my way, I probably would've majored in music, so no."

"Really…"

"Yeah. I was in a band when I was younger, much to my father's chagrin."

"What did you play?"

"Bass."

"Do you still play?"

"I dabble in it when I'm alone. But nothing on the regular." He stared down at his hands. "I envy you for pursuing what you love."

"But let's face it," I admitted. "Majoring in art is not the wisest career choice."

"Knowing that didn't stop you, though. That says a lot about you. You're willing to take a risk for the chance to do something you love." He looked into my eyes. "I think on some level, you know you have true skills, which makes it easier to take that risk. You must realize you're truly talented."

My face felt flushed. "I assumed you thought my monkeys were ridiculous."

"They are on the surface. But they're realistic as hell. And original. The more I think about it, the more impressed I am." He shrugged. "And I'm jealous that you're doing something you love."

"Well, thank you," I said, filling with pride. "Even if music isn't your career, can't you get back into it as a hobby?"

"I'm a little too busy right now for hobbies. Talk to me in thirty years."

"How old are you?" I asked.

"Twenty-eight." He arched a brow. "How old are you?"

"How old do you think I am?"

"Well, given that you're in college, I want to say... nineteen?"

My mouth dropped open. "Do I look nineteen?"

"Yes." He smirked.

I couldn't tell if he was serious. "I'm twenty-three, actually. Got a bit of a late start on the college front."

"Where are you from originally?"

"Cincinnati."

He nodded. "Are you hungry?" he asked after a moment.

"I could eat."

"Up for a midnight snack?"

"Always." I grinned.

Dorian stood, and I grabbed the popcorn bowl, following him out of the theater. On the way up the stairs, I couldn't help noticing how nicely his dark jeans hugged his ass. Attractive from every angle, apparently.

Once upstairs, Dorian looked around the large, all-white kitchen. "I haven't eaten here since I moved back. I have no idea what we have or where anything is."

"I'm due to go grocery shopping," I said. "So I don't have much to offer you from my personal stash besides Diet Coke."

We rummaged through the pantry, which contained several cans of the same exact item.

I reached for one and laughed. "Enough caviar?"

"My dad's favorite. Imported, made from sturgeon originating in the Caspian Sea. He always said it's the best."

"I've never eaten caviar," I said, scrunching my nose. "Not sure I'd like it."

"Well, no one else is gonna eat this." He took the can from me. "You wanna try it?"

"How do you eat it?"

"Usually crackers, but I don't see that we have any." He grabbed a bag of something in the corner. "Hot Cheetos?"

"Hot Cheetos and caviar?" I shrugged. "Why not?"

"I bet these were my dad's, too. He loved spicy shit." A look of sadness crossed his face as he stared down at the bag.

I interrupted his haze. "The reality hits in waves, doesn't it?"

"Yeah," he murmured. Taking a deep breath, he forced a smile. "Let's take these out to the table."

Dorian and I sat at the breakfast nook in the corner of the kitchen that featured a window overlooking the ocean. It was dark out now, so we couldn't see much. Through the glass, we could hear the waves crashing, though.

He opened a can of caviar and the bag of Cheetos. After dipping one of the cheese puffs into the caviar, he handed it to me across the table.

I took a bite and chewed for a while. "It's salty. But in an obnoxious way." Licking my lips, I added, "I feel like these two foods are a pretty accurate representation of the two of us. You're caviar, by the way. And I'm the Cheetos."

He took a bite. "I'm...overrated, obnoxious, and salty?"

"Basically." I smiled.

"And you're cheesy as all hell." He winked.

"You were supposed to tell me I'm *hot*."

His eyes seared into mine. "I don't need to tell you that."

My face felt hotter than the darn Cheetos now.

"Okay, hot's the obvious one." He lifted a Cheeto. "But from my observations, there are better reasons why you're similar to this Cheeto."

"Do tell." I wiped the corner of my mouth.

"You're bold. Moving across the country to follow your dreams and now having to face an uncertain future, yet with a smile on your face most of the time—that's a very bold thing. To smile in the face of uncertainty and tragedy is probably one of the greatest skills anyone can hold in life." He paused. "You also leave an impression. Just like these do."

"Heartburn?"

He shook his head and chuckled. "No."

"Well, thank you. I feel like I need to reciprocate—but I can't exactly call you fishy." I winked.

As we continued to munch and make easy conversation, I hoped this wouldn't be the last late-night snack session I'd get to have with Dorian. I enjoyed his company.

When I licked the spicy seasoning off my fingers, I noticed the way his eyes fell to my lips, following the motion of my tongue.

And suddenly my tongue wasn't the only thing burning up.

CHAPTER 5

A few days later, I was tucked into bed when my friend Janelle FaceTimed me. Janelle and I went to school together, but we hadn't crossed paths lately due to our class schedules. I'd just finished telling her about my late-night encounter with Dorian.

"You went on a date with him," she informed me.

"It wasn't a date. It was an accidental…moment in time."

"He ditched his potential hookup to watch a movie with you."

"He didn't ditch her. She was grossed out by Tess's asshole."

"What?"

"Never mind. But Dorian didn't mean to hang out with me. It was sort of a fluke."

"But he specifically found you again down in the basement, didn't he?"

"Well, yeah."

"After, you had a midnight snack together per his suggestion, correct?"

"Yes."

"Sounds like a freaking date to me."

I hated that she was getting me all riled up about this. The last thing I needed was to buy into some delusion that my secret crush on that man could actually go anywhere. Even if he did like me in that way, I needed to not complicate this living situation so I didn't end up out on the street.

"Doesn't mean anything, Janelle. Trust me."

"I googled him," she announced.

"Why did you do that?"

"I wanted to see what he looked like. He's totally gorgeous."

I felt my face heat, flashes of his fantastic face now all I could see.

"Dark and mysterious," she continued. "I love his vibe."

That was exactly how I thought of him. Dorian *was* a whole vibe. If there was a word to describe him, though, it would have to be *dangerous*. Crushing on a man like him would be like playing with fire and setting myself up for disappointment all at once.

"Let's change the subject," I insisted.

"Okay, then. How was the naked model you had to sketch?"

"Awful. I got a guy. Thought that was what I wanted, but then I was distracted the entire time, trying to make sure I wasn't staring at his dick for too long."

She laughed. "But aren't you supposed to stare to get the job done?"

"Yes. That's the problem. It didn't seem right in this case. So the drawing didn't come out as well as it could've."

"Will you have any more opportunities to get it right?"

"He'll be coming back a few more times, much to my chagrin. I'm more comfortable not using models and doing my art from memory."

"Well, I'm looking forward to seeing the finished product."

"There's not much to see." I yawned. "Anyway, I'd better go to sleep. It's late."

"Sweet Dorian dreams…" she teased.

Rolling my eyes, I vowed never to talk to her about him again.

Roughly fifteen minutes later, I fell asleep to the sounds of the ocean.

But in the middle of the night, I jumped awake to another sound, this one far from peaceful: the fire alarm. A rush of adrenaline shot through me. This was the first time the alarm had gone off since I'd lived here. Unfortunately, this very scenario was my biggest fear.

As I leaped out of bed and headed out of the room in a panic, I ran smack dab into Dorian's shirtless body in the middle of the hallway.

"Sorry." He wrapped his hands around my arms to steady me. "You okay?"

"Yeah. Let's get out of here," I said, grabbing his arm and attempting to get him to move faster.

"I don't smell smoke," he said as he followed me. "Probably a false alarm."

"We can't risk it," I told him, my voice shaky from panic.

The cool air hit my face as we made it outside.

"Stay right here," Dorian said before turning to head back in.

I ran after him. "What, are you crazy? Get back here!"

"I'll be right back," he said, darting inside.

My heart raced every second he was gone.

I let out a sigh of relief when he emerged again, carrying a throw blanket I recognized from the living room.

He placed it around my shoulders. "Here."

Benjamin emerged from the guest house. "The fire department is on its way." He looked at Dorian and me. "You guys all right?"

My teeth chattered. "I think so."

"Our alarm system automatically alerts them to come," Dorian explained. He turned to Benjamin. "I think it's a false alarm. I don't smell smoke."

I closed the blanket tighter around my body. "Better safe than sorry."

A minute later, the sound of sirens began in the distance and after a moment, two fire trucks and an ambulance arrived at the property.

Over the next several minutes, they surveyed the house as Dorian, Benjamin, and I waited outside.

It took a full half hour before one of the firefighters approached us. "Looks like there might've been a power fluctuation of some kind, which prompted the system to reset and go off. Probably what caused the false alarm."

"I'll call someone to fix that tomorrow," Benjamin said.

"Thank you for coming out," Dorian told the firefighter.

"Of course. That's my job. You should be good to go back inside the house." He nodded once. "You all have a good night."

"Thank you, sir," I said.

Benjamin spoke to the firefighter a bit more as they walked back toward the truck. The other fireman emerged from the house before climbing into the truck.

Dorian and I were left standing alone. The wind from the ocean blew my hair around.

"Come on." He placed his hand gently on my back. "Let's go back in."

Still a bit frozen in shock, I didn't move.

"Everything is fine, Primrose." He repeated, "Let's go inside where it's warm."

I nodded, forcing one foot in front of the other.

Once inside, we faced each other in the foyer. I walked over to the living room, returning the blanket to the couch.

His eyes narrowed. "What's going on? You seem really shaken by something that turned out to be nothing."

I didn't want to recall the horrible memory, but I owed Dorian an explanation for my behavior. "When I was younger, the house next door to us burned down," I told him. "Three members of the family passed away, including the girl who'd been my best friend at the time. Whenever there's a fire alarm, I get rattled, I guess."

He closed his eyes for a moment. "I'm so sorry. I had no idea."

"Thank you," I muttered.

"What was her name?"

"Lily. The first great tragedy of my life."

"Not the last unfortunately, huh?" He exhaled.

"No."

"Well, that certainly explains your reaction."

"Sorry for freaking out. I realize there was nothing to freak out about."

"No apologies needed."

"Thank you for risking your life to grab me a blanket." I smiled.

"You even *sleep* in crop tops, I see." Dorian gave me a once-over, sending a chill down my back.

"What else is there?" I smirked.

Our eyes caught for a long moment before I went toward the kitchen.

"You're not going back to bed?" he called from behind me.

I turned, walking backward. "I'm wired now. I won't sleep. Just gonna make some tea." Stopping, I tilted my head. "Wanna join me?"

He chewed his bottom lip for a moment. "I should try to get some shut-eye. I have to leave early in the morning."

Disappointed, I turned away from him again. "Okay, then. Goodnight."

"'Night."

Still feeling on edge as I made tea, I watched as the steam began to rise from the kettle, trying to catch it before the whistle went off. I removed it from the stovetop and poured the hot water into a mug.

After moving over to the breakfast nook, I sipped my tea while looking out at the dark ocean. It had been years since I'd been spooked by a fire alarm like that. I thought

I'd gotten over it, but trauma was a bitch. Dorian had been super sweet to go inside to get me that blanket. Despite my nerves, wrapping it around myself had felt like a warm hug.

About twenty minutes later, I heard footsteps and Dorian appeared, now wearing a black T-shirt over his gray sweatpants. Goose bumps peppered my arms at the sight of him.

His hair was tousled, his voice groggy. "Hey."

"I thought you were gonna try to sleep."

"Turns out I'm pretty wired, too. I guess it's contagious."

"Want some tea? I can heat up the water."

"Sure."

Dorian took a seat at the breakfast nook as I walked over to the stove.

I reached for the canister of teas and turned to him. "Darjeeling or Earl Grey?"

"Actually, got any whiskey? I've had that kind of week."

I couldn't tell whether he was serious. "Sorry, no."

"English Breakfast, then?"

"Don't have that, either."

"I'll take the Earl Grey."

"Coming right up."

While I prepared his tea and another for myself, I could sense his eyes on me. Especially after tonight's scare, it comforted me to know I was no longer alone in the house at night. Benjamin was always right next door, but after he and Patsy left for the day, it had just been me.

I slid a mug across the table to Dorian. "What's been going on that you'd need whiskey at four in the morning? Besides me freaking out over the fire alarm, of course."

He sighed. "I guess what's been going on…is the realization that this stay is really not temporary. That I might never be able to go back to my life in Boston. And that my feet may never be big enough to fill my father's shoes."

"Maybe you don't need to fill them. No one should be expected to step into someone else's life and be perfect at it. All you can do is your best. Find your own way. And if that's not good enough, then fuck everyone."

His mouth curved into a smile.

"What?" I asked.

"My mother used to say that. Well, a little more eloquently than 'fuck everyone.' She used to say, '*All you can do is your best. And if you've done your best, you should be happy with any outcome.*'" He grinned. "I kind of like 'fuck everyone' better though."

"Your mother was a wise woman."

"Sitting here in this spot reminds me of her. So it's weird that you said that on top of it. It's like she's coming through or something."

"Maybe she is, for all we know."

He steeped his tea as he looked down. "I used to get up in the middle of the night when I couldn't sleep and find her sitting alone here in the kitchen. Instead of telling me to go back to bed, she'd pour me some milk and we'd talk—right here in this same spot where you and I are now. It would calm me down, and I'd fall asleep easily after that."

A warm feeling came over me as my eyes began to water. "Mothers are the best."

He ran his thumb along the mug. "What happened to your mom?"

"Cancer. She was only sick for a short time."

He nodded. "My mother too."

"Yeah. Benjamin had mentioned that."

"Well, she struggled with it for a while. So it wasn't short. But it was cancer."

"That must've been so hard for both you and your dad."

Dorian looked away. "He loved her, but he didn't know how to be faithful. That's something I never forgave him for."

My stomach sank. This was the first I'd heard of Remington being a cheater. I wondered if Christina knew he'd cheated on his first wife. Had he been loyal to my aunt? I took a sip. "Why do men cheat?"

"I've been asking myself that question for years. But I think ultimately, it's ego—a feeling that you're somehow entitled to a certain amount of gratification, even if it hurts others."

I hesitated. "Have you ever cheated on anyone?"

He shook his head. "Can't cheat if you're not in relationships."

"You've never had a girlfriend?"

"Not since high school. And I didn't cheat back then, no. I was a nerd in those days. Lucky to even have a girlfriend, let alone play the field. Not sure I would've known how to be a player."

"I can't picture you as a nerd."

"I didn't grow into myself until my late teens."

"What about now? Are you a player?"

"I'm not interested in monogamy, if that's what you're asking."

That was a letdown; although maybe it was the reality check I needed to squelch any remaining delusion that something could happen between him and me.

"I'm the opposite, actually," I said. "A serial monogamist. I don't know how to just casually date someone. If I like him, I get attached, and I want him to myself. If I sense that's not what he wants, though, I detach myself for fear of getting hurt."

Dorian leaned his elbows on the table. "How many times have you had to do that?"

"Pretty much every time I've had a boyfriend, I've broken up with him before he had a chance to do me wrong. At the same time, I don't like to just date casually. So, there you go. Perpetually single."

"How do you know when to break up with them?"

"It's a feeling that I'm getting in over my head. The need to protect myself kicks in."

"Well, you're too young to be tied down anyway. You should enjoy your life a little first."

"I don't think it's about age," I said. "If you find the right person, you find the right person, whether you're twenty or sixty. But I agree that I could stand to let loose a bit more. I'm definitely too young to be staying in most nights."

His eyes widened. "You never go out?"

"Well, I wait tables a few nights a week and meet a lot of guys on the job. But I find I'm also not so good at picking up signals. It would be much easier if someone would just say, 'I'm flirting with you.'"

"Wouldn't life be easier if everyone gave clear signals? I'm lying to you. I'm cheating on you. I'm using you.

Instead, we're expected to blindly judge people based on instinct, which may or may not be influenced by what we *want* to see."

I nodded. "You're right. So often I want to see the good in people, but I'm consistently disappointed."

"So you surround yourself with monkeys instead." He grinned.

"You've got my number." I winked. "The monkeys in my head are far superior to humans, yes. Although I was forced to work on a human this week."

"That's right!" He pointed at me. "The nude portrait."

"Yep." I sighed.

"Didn't go well?"

"It didn't."

"Balls weren't low enough?"

I laughed. "The balls were okay. But apparently, I freeze when you show me a penis."

He bent his head back in laughter. "I thought you said you were up for that challenge."

"Yeah, well, I suppose it's different when you're slapped in the face with it."

"Not gonna touch that."

"Figuratively, of course." I took a sip of my tea.

"Was he...well-endowed at least?"

"He wasn't hard. So not sure what his potential would've been."

"*Potential.* That doesn't sound too complimentary."

"Take that how you may."

Dorian chuckled, and we continued talking until long after he'd finished the last of his tea. He eventually took his mug to the sink and announced, "I have to get going soon. I try to get into the office by six so I can get some work done before I have to deal with people."

"You've peopled enough in the middle of the night with me."

He smiled. "I didn't mind it."

I felt myself blush.

"Thanks for the tea," he said. "And the talk."

I held up my mug. "Here's to fire alarms."

Dorian saluted me. "Until the next strange encounter in the night, Primrose."

I'll be looking forward to it.

CHAPTER 6

A few nights a week I worked as a waitress at The Blue Wave, a waterfront restaurant. There certainly were worse places to work, given that it was right on the ocean. But on this particular night, it was so busy that I barely had a moment to breathe.

I got to table three and prepared to take their drink order. "Sorry for the wait," I said, taking out my tablet. "How may I—"

I stopped in my tracks when I got a look at the handsome man sitting across from his date.

His eyes widened. "Primrose..."

I gulped. "Dorian."

We hadn't crossed paths since the fire alarm incident almost a week ago. It was jarring to see him here in my place of work. The look on his face told me he hadn't known I worked here.

The blonde sitting across from him looked between us. "You two...know each other?"

"You could say that." Dorian closed his menu. "I didn't realize you worked here."

"Well, we never discussed where I work. This is where I waitress a few nights a week." I shrugged. "Obviously…"

He turned to his date. "Primrose is the niece of my late father's wife."

"I see." She sighed. "Good to meet you."

"You as well." I ran a hand through my hair.

"She's actually staying at the mansion," Dorian added.

The woman blinked as she turned to him abruptly. "With you?"

"Yes."

"We don't see much of each other, though," I added.

His mouth curved into a smile. "Unless the fire alarm goes off."

I tucked a piece of hair behind my ear. "Right."

"And *why* is she living with you?" his date asked.

Before Dorian could say anything, I responded.

"I lived there with my aunt before she and Dorian's father passed away. Dorian was gracious enough to let me continue staying there while I finish school."

"Shouldn't we all be so lucky to have wealthy relatives to live off of?" she chided.

The nerve of her. Wow. "We're not related," I clarified.

"Clearly," Dorian agreed. "Since I haven't an artistic bone in my body. Primrose is very talented."

Sensing my cheeks reddening, I lifted my tablet again. "Anyway…I should take your order. What can I get you to drink?"

"I'll have a glass of your best Chardonnay," she said.

I nodded and turned to my *relative*. "And you?"

Dorian flashed a mischievous look. "Surprise me."

I could barely think straight, let alone decide what to have the bartender make him. "Okay. Be right back." I rushed off, my mind racing.

Before I got to the bar, I ran into the girl working alongside me tonight. "Hey, Maddie, any chance we can switch tables, and you can take over number three?"

She shook her head. "I'm sorry. I actually just got a call that my sitter bailed on me, so I have to relieve my mom who's watching my daughter. I have to leave here in five minutes."

Great. So not only would I be serving Dorian and his date all night, we were about to be short-staffed.

"No problem. Sorry about your sitter," I murmured as I headed toward the bar.

I sucked it up and placed their drink orders, having a little extra fun with Dorian's request to be surprised. Served him right for putting me in this awkward situation.

The bartender handed me their drinks, and I headed back to Dorian's table. Of course, on top of everything, he had to look more gorgeous than ever tonight in a linen button-down, his hair parted a bit to the side. He seemed even more tan, and I wondered if he'd taken a day off and spent it at the beach with her.

I placed his date's wine in front of her and set down the mixed drink I'd had the bartender make for Dorian.

Dorian lifted the glass, examining the contents. "What is this?"

"An Alaskan Duck Fart."

His eyes went wide. "Excuse me?"

"You said to surprise you. I take that responsibility very seriously."

He took a reluctant sip. "What's in it?"

"Coffee liqueur, Irish cream, and whiskey. I know you like that, since you requested it instead of tea once. This drink is potent, but it goes down easy."

He ran his tongue over his bottom lip. "It actually tastes pretty good. Would've never guessed those ingredients went well together."

"Next time be specific, or be prepared for another surprise." I flashed my teeth.

His eyes were piercing. "You're definitely full of those, Primrose."

The woman I'd nearly forgotten sitting across from him cleared her throat. "Should we order?"

"Yes." He gestured toward her. "You go ahead."

She closed her menu. "I'm going to get the garden salad."

So predictable. What a waste. "The food's really good here. Are you sure?"

"I think I know what I'm in the mood for. Thanks." She pushed the menu aside.

What a bitch.

Dorian frowned.

I swallowed. "And you?"

"Is there anything you'd recommend?"

"Well, we don't have caviar and Hot Cheetos, so no."

He smiled. "That's a shame."

"I do like the filet mignon with asparagus, though," I added.

"That sounds delicious. I'll try that. Thank you."

Despite enjoying the inexplicable chemistry I had with Dorian, after I put in their order, I welcomed the breather. I busied myself waiting on other tables until their food was ready.

When I returned with their meals, I set the salad in front of his date, and she immediately ripped into me.

"This is not what I asked for."

"It's not?" I looked down at what was very clearly a salad.

"No." She shook her head. "I asked for the garden salad. This has cheese on it. I'm vegan. And gluten free."

"The garden salad comes with shaved parmesan. You never mentioned your food restrictions."

"Well, it didn't say anything about cheese on the menu, so I didn't think I had to. I need you to take it back immediately."

Dorian's brows drew in. "Why don't you just pick it off?"

"I think she should get me a new plate. I don't want cross-contamination."

I feigned a smile. "I'm happy to do that."

Gritting my teeth, I returned to the kitchen, dumping her old salad in the trash and requesting a new one. But when I returned to the table with it, she still looked like someone had pissed in her Cheerios.

She shook her head. "There are still croutons on this. I said I was gluten-free."

"You only mentioned the cheese."

"I said I was gluten-free, though. You should know that croutons are bread, and bread contains gluten. I shouldn't have to spell it out."

"I don't understand why you didn't just tell me about the croutons last time. I wouldn't have had the chef add them."

"Again, the problem is that neither the cheese nor the croutons were specifically mentioned on the menu. You should really speak to someone about greater transparency when it comes to the menu items."

Dorian's brows furrowed.

"I'll get right on that," I said, though I had no intention of going out of my way to please this woman.

"I'm sorry to send this back again."

"No, you're not," Dorian interjected, his face turning red.

She moved her shoulders back. "What do you mean?"

"You're being a bitch about it. You're not sorry at all," he seethed.

"You're calling *me* a bitch?"

"I am. You think you're better than her because she's a waitress. Is this how you treat everyone you encounter?"

"You've been flirting with this hussy who's freeloading off you since the moment we got here. If I'm a bitch, you're an asshole."

He turned to me. "Have I been flirting with you, Primrose?"

"If *that's* flirting, you really need to up your game, Vanderbilt. I mean, the moment you asked me to surprise you with that drink. Gosh, I thought I was going to have to change my panties."

His date gritted her teeth. "Okay. You know what?" Her chair skidded against the floor as she got up. "I've had enough. Have a nice life...both of you."

I watched her until she was out of sight, then turned to Dorian. "Sorry about that."

"Sorry for what? I should be thanking *you* for sparing me the rest of the evening with her."

"She was pretty, though. You could've at least gotten laid."

"Pretty ugly on the inside is what she is. And it takes a lot more than a pretty face to get me interested these days. That damn dating app should come with a bitch warning."

Someone in the distance called my name.

"I have to get back to work," I told him. "Are you staying?"

He gestured down to his plate. "Well, I have this delicious steak to eat."

"And a salad full of glutenous croutons."

"Even better." He winked.

I pointed to his empty glass. "Can I get you another drink?"

"Yes. But something other than the duck fart one, even though it was tasty. Might have a stomach upset with two of those things."

I chuckled. "How about a glass of red? Pairs well with steak."

"That sounds perfect."

"Be right back."

My heart fluttered. We'd joked earlier about *not* flirting, so why did every moment with him *feel* like it had a subtext? And how could I be giddy after the disaster that had just occurred at his table? Yes, I was happy his date had left. But I feared the false hope it gave me was going to lead to major disappointment. Dorian wasn't hanging out with me tonight by choice. It was only by default after a series of weird circumstances. He'd had more than one opportunity to ask me out after the couple of times we'd bonded. He'd chosen not to do that. From everything I could tell, he had decided to friend-zone me, so I needed to be careful about inferring anything from his behavior tonight.

As I waited for the bartender to pour Dorian's wine, I thought about how silly my damn crush on him was. Why was I thinking this way about a man who clearly went for women who were the complete opposite of me? Not only had both of his last two dates been tall blondes, they were both stuck-up. I was a petite brunette who didn't have a prissy bone in my body. Clearly, Dorian wasn't interested in women like me.

I walked the wine over to Dorian and placed it carefully in front of him. "Here you go."

"Thank you."

"I feel bad deserting you when your date left, but I have to get back to work."

"Well, because of you, I'm not *living* alone, right? I think I can handle half an hour in a restaurant."

"Flag me down if you need anything."

"Will do."

But he never asked for a single thing more. My attention diverted to him from time to time, and once I caught him watching me, but I tried to tell myself not to make anything of it.

After he seemed finished, I returned to Dorian's table. "Can I get you some dessert?"

"How about we have dessert together back at the house after your shift?"

A zap of excitement ran down my spine. "Okay." But I once again warned myself not to read into anything.

"Up for a movie, too?" he asked.

"Yeah. That'd be great," I answered.

You could at least not seem so damn eager to hang out with him.

"When do you get off?"

Get off, you say? "Ten thirty."

"You need a ride home?"

"No. I have a car."

"That little sky blue Beetle I see parked in the driveway is yours, right?"

"Yeah. It gets the job done."

"You look like you drive a Beetle."

My mouth dropped open. "I'll choose to take that as a compliment."

"You should." He laughed.

"You want me to pick up dessert on my way home?" I offered.

"I'll handle it. Anything you can't eat?"

"I'm vegan, gluten-free, and allergic to air."

"Liar. You ate the Cheetos."

"Good catch." I chuckled. "No food restrictions."

"Okay. See you tonight."

"Yep." I exhaled. "See you then."

I almost said, "It's a date." But that would've been stupidly presumptuous. Dorian was my roommate. I had no evidence that he was interested in anything aside from some very light flirting. I needed to calm my tits.

After he left, I checked the bill and noticed he'd left me a massive tip along with a note:

Neither blue, nor green. Aquamarine.
I stared at it for several seconds.
Hmm...

CHAPTER 7

That night, I entered the house to the most amazing smell. Apples and cinnamon, maybe? What the heck was going on?

I went straight to the kitchen to find Dorian standing near the oven.

I cleared my throat to announce my presence.

He turned and smiled. "Oh, hey."

"Have I just walked into The Billionaire Bakeoff?"

"It would seem that way, wouldn't it?"

I sniffed the air. "Apple pie?"

"Apple crisp."

My mouth went agape. "Dorian Vanderbilt baking apple crisp was certainly not on my bingo card this week."

"Don't get too excited. It's the one thing I actually know how to make. My mother's recipe. When I was little, she used to have me help her make it after we went apple picking. I never forgot the steps."

"Well, if you're only gonna know how to make one thing, apple crisp is a pretty damn good choice."

"I can agree with that," he said as he rummaged through the drawers.

"When you said dessert, I was expecting you to maybe pick up some Krispy Kreme donuts. I'm impressed that you took the time to make something."

"Well, consider it my official apology for putting you through the wrath of my miserable date."

"What was her name? You never introduced me," I teased. "How rude."

"That's because I knew from the moment I met her that I wouldn't be seeing her again. But her name was Eve."

"You said baking apple crisp was an apology for her. But, um, wasn't that enormous tip you left me enough?"

"No, it wasn't." Dorian grabbed a mitt and opened the oven to pull out the baking dish. The bubbling crisp looked just as amazing as it smelled. "It's going to have to cool off for a bit. Maybe we go pick out a movie and come back for it."

"Actually, I'd like to go upstairs and change real quick. Why don't you pick the movie while I do that? You seem to know my taste."

He removed the oven mitt. "Okay."

As I headed upstairs, butterflies swarmed in my stomach. I had no evidence that this was anything more than two roommates hanging out, yet I couldn't help how I felt. An attractive man with whom I felt intense chemistry had just baked for me, and we were getting ready to watch a movie together. I couldn't remember the last time anything had made me feel so giddy. It was pretty pathetic that some of the best "dates" I'd ever had were spur-of-the-moment encounters with Dorian Vanderbilt.

After taking off my work clothes, I slipped on a crop top I'd been dying all night to wear in front of Dorian and a pair of lounge pants. Normally I would've showered, but I didn't want the dessert to be cold by the time I returned. I fluffed my long brown hair in the mirror. My caramel highlights were fading to more of a blonde, but I kind of liked the contrast, even if it meant I was overdue for a touch-up at the salon.

When I got downstairs, Dorian was back in the kitchen.

"I set up the theater. Looks like this is cool enough, too." He served generous portions of the apple crisp onto two plates and handed me one with a fork.

I sniffed. "This looks and smells amazing."

"Well, don't judge it until you taste it."

"I never do." My cheeks burned as I realized how that sounded.

"Okay, then." His eyes fell to my midriff. "Interesting choice of crop top. That can't be a coincidence."

My shirt read: *Allergic to Stupid*.

"In honor of your annoying date. I couldn't wait to get home and put it on."

"That's awesome and timely."

We walked our plates of apple crisp down to the theater and each took a seat.

"What movie did you choose?"

"I didn't yet. Couldn't decide. We need to discuss it."

I dug into the dessert. My tongue tingled at the sweet combination of apples and cinnamon, complemented by a hint of salty butter. "This is delicious."

"I'm happy you like it."

"I can't remember the last time anyone baked for me," I said with my mouth full. "I most definitely wouldn't have imagined that the person to break the chain would be you."

"Because of the way I was the night you met me?"

I nodded. "You're supposed to be an elusive billionaire, not Betty Crocker."

He covered his full mouth as he laughed. "And you were supposed to be a slightly odd, crop-top-wearing monkey artist." He paused. "Well, you *are* those things, but in a good way. You're also someone I quite like spending time with."

I felt my face heat as I licked sticky apple off my lips. "I find myself enjoying your company, too, Dorian, which is interesting considering I feared the idea of you for so long."

"Well, I'm glad you don't fear me anymore."

"You haven't given me a reason to—yet. Doesn't seem like the dogs fear you, either. I haven't heard them barking lately."

"Hard to fear someone you've been sleeping with."

I stopped chewing. "Sleeping?"

Dorian shrugged. "I came home one night to find them in my bed. It was late, and I was too damn tired to kick them out. So I got under the covers and accepted that they were there. Now they won't leave me alone."

Laughing, I pointed my fork at him. "Let that be a lesson to be careful about the mixed messages you give women."

He licked the corner of his mouth. "Wanna know the strange thing?"

"What?"

"I've actually come to depend on their snoring to help me sleep."

"Your dad would be proud."

"Probably the only thing he'd be proud about."

"I highly doubt that. You seem to be doing everything you can to make him proud."

He shook his head. "He always found reasons to criticize me. My father and I had a very difficult relationship. Things might've been easier if I'd had siblings. At least some of his attention would've been dispersed among us. Being his heir apparent wasn't a responsibility I signed up for. There are a lot of people who think I should be grateful for the empire he built. But it comes with a lot of headaches."

"Don't you have the option to sell the business and just live your life?"

He let out a long breath. "That's easier said than done. The need to please him doesn't just end because he's not physically here anymore. I'd feel a lot of guilt for throwing away everything he built. Not sure I could live with myself. I'm better off trying to figure out a way to put my own stamp on things while keeping it going, even if it kills me."

"I hope it *doesn't* kill you." I frowned. "Stress is no joke."

"I know," he said with a sigh.

"You're brave for taking it on when you could've walked away."

"A less-than-perfect life is better than no life at all. I've tried to just be grateful to be alive since they died. To pause and appreciate the little things."

"Like apple crisp late at night in the theater."

He smiled. "Like an unexpected connection with a mysterious artist."

That gave me chills. "You find me mysterious?"

"I do. You haven't shared too much about yourself. You come across as this carefree, creative, and caring person. While you appear to be an open book at first glance, you haven't offered me too much about your life before you came here."

I sighed. "The truth might not match up with your preconceived notions."

"That's okay." He set his plate on an adjacent chair. "I want to know anyway." He reached for my empty plate and set it atop his. He looked into my eyes, waiting for me to speak.

"I was a very sad and depressed person before moving to Orion Coast," I admitted. "Well, you know I'd lost my mom. It was hard for me to be back in Ohio without her. It's a weird feeling to have no family left. I'd always believed the only people to truly love you are your family. I had a few friends back home, but they were all busy with their boyfriends or jobs. For the first time in my life, I felt totally alone, like an adult orphan. It's strange to feel like if you died tomorrow, no one would be particularly devastated."

"I feel that in my soul, Primrose." He placed his hand on my arm. "I really do."

The contact sent shivers through me. "The decision to sell the Ohio house and move here was the easiest one I'd ever made."

"Did you feel less lonely here?"

"A little. Christina and I were never close enough for her to be anything like my mother. But the fact that she was my mother's sister made me feel closer to my mom." I took a deep breath. "The ocean brought me some peace, too. It was all so different from home, and that was what I needed at the time."

He rested his chin on his palm. "It was good for a while—until it wasn't, huh?"

I nodded. "After they died, I had to adjust to yet another new reality."

"I'd ask how that's going, but I understand, because I'm living it."

"I throw myself into my art. That's pretty much how I handle it. And I'm grateful to still have school to distract me. That's thanks to you for allowing me to live here, since I might've had to drop out if I had to pay for an apartment." I paused. "Anyway, I'd stopped practicing my craft for a while back in Ohio, but enrolling in art school ensures that I stick to it."

"What do you hope to achieve long term?"

"I don't expect miracles. If my art ends up in some big gallery someday, I wouldn't be mad at that." I smiled. "But honestly, I'd be just as happy as an art teacher. As long as I could still draw and paint for *me*, I'd be happy."

He stared at me so intently that I had to look away. "Should we start a movie?"

He looked over at the screen. "I almost forgot we were supposed to be watching one."

"We don't have to, if you'd rather keep talking."

"That's the weird thing, Primrose. I *do* want to keep talking, and normally I hate talking. But this isn't small talk. It's more meaningful. I could talk to you all night."

Dorian settled into his seat, turning toward me. My arm leaned against his a little, and I could feel the heat of his body. This had started to feel intimate, though not necessarily in a sexual way.

He went on to tell me stories about his childhood, growing up in the mansion. He said after his mom died, Benjamin was almost like a second father to him, since his dad worked so much. He told me his mother used to have a beautiful rose garden out back, but after she died, no one kept it up. He felt sad that he hadn't tried harder to maintain it in her memory.

I talked about my childhood, too, admitting that it wasn't the greatest. My mom had a lot of boyfriends, none of whom ever turned out to be the one for her. Watching her bad luck in the love department had made me wary of trusting men in general.

Dorian and I stayed in the theater talking well into the middle of the night.

And the movie never happened.

CHAPTER 8

The following morning, Patsy looked down at the apple crisp still on the stove.

"What is this dessert?"

Crap. Neither Dorian nor I had returned to the kitchen last night to put it away. I wasn't sure he'd want me spilling his Betty Crocker secrets. But considering I was a terrible liar and Patsy was staring at me, I decided to tell the truth.

"Dorian made it."

Her eyes widened. "Dorian?"

"Yes."

"Interesting. I wouldn't have taken him for a baker."

"Dorian made his mother's apple crisp?" Benjamin asked as he entered behind me.

"You knew about that recipe?" I smiled.

"Sure." Benjamin peeked into the tray. "Not a bad effort."

After he left the kitchen, I noticed Patsy looking at me funny.

"Hmm..." she said.

"What?"

"Nothing."

"Patsy, what is it?"

"Something going on between you and Mr. Vanderbilt?" she finally asked.

It sounded funny to hear Dorian referred to as *Mr. Vanderbilt*. Remington would always be the only Mr. Vanderbilt to me.

"Dorian and me?" I snorted uncomfortably. "No."

"But he made this for the two of you, yes?"

I'd never said anything about who he made it for, but perhaps the guilty look on my face gave me away. "Yes, but it was just a friendly gesture."

Patsy looked around then whispered, "You should be careful."

My stomach dropped. "Why do you say that?"

"Just that...if he's anything like his father, you should be careful about getting too close to him."

My chest tightened. "What *about* his father, specifically?"

Patsy's eyes began to water.

What the fuck? "What's going on?" I asked, looking over my shoulder to make sure we were still alone. "Why are you upset?" When she didn't clarify, I placed my arm gently around her. "Let's go sit."

We went to the breakfast nook.

Patsy stared out the window at the ocean. "There was a time before Remington married your aunt when he and I...got close."

Got close.

Oh.

Okay, for some reason, this was *not* where I'd thought things were going, even if the tears should've clued me in.

"You had a relationship with him?"

She nodded. "If you want to call it that."

Wow. Patsy and Remington Vanderbilt...

Holy shit.

Did not see this coming.

Was I naïve that this seemed so surprising? Despite only ever seeing her in a housekeeper's uniform, I knew Patsy was an attractive woman. She was older than my aunt, but I could certainly see why Remington might've been interested.

"How did it happen?"

"One night, I was working late. He asked me to stay and talk. I'd always had a secret crush on him. I mean, who wouldn't? He was a handsome guy, just like Dorian is. But I never thought he saw me in the same light."

"Why wouldn't he? You're beautiful."

"Well, thank you." She sighed, looking back out toward the ocean. "Anyway, that one night was the first of many where I stayed late. It wasn't sexual at first. He opened up to me a lot about his first wife, Dorian's mother, and his regrets when it came to her. He talked about how he got started in his business. He seemed very comfortable around me, and I think he trusted me." She paused.

My stomach tightened. This sounded a heck of a lot like what I'd been experiencing with Dorian.

"Eventually, one thing led to another. And things continued like that for several months."

"You were basically dating or..."

"Well, if you want to call it that. He never took me anywhere. That should have been the very first red flag. And he was careful never to define anything. But I was all too eager to play along because being with him was the most exciting thing that had ever happened to me. I wish I'd had the self-esteem to insist on better, but I just didn't at the time."

"So it went on for months, and then what?"

"Then one day, like clockwork, he stopped asking me to stay after my shift. He started working at the office later and avoiding me at home. When I confronted him about it, he admitted that he was sorry, but he couldn't continue what he'd started with me. He explained that he wasn't in any way ready for a relationship. He said he'd thought we were just enjoying spending time together, but he sensed I was getting attached, so he needed to nip it in the bud before I got hurt. He said he didn't want to continue to send me false messages about where things stood between us."

I felt so bad for her. "That must've been hard."

"He told me he hoped I wouldn't leave my position. And I made the difficult decision to stay. I didn't need to lose my job on top of everything else." She closed her eyes for a moment. "A few weeks later, he brought your aunt home for the first time."

"No…" My mouth dropped open in shock. "He left you for her?"

"He was never really *with* me. I believe now that he was just using me to pass the time until something better—in his eyes—came along. Someone he deemed worthy of him." She shook her head. "The truth is, men like the Vanderbilts don't stay with good women like you and me.

They end up with their own kind: rich, entitled—people with the same pedigree. They have a type. It's ingrained in them, whether they know it or not."

That assertion confused me a bit. "My aunt didn't come from money, though…"

"No. But she was successful when he met her and presented herself as worldly. She was glamorous and very good at adapting to his life. She was also thick-skinned and fit in well with the people he surrounded himself with. She was a level of beautiful that matched the image he wanted to portray to the outside world." Patsy smiled. "Don't get me wrong. You're just as beautiful as your aunt. But Christina was tough. She gave me the impression that if things didn't work out between them, she would just move on to someone else. You strike me as more like me: sensitive and vulnerable to the pain that comes from falling for a man who can never be with one woman."

Ouch.

Those words were hard to swallow. Mostly because she might've been right. Patsy was definitely pushing my buttons right now, bringing to the surface all the insecurities I had about my developing feelings for Dorian. This made me feel like my hopes were foolish. Perhaps any kind of future with Dorian was nothing more than a pipe dream.

"There's nothing going on with Dorian and me," I finally said.

"If you say so. I just want you to be careful. I don't know him well enough to understand what he's like. But I'm looking out for you."

It brought me some relief to know she didn't have any real basis for distrusting Dorian. But it made sense based on her experience with his father.

"I appreciate you sharing that with me, Patsy. I'm honestly still shocked. Does anyone else know?"

"I confessed everything to Benjamin some time ago. He picked up on the change in me after everything went sour. I needed to tell someone."

"Was he as surprised as I am?"

"Benjamin has been around here a lot longer than I have and has seen a lot of things, apparently. He said *nothing* surprised him when it came to Remington."

Interesting. "I don't understand how you were still able to work here, especially once he married my aunt. I don't think I'd be able to do that."

"A few reasons," she explained. "First, I really needed the job. I have a mortgage to pay. Second, I didn't want to let him win, which he would have if I'd cowered and run away. But I'm ashamed to admit, there was a part of me that still had feelings for him, even if they couldn't go anywhere after he married Christina. I wasn't ready to let the idea of him go."

Dread rose in my stomach. "And nothing happened between you and him once he was married to Christina?"

She reached her hand across the table. "I wouldn't have done that, Primrose. I hope you know that."

I let out the breath I'd been holding. "Well, I'm relieved to know he didn't try anything."

"He didn't try anything with me. But he wasn't faithful."

Nausea quickly returned, my stomach like a rollercoaster. "You know that for a fact?"

"Benjamin knew." She frowned. "Marrying Christina didn't change him."

"Wow. Okay. I suspected that maybe he'd cheated on my aunt after what Dorian told me about when Remington was married to his mom. But this confirms it."

Patsy sighed. "Every woman thinks she's gonna be the one to change a man. But you can't change who someone is. You're either a cheater or you're not." She shook her head. "And I didn't mean to imply that Dorian is automatically a cheater because of his dad. I'm just concerned for you. That's all."

If I were honest about my feelings and how fast I was falling for an unattainable man, I would've been concerned for me, too.

CHAPTER 9

A few days passed before I ran into Dorian again. It was especially unusual to see him home on a Saturday afternoon—with a guest.

When I entered the kitchen, I froze upon finding him standing with another man.

"Oh, hello." I waved.

"Hi there." The guy's face spread into a smile.

"Primrose, this is my buddy Chandler." Dorian looked over at him. "We grew up together."

"Oh wow. Nice to meet you." I smiled, offering my hand.

He took it and grinned. "The pleasure is all mine."

Running a hand over my hair, I turned to Dorian. "What are you guys up to?"

"We were just gonna hang out by the pool," Chandler answered.

My eyes widened. "Dorian is taking a day off to hang out by the pool?"

"I know, right?" Chandler laughed. "It's only because I've been calling him every day, torturing him to get together until he finally gave in. It's not easy getting this guy to give up a day of work."

"Well, enjoy your time together. I'm just gonna grab a drink and take it up to my room."

"Nonsense," Chandler said. "You should hang out with us."

No way was I going to join them unless Dorian invited me. I shook my head. "I wouldn't want to interrupt your guys' day."

"It's not a guys' day, actually. My wife, Candace, will be here soon," Chandler explained. "She's coming straight from an appointment, so we took separate cars. I think she'd appreciate some female company."

"Oh, I see."

It surprised me to learn Dorian had married friends. He seemed to be the quintessential bachelor. I'd assumed most of his friends were the same.

"You should join us," Dorian finally said.

In that case, sure. "Okay." I nodded. "I'll go get changed."

I had stuff to get done today, but I couldn't pass up the opportunity to meet Dorian's friends, even if just to satisfy my curiosity.

My stomach felt a bit unsettled as I headed upstairs, and I could identify a variety of possible reasons. Getting into a bathing suit in front of Dorian was at the top of the list. Not to mention meeting his friend's wife. Would we get along? Lord knows every other woman Dorian had brought around me had turned out to be a disaster. What if she was judgmental? I thought about my conversation with Patsy, how she was so sure men like Dorian went for a certain type of woman—one that wasn't anything like me. Chandler seemed nice enough, but he might've had the same taste.

Once upstairs, I slipped into a basic black bikini and threw a light, beachy dress over the top. I would not be taking it off unless I felt fully comfortable around them. I'd have to play this whole thing by ear. After finding some black flip-flops, I headed downstairs.

Outside at the pool, I was surprised to find that Chandler's wife had already arrived. She wore a scarf around her head. I thought maybe it was a style choice until she walked over to introduce herself.

"You must be Primrose." She beamed.

"I am. So great to meet you. Candace, right?" I offered my hand.

"Yes." She shook with me. "I have cancer. That's why I'm wearing the head wrap. Just thought I'd let you know, so you didn't have to wonder or ask me about it."

I couldn't help but admire her candor. I nodded. "How many times have you had to explain that to people?"

"I do it at the top of every introduction. Makes me feel better to get it out of the way."

"I totally get that."

"I normally wear a wig, but it's too damn hot today, and this cotton is pretty cool, while still protecting my head from the sun."

"Thank you for being so open. It must be exhausting feeling like you need to explain the situation to strangers."

"Well, thank *you* for not saying 'I'm sorry' when I told you I had cancer."

"There's nothing to be sorry about if you're happy and staying present." I smiled. "And you seem to be doing well, despite everything?"

"I am. I try my best not to let my mind go to the dark places. I'm living my life as Candace as best I can, not as a patient. It's important to stay busy and distracted. But most important, I have to surround myself with positive people."

I nodded. "When my mom had cancer, we had to shut out some friends who were real downers."

"Yeah…the ones who always feel compelled to tell you that their distant relative died of the same disease you have."

"That's the worst." I rolled my eyes.

"Is your mom…okay?"

My stomach dropped. "She passed a few years back." It killed me to have to admit that.

Her expression fell. "I'm sorry."

"It's okay."

Chandler walked over, interrupting our conversation. "It didn't take long for my beautiful wife to charm you, did it, Primrose?"

"Maybe all of thirty seconds."

Dorian grinned from behind him.

Candace and I moved to sit on lounge chairs while Dorian and Chandler opened the barbecue grill. She told me she and Chandler had both grown up with Dorian. They were all friends in school. I got the impression that Chandler and Candace also came from wealthy families, particularly since they went to the same private school.

Her eyes lit up when I told her I was an artist, and her excitement only grew when I showed her some photos of my paintings on my phone. She was so easy to talk to, and it was a huge relief to realize I might enjoy this afternoon instead of having to put on a front. I'd been planning to fake my way through the entire thing, but she made me feel so comfortable.

At one point, I went inside to use the bathroom, and I found Dorian alone in the kitchen, looking through the refrigerator.

I snuck up behind him. "Whaddya looking for?"

"Chandler brought a bunch of meat to grill, but we have no condiments. That was poor planning on my part. I'm gonna head to the market." He closed the refrigerator. "Wanna take a ride with me?"

I raised my shoulders. "Sure."

He told his friends we'd be back in a bit, and he and I got into his Porsche.

As he pulled out of the driveway, I turned to him. "They're really awesome. You have some nice friends there."

He glanced in my direction. "You're shocked I have *any* friends, aren't you?"

"I didn't say that. You did." I chuckled. "But yeah. You hadn't brought anyone around besides that one woman you said you used to hook up with, so I assumed maybe you'd lost touch with most of your friends from here."

"It doesn't get any better than Candace and Chandler. Truth is, I *have* lost touch with a lot of people over the years. But those two? They don't let you get away. I couldn't lose them if I tried. And I'm a lucky guy for it."

"Those are the best kind of friends," I said. Most of my friends from back home had gone by the wayside.

"I'm a bit ashamed, actually, that I didn't reach out to them as soon as I got back out here."

"Doesn't seem like they're mad about it…"

He suddenly pulled into a coffee shop drive-thru.

"You're getting a coffee?" I asked.

"I didn't have enough this morning, and I'm getting a headache. What do you want?"

"I'll take an iced vanilla latte. Thank you."

After he made it through the drive-thru, he parked.

"Shouldn't we be heading to the supermarket, so we can get back to your friends?"

"Yeah. I just wanted to enjoy this in peace for a bit and talk to you first."

Ah. Perhaps there was another purpose to this drive. "Talk to me about what?"

"About Candace, actually."

"Oh. Okay…"

He leaned his head on the back of the seat. "I feel like shit."

I stopped stirring my drink. "Why?"

"I think I was subconsciously avoiding seeing them because I was afraid I'd treat her differently and she'd see through it. I never want to make her uncomfortable. This is my first time seeing her…since the diagnosis."

"Why did you think you'd come across that way?"

"I get triggered around people with cancer because of my mother. I do my best not to let it show, but I'm not the best actor. That was partly why I avoided seeing them. But now that they've come over, I'm glad I didn't put it off any longer." He pulled back the lid on his coffee. "Not sure why, but I wanted to explain that to you. Maybe you can help keep me in check. Let me know if I'm coming across as weird at any point."

"Well, I've thought you were weird from the moment I met you." I winked. "Kidding, but did we even need condiments, or was this just an excuse to talk?"

"We did, actually."

"Okay." I sighed. "Candace told me she appreciates it when people treat her normally and don't make a big thing about her diagnosis. She doesn't want her life to be about the disease. I didn't ask her what kind of cancer she has. Do you know?"

"Ovarian." He stared out the windshield. "Same as my mother."

Now his reaction made even more sense.

"Oh." I nodded. "Have they mentioned her prognosis?"

Dorian shook his head. "She and Chandler don't like to talk about the details. I don't blame them."

"I think the best thing you can do is to stop avoiding them. Don't worry so much about how you're coming across. Just be present and enjoy your friends without trying to be perfect."

"You're right." He lifted his drink in a salute. "And I'm glad you happened to be home today, so you could join us."

"Me, too."

Trying to ignore what felt like a massive swarm of butterflies in my stomach, I stayed in the car and continued to sip my coffee as Dorian ran into the adjacent supermarket to grab the needed items.

When we got back to the house, Chandler wasted no time busting Dorian's balls.

"Where the heck did you go to get barbecue sauce, Timbuktu?"

Candace laughed as she sat at the edge of the pool, moving her feet around in the water.

Since she'd taken off her cover-up to reveal her impressive figure, I decided it was safe to take off my dress and join her. I couldn't help but notice Dorian's eyes veer in my direction as I sat down next to Candace.

"So..." she said, splashing the water with her toes. "You and Dorian?"

Quick to debunk her theory, I shook my head. "Oh no. No, no. We're just friends. I guess? Roommates..."

"You don't sound too certain about that," she noted. "Nothing *else* happening there?"

"Nothing." I grinned. "Is there a reason you thought it was more?"

"I just figured...two attractive people living together. It made sense that maybe things might've gotten...interesting." She shrugged. "I asked Chandler, but he said he wasn't sure. Dorian denied it, but Chandler still got a vibe."

Dorian denied it.

I cleared my throat. "Why does Chandler suspect something?"

"Dorian seemed a little coy when my husband asked him about it."

"It's not more than friendship right now," I repeated.

"Right *now*." She smirked. "Okay. I'll check back in a month, then."

I felt my cheeks burn. Why had I worded it like that?

Candace giggled. "Oh my gosh. I'm totally embarrassing you."

"Uh-oh. Why? Am I red?"

"Yes." She laughed. "I'm sorry. I was just being nosy."

Naturally, Candace's words regarding Chandler's *vibe* from Dorian weighed heavily on my mind all afternoon.

As the four of us eventually got in the pool together, I caught Dorian looking at my chest. And I might've noticed how well his wet swim trunks clung to him as well. Still, I warned myself not to get my hopes up. He'd given me no direct hint that he was interested in me as more than a friend.

After our swim, we enjoyed an impressive barbecue of steak, chicken, and shrimp, along with a delicious potato salad Candace had made.

It was one of the most fun afternoons I'd had in a long time. It felt like life had returned to this mansion for the first time since Remington and Christina died.

As the sun set, we returned to the lounge chairs after dinner. The mood of the evening changed in a way I never could've predicted when Candace uttered a simple sentence:

"Let's play a game."

CHAPTER 10

Who knew there was an entire stash of games in the pool house? Everything from old board games to various decks of cards. Candace had brought out a pile for us to choose from.

The four of us ended up playing Pictionary, which was innocent enough. There was another game in the bunch, though, that seemed anything *but* innocent. And while we'd all gotten a good laugh about it, we'd steered clear of that one.

After Candace and Chandler left, though, Dorian and I stayed out by the pool. It was dark now, the moon casting a glow over the patio. And the rainbow lights that lit up the pool at night created a sexy vibe.

"Who do you think is responsible for the sex card game?" I asked, gesturing to the box on the table.

It was called Toe the Line, a truth-or-dare-like game of sexually provocative questions. We had joked earlier about who it might've belonged to, but no one seemed to know.

Dorian stretched his legs out on the lounge chair. "What's your guess?"

"I'm gonna say it had to be Christina's."

"Maybe. Although I can't picture my father playing that game."

"But they had to have played it together. Who else would it belong to?"

"Maybe it's Benjamin's," Dorian suggested.

We both cracked up at the idea of straight-laced Benjamin stashing this game away.

I'd read the rules. You had to ask your opponent a sex-related question, and if they didn't want to answer, they were required to do a dare, one I assumed had to be sexual in nature.

I reached over and opened the box. "I must've had a little too much to drink because I would totally play this right now."

Dorian shifted in his seat. "I'm not sure that'd be a good idea."

"It would be a *terrible* idea," I agreed.

He looked up at the dark sky. "How bad do you think the questions are?"

"I guess there's only one way to find out." I took out the cards. Flipping over the first one, I read it in silence. "This isn't that bad," I said. "It's dumb, actually."

"What is it?"

I read from the card. "What's your favorite sexual position and why?"

He stared out toward the pool. "That's predictable and lame."

"Right?"

I let out a breath and waited, looking over at him.

He turned to me. "Are you asking me to answer it?"

"Only if you want to play."

"What's the dare option?"

I laughed a little as I read it. "Try to turn someone on just by looking at them."

"So...stare at you like Zoolander and expect you to get hot and bothered?"

"Basically."

"I'll answer the question."

"Thanks for sparing me."

He scratched his chin. "My favorite sexual position is holding a woman up with her legs wrapped around me, one hand around her ass, and the other pulling her hair while I fuck her."

Holy crap.

Hearing those words exit his mouth—particularly "*fuck her*"—made the muscles between my legs tighten. If I'd thought I was hot and bothered before, now I was a goner.

I swallowed. "That's...nice."

"What about you?" he asked.

Your favorite position sounds pretty damn good to me. "That's not how the game works," I replied. "You answer the question, and you get a point. I don't answer the same question. Now you pick a different card for me to answer."

"All right, then." He sat up, reaching for a card. "This one is even lamer."

I sat up. "Oh good. I'm counting on lame."

"You cannot get *any* lamer than this one," he said before reading it. "Name three things that turn you on that have nothing to do with sex."

How did I get so lucky? I giggled. "I don't need to know the dare. This is easy."

"I'm listening." He threw the card aside.

"One is…men reading," I said.

Flashing me a look of disbelief, he crossed his arms. "Really…"

"Oh my God, yes. There's something so sexy about it. Related to that, men in glasses." I shivered. "That's number two. And number three is…libraries."

"I'm sensing a theme here. But the library? Doesn't exactly scream *sex* to me."

I sighed deeply. "There's something about a library. The echo. The windows. The smell of the books. It reminds me of sex, even though it has nothing to do with sex. I have this fantasy where I'm browsing the book aisle in an empty library, and a man comes up behind me, pulls my hair, and kisses me. Then we…you know…up against the bookshelves."

"Very interesting."

"You don't think that's weird?"

"No. I don't judge anyone for what gets them off. We can't help what we like. It's nature."

"Do you want to keep playing?"

"I never said I wanted to play in the first place."

"Okay, hardass. I'll put the game away." I stacked the cards to put them back into the box.

"But actually, I'm enjoying it. So let's keep going," he said.

"Okay." My skin tingled as I took one of the cards. *Oh boy*. I felt my face blush as I read the sentence aloud. "What did you think about the last time you masturbated?"

He rubbed between his brows. I assumed he was pondering the answer. But instead, he asked, "What's the dare?"

Feeling my pulse race, I gulped as I looked down at the dare section. *Oh my*. "Do a body shot off of your opponent."

"I see." His jaw tightened.

He didn't say anything else. Adrenaline coursed through my veins with every second that went by.

I cleared my throat. "Well?"

"The body shot is not exactly my decision to make. You'd have to consent to that. If you're okay with it, I'd like to take the dare."

All the blood in my body rushed to my vagina. "Yeah, I don't care," I said nonchalantly, trying my best to keep calm at the prospect of Dorian's mouth coming anywhere near me, let alone *on* me.

"Hope you'll join me for a shot, though. Tequila or vodka?"

"Tequila. Always."

He stood from his lounge chair and went to the small bar at the corner of the pool area. A mild evening breeze blew through my hair as I waited, my body brimming with excitement.

Dorian returned, carrying a few items. He handed me a shot glass filled with tequila blanco. I downed it and handed it back. He then filled it again.

"Lie down," he commanded.

"No hands. That's the rule," I teased.

"I know how to do it," he assured me.

Goose bumps covered my body as I did as he said, lying back on the lounge chair. Dorian placed a lime wedge in my mouth, which I held between my teeth. My chest heaved as I waited for what was to come.

Next, he sprinkled salt along my neck. It tickled. *Is he really gonna lick me?*

Dorian then poured a shot of tequila in a slow stream into my belly button. The alcohol stung my skin. But the feeling was nothing compared to the arousal building in me at the thought of what he might do.

He knelt beside my lounge chair. Desire pooled between my legs as his mouth lowered to my neck. I flinched at the first contact. Dorian ran his tongue along the nape where he'd placed the salt, the heat of his breath practically lighting me on fire. *Oh. My. God.* The feel of his tongue on my skin was indescribable. Yearning to pull on his inky black hair, I closed my eyes, relishing every second of the electrifying feeling. When I'd watched people taking body shots before, everything seemed to move a lot faster than this. But Dorian was taking his time. And I didn't mind one bit. I opened my eyes and watched him lick his lips as he moved away from my neck.

The wait for something else felt like torture. But I knew nothing yet. Because a moment later, he lowered his mouth to my stomach. The sensation of his tongue lapping up the tequila in my navel was next-level arousing. He sucked my skin to sop it all up, then licked the last remnants with his tongue. I writhed, wishing he'd go lower, even if that certainly wasn't part of the task at hand.

His breathing grew faster as he moved off my stomach and brought his face to mine, lowering his mouth to my lips and gently sinking his teeth into the lime. Somehow, he managed not to even graze my lips. Was he intentionally torturing me? My loins quivered as I watched him suck on the lime, my body desperate for more.

Then he tossed the lime aside and suddenly stepped away. It seemed we'd reached the end. Except my body hadn't gotten the message. My nipples were stiff, alert, and waiting for more. My bikini bottom was soaked. I'd never wished harder for someone to go down on me.

But Dorian returned to his seat as if nothing had happened—as if he hadn't just rocked my world. He deserved an award for bouncing back into a composed state.

I wanted to continue lying there, but I forced myself to sit up. Trying to seem unaffected, I cleared my throat. "Are we done with the game?"

He licked his lips. "I could keep going."

This might kill me. "Your turn to ask a question, then."

He reached for a card. "Have you ever had a fantasy about an inappropriate person?"

Another easy one for me.

"My high school teacher, Mr. Eaton. I used to fantasize about him. He wore sweater vests and glasses." I tilted my head. "What about you?"

"You're forgetting the game doesn't work that way. I don't need to answer that." He grinned. "I'm kidding. I don't care. It was my friend Evan's mother, actually."

"Really. She was hot?"

"Very. I fantasized about her a lot when I was a teenager."

My cheeks burned with jealousy. I wanted him to want *me*, not "Evan's mother," and I was more confused than ever right now. I knew he thought I was attractive, but this man could likely have any woman he wanted and had given me no reason to believe he'd ever try anything outside of this game. As erotic as that body shot had been, he'd stuck to the rules when he very easily could've taken advantage of me. Lord knows, I'd hoped he would.

"What was the dare that I missed, by the way?" I asked.

"You would've had to send a naughty text to someone in the room. Given that it's just me here, I suppose I missed out." He winked.

I wondered how I would've handled that. Would I have told him once and for all how much I wanted him and watched as he pretended I was kidding when I really wasn't?

It was my turn to ask a question, and I reached for a card. "How many times a week do you pleasure yourself?"

"How many times a week or how many times a day?"

Okay, then. I let out a shaky breath. "I guess either?"

"What's the dare?"

My heart began to race. "Slowly and seductively kiss someone in the room."

Pick the kiss.

Pick the kiss.

Seconds passed, and this felt like the longest silence of my life. My heart pounded, my body begging for the right answer.

"I would say I do it about once a day," he finally said.

Fuck.

I felt like I was a balloon and he'd just popped me, leaving me deflated. His response brought on a mix of emotions. On one hand, it felt like a slap in the face, since he'd clearly chosen *not* to kiss me. On the other hand, the visual of him pleasuring himself got me hot and bothered all over again.

I cleared my throat. "So, seven times a week."

"Give or take. If I have a particularly stressful day, I might do it more than once."

I needed this game to end—not only because I somehow felt rejected, but because I wanted to go relieve *myself* right now. He'd gotten me all worked up. I hadn't been this aroused in as long as I could remember, my body aching to be kissed, licked, sucked.

But he'd made the decision to do none of those things.

Before I could excuse myself, though, Dorian made an announcement.

"We should really go upstairs."

Wait.

What?

It aggravated me that I didn't know whether he was propositioning me or explaining that he wanted to go to sleep.

I knew what *I* was hoping for—which was crazy. He and I *lived together*, for Christ's sake. Crossing the friendship line would be a terrible idea. Maybe I was delusional about the possibility of a deeper meaning to *go upstairs*? But the way he'd said it...

I closed up the game and returned it with the rest of them to the pool house because I needed a breather.

After, we left the patio together, and I followed him upstairs, my heart pumping faster with each second that passed. The vibe was still unreadable.

I decided to take a chance, not immediately heading to my room, but stopping at his room when he did. The sight of Tallulah and Tess sleeping soundly at the foot of his bed caused me to smile despite my nerves.

"You weren't kidding. Look how comfortable they are," I said from the doorway.

He didn't say anything, and the anticipation nearly killed me. I still had no idea what was happening here. Were we about to continue our evening together in a *different* way, or was that all in my head?

If you leave, you'll never know.

Dorian slipped his hands into his pockets as he stood across from me.

Is he waiting for me to go? Or is he thinking about whether taking things further is a good idea?

I had heard him say we should go upstairs, right?

Never in my life had I made the first move. But also never in my life had I wanted someone as much as I wanted Dorian Vanderbilt right now. He'd gotten me so riled up tonight that I was apparently willing to risk humiliation for the chance to satisfy this unprecedented hunger inside me.

The words escaped me before I could think better of them.

"Would you...want to come to my room?"

His eyes widened as he stood there, mouth open.

Oh no.

I really needed to learn to read people because I was dead wrong about him being interested in more than just a game.

Shit.

"I can't, Primrose," he said.

Backtrack.

Backtrack.

"Of course! That was dumb." I shook my head. "Goodnight."

"Wait!" he called after me.

I fumbled over my words, continuing to hurry away. "You're right. It's late. Goodnight!"

After running down the hall to my room, I closed the door and leaned my back against it, trying to calm myself after the horror of the situation I'd put myself in.

Eventually I forced myself to crawl into bed, pulled the covers over my head, and prayed for sleep to claim my humiliation.

CHAPTER 11

For an entire week, I'd done nothing but go straight to my room after entering the house each day. I'd also been making sure Dorian's car wasn't in the garage and would bypass the kitchen altogether to avoid running into him. I'd pop in there to say hello to Benjamin or Patsy briefly, but that was only if I was absolutely sure Dorian wasn't home. I hated being outside of my bedroom too long on the off-chance he came home unexpectedly.

Since it was unlike me to be so withdrawn, I'd told the staff I was busy working on a new art project, which technically wasn't a lie. That left me free to stay in my room all night until it was time to leave for class the next morning.

My friend Janelle and I were eating lunch outside on campus this afternoon when I'd finally filled her in on my judgment faux pas with Dorian last week.

"Maybe he has a good reason for not wanting to go there with you," she suggested.

"That doesn't take away the humiliation and my fervent wish that I could take it all back."

She ate a spoonful of yogurt. "How the hell are you managing to avoid him?"

"It's not hard. He's almost never home. The only chance of running into him is if I use the theater or the kitchen. So I've been careful to avoid both." I picked at my salad.

"How do you avoid the kitchen, though?"

"I just eat out or starve. Takeout coffee is my friend. I do miss my tea at night."

"Damn. You can't live like that forever, Primrose."

"Watch me." I exhaled. "I'd move out if I could afford it. Anyway, if he wanted to talk to me, he knows where my room is. He could knock on my door. But he hasn't. All the more reason I don't regret avoiding him." Still so angry at myself, I shook my head. "The one time! The one time in my twenty-three years that I decide to take my shot, and look where it got me."

She shrugged. "I'm still proud of you for taking a chance. It takes balls to do what you did. And why should women always stand by and wait for men to make the first move?"

"Because they could get shot down and have to hide from the world after."

"He was the one who encouraged the body shot, though, right? I would've totally bet he was down for more after that."

"Well, clearly he wasn't. He was just playing the game."

"At least you know where things stand now instead of wasting weeks pining over him, thinking something's going to happen."

I thought back to Patsy's confession and advice. She was right. *Men like Dorian and his father don't go for ordinary women.* What other reason could he have for turning me down? He'd told me he thought I was attractive, and yet when given the opportunity—nothing.

I looked away, thinking back to better times, before my embarrassing rejection. "The anticipation had been kind of fun. I miss the excitement of wondering whether he and I would run into each other. But you're right. The letdown would've been worse if more time had passed. Apparently, I'd been living in a delusional state."

She perked up. "How about we go out this Friday? Help you forget about what's-his-name billionaire?"

"I don't know." I sulked.

"It's a good excuse to get out of the house," she said, scraping up the last of her yogurt. "Even less of a chance of running into him."

"Now that you put it that way, yeah. Sure, why not?"

• • •

That evening, I decided to make myself productive at home.

One of the things Dorian and I had discussed over caviar and Hot Cheetos a couple of weeks ago was what to do with my aunt's clothing, handbags, and shoes.

He'd asked if I would be willing to go through everything, figure out what I wanted to keep and what should be donated. I'd told him I'd be happy to, but I hadn't yet done it.

Since I hadn't heard the garage door open, that meant Dorian was not home from work. I took the opportunity to leave my room and head down the hallway to her old bedroom.

Remington and Christina had shared an enormous walk-in closet. Her clothing was on one side and his on the other. Even though it was *supposed* to be a closet, the space was pretty much an entire room—at least the size of my bedroom, if not a bit bigger.

A chill ran through me as I glided my hand across Christina's clothes. Some of the items still smelled like her perfume. Everything was organized by category. There were a dozen gowns, many with sequins, all in a row. She loved blazers and silk scarves. And the shoe collection? Nothing to scoff at. Mostly designer heels, each pair with a dedicated shelf featuring its own recessed lighting.

As beautiful as the closet was, there was nothing happy about this experience. I hadn't properly prepared myself for how emotional it would be to look through her personal items. It was sometimes possible to forget what had happened, but being in here, immersing myself in all of her things, served as a harsh reminder that she was no longer here to enjoy them. Life was unfair.

What good was having wealth if it could all end in an instant? You can't take any of it with you. And I suppose none of it matters if you're not happy in life. Christina may or may not have been happy in her final days. She and I weren't close enough to delve that deep. If what Patsy said was true—that Remington wasn't faithful to my aunt—

Christina might've been hiding some pain. Either that, or she was being lied to. I'd never know.

The more I sifted through her clothing, the more I felt wrong about keeping anything that wasn't rightfully mine. I didn't want to inherit something from my aunt solely because she'd died. I decided the best course of action would be to give all the clothes and shoes to charity, rather than picking out certain things. The latter felt like greedy entitlement. It also felt easier to give it all away and not have to think about each item and the memories that would never be made.

I froze at the sound of footsteps.

Then came his voice from behind me. "Well, of all the places I imagined I'd find you tonight, this wasn't on my list."

Shit. I turned slowly. "How did you know I was in here?"

"I noticed the bedroom door open. Thought that was a little weird. So figured I'd check things out."

"You aren't supposed to be home at this time."

"Spoken like someone who's specifically trying to make sure she avoids me."

"I'm not gonna deny that."

"You shouldn't. You're a master at it lately."

"Apparently not anymore."

"Actually, I came home early hoping I'd catch you. I knew you wouldn't be expecting me, and I figured your guard would be down."

"Why do you want to see me?"

"I think you know why."

"It's not necessary to talk about it."

"I think it is. You ran off before you let me explain *why* I said no to you."

Cut right to the chase, why don't you? Cringing, I took a seat on the floor and crossed my legs. "I don't need to be reminded of that night. But you reminded me there's a very good reason I'd never made the first move before."

"I *loved* that you made the first move."

"I could tell," I said sarcastically.

He joined me on the ground and situated himself on the side of the closet that housed his father's clothes. A waft of his amazing scent registered, and I felt my body tingle. *Damn it.*

"Technically, it wasn't the first move, though," he said. "That was all mine when I licked that body shot off of you."

My nipples stiffened.

"I was having a little too much fun with that game," he added. "And the last thing I wanted to do was continue to take advantage of the situation. We'd both been drinking that night."

"Nice try. But we weren't drunk. Just buzzed. I knew what I was doing."

"Me, too. But any amount of alcohol messes with your inhibitions."

He had a point, but unfortunately, I hadn't been anywhere near under the influence enough to forget my humiliation.

"There's so much more to why I didn't take you up on your offer, Primrose." He exhaled. "I don't know if I've properly articulated just how hard it was for me to come back to California. It took me a month to leave Boston and face everything. I'd imagined that coming back to this empty place and getting thrown headfirst into my father's unfinished business was going to be the most horrible experience of my life. But then there was you, an unexpected light in this miserable darkness. Someone who not only had also just been through losing someone, but who seemed to make me smile at every turn."

I listened quietly, unable to come up with anything to say.

"No one has captivated me like you have. Every time I talk to you, it's the highlight of my day. I look forward to the moments we run into each other."

Desperate to get the formal rejection over with, I interrupted. "Fine. So you want to be friends. You like me, but you're not attracted to me in a physical way. No need to say more. I said it before you had to. I get it. Really. You don't need to explain any—"

"That could not be further from the truth. I think you're stunning." His eyes seared into mine. "But you said yourself that you're a serial monogamist. And I'm not relationship material—at least at this point in my life. Given that we live together, becoming anything more than friends would make our lives very complicated. I know you're not the type to just fuck and forget about it. Nor do you deserve that. I want you to have everything you truly desire. I'm just not the right person to give it to you."

What he said made a lot of sense.

After a moment, I nodded. "I'm sorry I put you in a position to have to reject me."

"It wasn't rejection. It was restraint." He looked into my eyes. "What about my licking your body made you think I wasn't interested? I *did* want to go to your room. More than anything I'd wanted in a long time. For once in my life, though, I'm trying to do the responsible thing when it comes to a woman I've grown to care about." He leaned toward me. "Make no mistake, I *do* care about you, Primrose, even though we haven't known each other that long."

I sighed. Maybe this whole thing was for the best. I didn't want to lose him, either. There was no one else on Earth who understood the loss we'd both endured. I needed to grow up about this and be happy *one* of us was being mature.

"I can respect that. And I'll try not to take it personally."

"Can you? Because you constantly checking to make sure I'm not home sucks. I feel like if I hadn't come home early tonight, I might not have seen you for another week."

"If you're barely home, how could you be so sure I was avoiding you?"

"There are cameras all over the house. Do you know how many times they've alerted me that someone was in the garage? And then I'd check it to find you peeking at the bay where I park."

"Shit." I closed my eyes briefly and had to laugh at myself. "I'm sorry if I've made things uncomfortable."

"It doesn't have to be that way unless we make it so."

"I don't want to avoid you anymore," I muttered.

"Good, because I miss running into you."

"And *I* miss my tea in the kitchen."

"Ouch." He laughed. "You've been avoiding the kitchen because of me?"

"Somewhat. I'm excited to make my triumphant return." I sighed. "I'm glad you found me in here tonight. The hiding did need to end."

"Were you looking for another hiding place or going through your aunt's things?"

"Finally garnered the courage to look through her stuff. I decided I'm just gonna donate it all."

"There's *nothing* you want to keep?"

"I don't need any of it."

"I think you should keep at least one thing. You might regret it if you don't."

"Are you keeping anything of your father's?"

"Well, he's left me an entire mess of a company. So I don't feel like I need a Brooks Brothers shirt…or a set of cufflinks." He stood and flipped through his dad's clothes. "But I probably will keep a couple of things that remind me of him specifically. I'd been putting off coming in here, too. If I hadn't noticed the light on in the room and the door slightly open, it might've been months before I ventured into this closet."

I looked down at a pair of leather boots. "It's eerie being among their things, isn't it?"

He nodded. "Absolutely."

"It makes you feel like they're coming back," I whispered.

Dorian ran his hand along his dad's shirts. "I think I'm gonna follow your lead. Spare myself the misery of having to go through it all piece by piece." He turned to me. "We should donate it all this week. I'll have Benjamin hire someone to come in and take everything." He paused. "And then I think you should use this space as an art room.

Move into the main bedroom. That way you can have all your stuff in one area of the house."

My eyes widened. "What?" *Jesus*. Was this the consolation prize for being turned down?

"The shelves in here can easily house your supplies, and it'll be a better use for the space."

Guilt washed over me as I looked at the shelves that currently held my aunt's large shoe collection, unable to imagine canisters of paint and brushes replacing them. But it was hard to turn down the offer. The lighting in here was superb, and I could really use a space of my own to work.

"Are you serious?"

He nodded. "This is the best bedroom in the house. It shouldn't go to waste. Unless you're not comfortable sleeping where they did. I'd understand that, too. I'll have Benjamin order you all new linens."

"That's generous of you, but it's not necessary. The linens are beautiful."

"Nothing else will become of this space if you don't want it."

I didn't have to think too hard. "Okay, then I'm gonna take you up on that. Thank you."

"You're welcome."

Dorian took one of Remington's shirts off the rack and stared down at it for a moment.

My emotions got the best of me as I blurted, "I hope they're in a better place."

He looked up at me. "Me, too."

"I guess *we're* the ones left to feel the pain, huh?"

"I haven't let myself feel much of anything." Dorian smiled sadly as he looked down at the shirt again. "I gave him this for Christmas years back. I'm surprised he still had it. I remember being all proud that I'd picked it out because I knew it was his taste. When Dad opened the box, I remember him telling me what he *really* wanted for Christmas was for me to get a four-point-oh." Dorian shook his head. "I had a three-point-fucking-nine."

"He was really a perfectionist, huh?"

"A brilliant man and a perfectionist when it came to himself or anything he considered an extension of himself, yeah." He shook his head. "It was like he looked at me and saw all of his own imperfections amplified."

"Well, I think a three-point-nine is pretty freaking great."

"I thought so, too, until he rained on my parade. The next semester I had a four-point-oh though. Pleasing him was always my biggest motivator. Maybe because he was so hard to impress. Getting his approval always felt like a huge victory."

He hung the shirt back on the rack and sat back with me on the ground. The nearness of his body was immediately all I could think about. I didn't know how to feel anymore. On one hand, he'd closed the door on anything happening between us. On the other, he'd admitted he wanted to sleep with me. I really needed to detach from that glimmer of hope.

"Well, wherever your father is now, I'm certain he sees that the need for perfection was just the ego playing tricks."

"You think he's looking down with a different attitude?"

"I don't know for certain, but I can't imagine anything that happens here on Earth carries any weight when you get to the next phase of existence—certainly not perfect grades or money. I feel like superficial things are just tricks to see if we can overcome temptation and realize that the only important things are the people we care about."

"I wish I could believe that. I still feel so imprisoned by the need to ensure that he'd be happy with me. As if he has nothing better to do than continue judging me from the afterlife."

I nodded. "Ingrained beliefs are pervasive. Wanting to please your father is one thing. Making yourself sick in the process or feeling like even your best isn't good enough is a losing game, though."

Dorian shook his head. "How the fuck are you so wise at twenty-three?"

I shrugged. "I had to grow up fast when my mom died. When you're alone, you have no choice but to find strength from within. You have to be your own biggest supporter, learn to talk to yourself a lot. I had to let go of the false beliefs holding me back because I no longer had the energy for them."

"I wanna be you when I grow up."

I smiled, my gaze wandering over to a sparkly, emerald green gown. The lighting made the sequins shimmer. I stood and walked over to it. "This is beautiful, huh?"

"You should try it on."

I looked back at him. "Wouldn't that be weird?"

"Not at all. Someone will end up wearing it. Why not you?" He stood and turned so his back was facing me. "Try it on and tell me when."

The way he'd indirectly encouraged me to disrobe made my body come alive. *Foolish*.

And yet I listened, my nipples hard from merely his voice, the memory of his tongue on my skin all too fresh. After I pulled my crop top over my head, I kicked my pants off. Slipping into the silk-lined, beaded gown felt surreal. It was even heavier than it looked, practically weighing me down. I began to zip the back but couldn't get it all the way up.

"It's safe," I said.

Dorian turned around and smiled. "You look absolutely magnificent in that dress, Primrose."

I didn't *need* to zip it all the way up, but I was a glutton for punishment who wanted to feel his hands on me, even for a moment, and even if that would be torture.

I cocked my head. "Do you mind helping me with the zipper?"

His Adam's apple bobbed. "Of course."

Dorian took a few steps toward me and I turned around, giving him my back. The heat of his body made my skin prickle. As his hand slid up my spine to close the zipper, I shut my eyes, imagining that he was touching me for other reasons, imagining his tongue on my body again, this time drawing a line up my back.

"Sorry if I pulled your hair," he said as the zipper snagged for a moment near the top.

"I don't mind my hair pulled," I blurted, wondering instantly whether I'd meant to be so suggestive.

Dorian cleared his throat as he finished zipping me up.

I turned to face him, all too pleased by the sight of his eyes traveling the length of my body. He might not have been touching me anymore, but his eyes devoured me. If they were any indication, he was second-guessing his decision to turn me down.

I moved over to look at myself in the floor-length mirror. "I'm a little curvier than she was. Shorter, too."

Dorian stood behind me. "Nothing wrong with that."

"Nothing the right bra and a good hem can't fix, I suppose." I brazenly pushed my breasts together, enjoying the way his Adam's apple bobbed again.

He cleared his throat. "I think you should keep this gown."

After a moment, I nodded. "Wearing it could be something to look forward to in the future."

"Why in the future?"

"I don't have anywhere to wear this now." I turned to him. "But maybe if my art sells big someday, and I get invited to some fancy gala, I can wear it."

"*When* your art sells big. Not *if*."

"Don't even think about buying my pieces out of pity, Vanderbilt."

He laughed. "What made you think I was thinking that?"

"I don't know. Maybe because you also offered to pay my tuition."

He shook his head. "I wasn't thinking I could buy your art."

"Oh…" Well, now I felt dumb.

"I was thinking I could probably buy you a gallery of your own."

My mouth fell open. "Please don't do that. And don't ever buy my art, either. I'd never know if it was any good if someone I knew bought it."

"Trust me. You're good. I get it, though. I won't buy it if that upsets you."

I decided to go out on a limb. "Well, now that you've promised you won't buy my art, I can invite you to the Institute's art show. Don't feel obligated. But I figured I'd mention it, since I don't have any family here or anyone else to ask." I chewed my bottom lip.

"When is it?"

"Thursday night."

He pulled up the calendar on his phone. "I'll be there. Thank you for telling me."

"I don't want you going out of pity, though. Go only if you want to."

He looked into my eyes. "I promise you. I want to go."

"Okay."

"What are you showing?" he asked.

"The monkeys. And also a flower series you haven't seen."

He smiled. "I'll be looking forward to it."

CHAPTER 12

The exhibition hall for the art show was starting to empty. Most of the people who remained were either staff or students. And me? I was crushed.

"Why do you keep looking at the door?" Janelle asked.

Trying to keep my eyes from welling up, I played dumb. "Am I?"

"Yeah."

"Didn't realize it."

There were only a few minutes left of the show, and Dorian hadn't come. I didn't realize how much him being here mattered until he apparently stood me up. Almost every person here had someone who'd come to cheer them on—except for me. It cast a spotlight on something I'd tried to bury: the painful fact that I was essentially alone in this world. I'd made it seem like it didn't matter whether or not he came, yet I still couldn't help feeling let down. In my head, Dorian was my person, someone I could count on, even if things weren't romantic between us. But that was just another delusion.

"Hey, Primrose."

I turned to find Brandon Wright standing next to me. Brandon was a fellow artist who had graduated from the Institute several years back. He now served as a student advisor and mentor. I knew he had done really well in the industry, having sold several paintings, some to celebrity clients.

"Hi." I managed a smile.

"I didn't want to interrupt you earlier. Every time I looked over, someone was talking your ear off. But I didn't want to leave without congratulating you on the show. Your pieces are exquisite."

"Thank you," I said, forcing myself to perk up. "That means a lot coming from you."

"You should look happier than you do this evening," he told me.

"Oh..." I shook my head, ready to deny it.

"This business—it's a marathon, not a sprint, you know? I know how hard it is to stay the course when some days it seems like the only person you're creating for is yourself. There's little reward for most people, but I believe those who are talented will find success. So even if your paintings didn't sell tonight, just know that the longer you stay the course, the better things will get."

"Like you..." I nodded. "You're doing so great now."

He shrugged. "I'm hardly successful, but I'm getting there."

Brandon had long brown hair past his shoulders and a beard. He was handsome and sort of resembled Johnny Depp's character from *Pirates of the Caribbean*.

"I saw your exhibit on the faces of homelessness at the gallery in downtown L.A.," I told him. "The people you created look so realistic. And the message was obviously profound."

"When did you go?"

"When it first opened. I think on the second day."

"You should've let me know. I would have met you there." He paused. "Actually...are you busy tomorrow night? I'd love to hang out, talk more, if you're around."

Caught off guard, I waited before responding, unsure whether he was asking me out. But I shouldn't pass up the opportunity to connect with him in any case.

"I had plans to go out with a friend to Juno Bar," I finally answered.

"A *guy* friend or...?"

So he *was* asking me out.

"A female friend. You know her. Janelle Ainsley." I looked around. "She's still here somewhere."

"Ah." He nodded. "Would you want some company, then?"

I hesitated a moment because I wasn't a hundred-percent sure I wanted to *go there* with Brandon. But ultimately, I had no reason to say no.

"That'd be great, yeah," I said.

"Perfect." He smiled. "I'd love to get to know you better."

"That would be nice."

He rubbed his hands together. "Cool."

"We're supposed to be meeting there around eight."

"Eight's great. I'll touch base with you by text tomorrow to make sure everything is still on."

After we exchanged numbers, I said, "I really appreciate you coming out tonight, Brandon."

"I wouldn't have missed it."

Then one of my professors came by to say hello.

Brandon whispered, "See you tomorrow night," as he excused himself and left.

The moment he was gone, Dorian's absence returned to the forefront of my mind. As I finished talking with my teacher, I decided that if I ran into Dorian at the house later, I wouldn't even say anything. I'd let him figure out that he'd forgotten. Or maybe he didn't. Maybe he simply decided against coming. He probably didn't want to lead me on any more than he already had. Either way, I had to play like it didn't matter. I wouldn't give him the satisfaction of knowing it had hurt me.

. . .

The longer I could stay out of the house the better, so I asked Janelle if she wanted to stop at a bar after the event. She agreed, and then I spent most of that time out stewing in silence over Dorian's absence this evening.

When I finally got home, it was late, and I was shocked to find Dorian sitting in the living room. He stood the moment I entered, as if he'd been waiting for me to come back.

"Hi..." I said, trying to appear casual. It was comical that I'd ever thought I could hide my feelings from him. My emotions were about to explode out of my head, so I was certain they were written all over my expression.

"I thought you'd never come home."

"I went out," I said.

"Were you out with that Jesus-looking guy I saw you with at the art show?"

My eyes widened. "What?"

"I'm so sorry about tonight, Primrose." He shook his head. "If I'd had your number, I would've called. Why the fuck don't I have your phone number?"

"Wait." I blinked. "You came to the art show?"

He scrubbed a hand over his face. "I had meetings all day in L.A. Traffic was absolute hell getting back from the city to Orion Coast. I even left early, but there must've been like three accidents. I got to your event just as everything was ending. When I walked in, you were deep in conversation with some man, and I felt awkward interrupting you, especially when they were closing down the event. I'd already missed it. So I opted to leave and explain the situation to you later, rather than interrupt your conversation. Except *later* was much later than I thought it would be."

I expelled a breath. "I came home tonight determined to not let you see how upset I was that you weren't there. I was never gonna mention it to you. I feel like a fool for assuming you didn't care enough to come." I sighed. "But you absolutely should've interrupted my conversation."

"It didn't feel right for some reason. In retrospect, though, I agree. I should've let you know I was there. I've been anxious all night that you thought I'd forgotten or chose not to show." He hesitated. "But I got a vibe that something might've been going on with you and that guy. I didn't want you to have to explain me to him or have him make assumptions." He paused. "Who is he?"

"Brandon Wright. He's a local artist."

"*Would* I have been interrupting something?"

"He did ask to go out tomorrow night."

Dorian swallowed hard. "I was right, then."

"You still could've interrupted."

His face reddened. Or maybe it was my imagination. Maybe I wanted to *believe* Dorian was jealous, that it served him right after rejecting me. It also could've been in my head. In any case, the fact that I cared so much about what he thought was unfortunate.

I tried to downplay it. "It's not really a date. I'd planned to go to Juno Bar with Janelle anyway. When he asked me if I wanted to hang out, I told him I'd be there if he wanted to stop by."

"Seems like a date to me," Dorian insisted, wearing an unreadable expression. "You like him?"

I like you. I shrugged. "I don't know much about him, other than he's a talented artist."

"He'd be a good fit for you, then, right?"

"Not necessarily. I've never dated another artist. They tend to be moody and unpredictable."

His eyes stayed on mine for a moment. "Anyway... Big lesson learned tonight. I should have your phone number. I hadn't realized I didn't until I couldn't reach you."

I handed my phone to him. "Enter your number. I'll send you a text so you can program me in."

As he took the phone, the brush of his hand sent a flash of desire through me. I watched as he entered his information. When he gave it back to me, I texted him the middle finger.

He looked down at his phone. "Lovely. Thank you. Is that because you still somehow think I stood you up?"

"It's for being dumb and not coming to say hello just because you saw me talking to someone." I should've stopped there, but instead I added, "Do you think I'm hung up on you or something because of my stupid mistake of a proposition? Is that why you thought your presence would trip me up in front of Brandon?"

"No," he murmured.

"You don't need to worry." I looked down and muttered, "I'm over that."

If Dorian was smart, he'd see right through me. He'd see that all of this was for his benefit because I was indeed still hung up on him, and the fact that he'd rejected me still stung just as much as it had when it happened. And that was so very bad. I needed to protect myself from getting hurt even more. An idea occurred to me.

"In fact…" I continued. "I think the sooner we become more comfortable with this living situation out in the open, the better we'll be. There's nothing to hide. I think you should meet us tomorrow night at Juno Bar. Bring a date."

Dorian narrowed his eyes, seeming perplexed. "I don't know."

"Don't tell me you don't have a date on a Friday night."

After a brief pause, he proved me right. "I was supposed to meet someone for dinner."

Of course you are. A rush of jealousy shot through me. *Why am I like this?*

"So bring her to Juno Bar. We'll be there around eight."

"Will you be offended if I say no?"

"Yep." I smirked. "Plus, you owe me for flaking tonight, even if it wasn't your fault."

"I guess you have a point there. I wouldn't want to disappoint you twice."

"Great, then. I'll see you tomorrow night. And if something comes up, you now have my number."

"I do."

"Good." I pointed my finger against his chest. "Use it."

"I will."

Boy, did I know how to torture myself. Now I was pseudo-flirting with this guy? I walked toward the stairs.

"Heading to bed?" he asked.

"Yeah." I turned, pretending to yawn. "I'm kind of tired, so..."

"Okay." He nodded. "Can I show you something first?"

"Sure."

We walked upstairs together, and he led me into the primary bedroom closet. I was shocked to find everything...gone.

I gasped. "Wow."

"Benjamin took all their belongings to the donation place today. He left you the green dress. So, the closet and bedroom are ready for you whenever you want them."

My mouth hung open as I looked around at the space. "It looks so empty."

"That's because it is."

"I'll move my stuff over the weekend. I really appreciate you letting me have the space."

"It'd go to waste otherwise. But again, only use it if you want to. Don't feel like you have to."

"I genuinely want to. Thank you again."

"You don't need to thank me."

"Maybe I won't thank you verbally again. But I'll have to create something for you in this space as a token of my appreciation."

"I'll accept that."

I continued to look around. Then I turned to him. "You said you went to L.A. today. Do you normally have a lot of meetings there?"

"No. I can usually handle everything remotely from the Orion Coast office. But there was a potential investor in town from China. He wanted to meet with me personally before he went back."

"Are things getting any easier at work?"

"In some ways, yes. And in some ways, no."

"Why is that?"

"I'm getting more used to the job and dealing with some of the people who worked for my father. But there have also been some surprises—deals he made I wasn't aware of. Things I don't necessarily agree with in his business practices." He sighed. "It is what it is."

His eyes lowered to my chest and moved down the length of my body. "You look beautiful tonight, Primrose."

I looked down at myself. I was wearing a black dress with a sheer lace design at the top. "Are you just saying that because I put on something other than a crop top?"

"Not just that. You were glowing when I saw you talking earlier, clearly in your element."

"Jesus. How long were you watching me and not saying anything?"

"Not that long."

"You'd never know I was bummed that you didn't show, huh? I guess I'm a good actress."

"You were that upset?" He cringed. "Again, I fucked up in not letting you know I was there."

"Now that I understand what happened, it's not a big deal. I'm not sure why it upset me so much. I guess I wanted you to see a bit of my life outside this house. I wanted to impress you."

"You already impress me. Every day."

Feeling shy, I looked away for a moment. "Why do we always end up talking in this closet?"

"Because you make it easy." He grinned. "I used to hide in here, actually."

"What do you mean?"

"When I was younger. When I wanted to be alone, I'd go right to my mother's closet. No one would ever think to look for me in here. I'd fish in her pockets for breath mints."

"Did you find them?"

"Sometimes. Other times, I'd find things I wasn't meant to."

"Like what?"

"Like a business card to a private investigator, along with photos of my father kissing another woman." He grimaced.

My stomach sank. "That must have been hard. Were you old enough to understand?"

He nodded. "I think I was about ten. And, yeah, unfortunately, I did understand. I remember mourning the life I thought I had, figuring out that nothing was really the way it seemed. I also remember feeling this relief that my mother knew, and it wasn't a secret I had to keep. I couldn't imagine doing that. I was proud of her for not letting him pull the wool over her eyes."

"Did you say anything to her?"

"No. But I do remember secretly wishing she'd give him a piece of his own medicine. Kind of a strange thing to hope about your mom, I guess."

"Do you think she ever did?"

"I don't know. It was only a few years later that she got sick. And then a few years after that, she passed away." He let out a long breath. "I often wonder if it was the stress of my father's affairs that made her ill. Stress can do a number on the body." Dorian stared up at the ceiling. "I remember thinking there was no braver thing than what she did—staying married to him when she could've just taken him to the cleaners. They didn't even have a prenup."

"Do you think she loved him, or she stayed married to him for you?"

He pondered that a moment. "I think it was the latter. And I regret that. I wish she'd been with someone who respected her more."

"Isn't it also possible that she stayed with him because she loved him? Both things can be true, can't they?"

"I don't know. I don't understand how you can love someone who does that to you."

"When we first met, though, you said you believed your father only ever loved your mother. That's why he couldn't have possibly loved Christina…"

He waved that away. "I was talking out of my ass the night we met. I don't know whether my father truly loved my mother. And I never will. I know he was pretty upset after she died. I just never knew whether it was guilt or whether his heart was broken. But not sure how you could do something like he did to someone you truly love." The sadness in his eyes was palpable.

"You think having money turns some good people bad?"

"It definitely doesn't help." He paused. "I remember as a boy wishing so badly that I just had a normal family, you know? One where the father wasn't a cheater. Where there wasn't so much money that you never knew whether someone was using you." A pained look crossed his face. "But after Mom died, I regretted ever wishing for anything other than the life I had with her. She really was a great mom. And how much more did I need, you know?" He rubbed his temples. "God, how the fuck did I get to this place of vulnerability yet again in this fucking closet?"

"I think this stuff just needs to come out sometimes."

"It scares me how easily I open up to you, Primrose."

"I'm glad I'm here so you don't have to go through this experience alone. I'm always happy to listen."

"You say that, but I just complained to you about having a privileged childhood. How fucking tone deaf is that?"

"You still have a right to your feelings. Your wealth doesn't take away the fact that you were hurt by your father's actions, that you expected more, and also that having money sometimes can be a curse."

He searched my eyes. "You said your father wasn't around when you were growing up, but did you know him at all?"

I shook my head. "When my mother told him she was pregnant with me, he left and refused to believe he was the father. He didn't want to deal with it. Rick continued to deny I was his, even though he was the only person she'd been with."

"Did you ever meet him?"

A wave of overwhelming sadness came over me. My voice shook. "I met him once."

"You don't have to elaborate," Dorian said.

"I never told anyone, not even my mother, that I went to see him. She died not knowing."

"Will you tell me about it?" he asked softly.

I exhaled. "My mother had always been open with me about who my father was. I'd known his name from a very young age, but it wasn't until I became internet savvy that I was able to look up his information—where he worked, that kind of thing." I let out a breath of frustration. "I don't know what I was thinking...that maybe if he saw my face, saw the resemblance, he'd finally acknowledge me." I swallowed hard.

"What happened?"

"I found out he worked in construction for a contractor about thirty minutes away. I told my mother I was going to a lake for the day with my friend Brittany and her family. Instead, Brittany asked her older brother to drive us to the construction site." I shut my eyes. "I thought if I wore the prettiest dress I owned and got myself all dolled up, maybe he'd be happy to see me." I shook my head. "It was delusional."

"You thought maybe he wasn't the person your mother thought he was..."

Nodding, I shut my eyes as I felt tears start to form.

"You don't have to finish the story."

I felt his hand on my arm.

I opened my eyes. "It's just hard for me to go back to that place. There's no worse rejection than that which comes from the person responsible for your existence. Whenever I look at myself in the mirror, I see him—the face of the man who looked me in the eyes and called me a liar and told me to leave. How do you love yourself when all you can see in that mirror is someone who hates you? When people tell me I'm beautiful, I feel like they're lying."

"That's fucked up," he muttered. "I'm so sorry."

"The pain that comes from rejection by your own parent is not something that can ever be healed."

He looked at me a long moment. "You've said before that you try to beat men to the punch, breaking up with them before they have a chance to hurt you. Is that because you think they're all like him?"

I nodded. "I'm sure that's part of it."

"Your father is a shit human. And I hate that you see him when you look in the mirror. I obviously don't know what he looks like, but when *I* look at you, I see the kindest eyes and the most beautiful face. It's *your* face, no one else's. You can give someone your genes, but that doesn't mean anything. Your spirit is nothing like his."

His words felt like a warm blanket.

"Thanks," I said. "There's one good thing that came out of that meeting, though…"

"What?"

"That night I went home and drew for the first time. Despite the pain of the experience, it was the start of a new way to express my feelings. Now I rarely do that any other way than through art."

"Except when someone like me forces you to talk about it." He offered a sad smile.

"I'm glad you did, because every time I do, it's a reminder that talking about it won't break me. I can talk about it and move on. It's important to let stuff out." I wiped my eyes. "Anyway, thanks for the closet chat."

"I should be thanking you for letting me share first. An eye for an eye." He chuckled. "Or an ear for an ear."

My emotions threatened to overwhelm me, so I walked out into the bedroom. "I'll see you tomorrow night, right?"

"Yeah." He hesitated. "I'll see you then."

I wondered, though, if I actually would.

Back in my bedroom, I pondered what I was going to wear tomorrow. As I flipped through the closet, I knew my concern had nothing to do with impressing Brandon and everything to do with stealing Dorian's attention. That was a game I apparently didn't mind continuing to play. I just hoped it didn't end with me getting burned.

CHAPTER 13

"You look absolutely stunning, Primrose," Brandon said as he moved in to kiss me on the cheek.

Janelle and I had arrived at Juno Bar a bit early and had already ordered a drink by the time Brandon showed.

I'd worn a black crop top paired with black leather pants tonight. The shirt was a shimmery material and was as fancy as it got in my half-shirt collection. I'd spent extra time on my hair and sprayed a fresh burst of perfume before I left the mansion. And if pressed, I'd have to admit that it was all for my roommate, no one else.

But that was *if* Dorian even showed up. It wouldn't surprise me one bit if he bailed again. In fact, I was almost expecting it. Or at least I had to expect it to protect my feelings. I really wished it didn't matter so much.

After chatting for a minute, Brandon asked, "Can I get you ladies another drink?"

I lifted my glass. "I'm just gonna nurse this one."

"Actually, I'll have another cosmo." Janelle smiled.

"You got it." He made his way over to the bar.

She elbowed me. "You should bring guys along more often when we go out. Can't say I mind getting my drinks paid for."

"That's obviously not why I invited him, but noted," I said, glancing at the door.

"Why do you keep looking over there?"

This was like déjà vu of the art event. I'd spent that entire evening checking the door, and Janelle had called me out on it then, too.

"I invited Dorian to meet up with us," I admitted. "Just seeing if he showed up."

Her mouth went agape. "What? Why did you do that? You gonna have a threesome or something?"

"Hardly. Like I said, he's not interested in me that way. I told him to bring a date. And your reaction is exactly why I put off telling you for as long as possible."

"Why would you invite the guy you're crushing on to bring a date while you're on a date with a guy who is clearly into you? Seems too complicated."

"First of all, I'm not even sure this *is* a date with Brandon. It's just a casual meet-up. Second, the sooner Dorian and I get comfortable with the reality of our relationship, the better. He's my roommate. He's also come to mean a lot to me as a friend. I don't want to feel strange if he brings a date around. Nor should he feel weird if I do the same. I have to move on with my life."

"Well, that sounds dandy, except for the fact that you still like him. Are you kidding yourself?"

"Any lingering feelings I may have are exactly *why* I need to do this."

"Okay." She sighed. "Whatever."

Brandon returned holding a beer and Janelle's cosmo. He gave it to her and looked over his shoulder. "There's a table over there that just became available. Should we steal it?"

"Absolutely." I started over, grateful for the opportunity to sit down, since the stiletto booties I'd worn tonight were killing my feet.

As we sat at the table, Brandon took a sip of his beer. "You said in your text that your roommate might be meeting us?"

"A friend." I nodded. "I'm not sure if he'll show."

Janelle smirked. I glared at her.

A live band that had been setting up now started to play in the corner of the room. It was already nine, an hour past the time I'd told Dorian we'd arrive, and there was still no sign of him. Looked like this was going to be a repeat of the art show.

I'd been saving my second drink in case I needed it after Dorian showed, but I finally gave in and let Brandon fetch me another white wine from the bar. I was looking over at Brandon waiting in line when a voice startled me.

"Is there room for two more at this table?"

A rush of adrenaline shot through me as I turned to find Dorian and a gorgeous brunette—that was a change. I swallowed the lump in my throat, forced a smile, and pretended to be delighted to see them. "Hey!"

Dorian gestured to his date. "This is Meena." He turned. "Meena, this is my roommate, Primrose."

Janelle cleared her throat, prompting me to remember she was here. I needed to get my head out of my ass.

"I'm sorry." I pointed to my friend. "Dorian and Meena, this is Janelle. She's my closest friend here in California."

He nodded. "Very nice to meet you, Janelle."

Janelle smiled.

Of course, Dorian had to look and smell freaking amazing. He was dressed more casually than usual, with dark jeans and an olive green Henley that fit against his muscles like a glove. Why did he have to be so freaking hot?

Meena took a seat across from me, next to Janelle.

"Is your date here?" Dorian asked.

"Yeah. He's at the bar."

"Looks like we need one more seat, then. I'll see if I can find one."

A moment later, Dorian returned with a chair, positioning it at the end of our table.

Brandon returned shortly thereafter, setting my wine in front of me and reaching his hand out to Dorian. "Brandon Wright. You must be Primrose's roommate?"

They shook.

"Dorian Vanderbilt." He turned to his date. "And this is Meena."

"Nice to meet you, Meena." Brandon grinned.

She smiled and took his hand.

Dorian stood. "I know you just got wine, Primrose. Does anyone else want something from the bar?"

Janelle jumped at the chance for another free drink. "I'll have a cosmopolitan, if you don't mind."

She wasn't even done with her last one.

Dorian nodded. "Of course."

I guess I'll be driving home.

Meena asked for a vodka seltzer with lime before Dorian left the table.

After a moment of awkward silence, I twiddled my thumbs and turned to Meena. "So...how did you meet Dorian?"

"We met on an app. This is our first date."

"I see."

Meena tilted her head. "He said you're an artist?"

"Yep." I nodded and took a long sip of my wine.

"That's very cool," she replied.

That was the extent of our riveting conversation.

Janelle had bumped seats with a man behind her, and now she was chatting him up. He appeared to be the fifth wheel to another set of two couples, and he and Janelle were joking about having that in common.

Dorian finally returned. "I thought I'd never get out of that line. This place is packed." He set the drinks down before turning to Brandon. "You guys met at school?"

"Yes..." he answered. "But I'm not a student. I graduated a few years back."

"Brandon is an advisor and mentor," I added.

Dorian stirred his drink. "Are you a full-time artist?"

"Yes. I do well working on commission."

"Impressive." Dorian took a sip.

"And what do you do?" Brandon asked.

"I run a technology company."

"That's right. Primrose mentioned that you lost your dad and had to take over. I'm sorry to hear that."

"Thank you."

Brandon turned to Dorian's date. "And what do you do, Meena?"

"I'm a buyer for Sheldon's."

"Oh nice." I feigned interest. "I love their...crop tops."

"I'm sure you do." Dorian grinned mischievously over at me as I felt my cheeks heat.

Maybe I was kidding myself, but it felt like from the moment he'd walked in, Dorian's eyes had mostly been on mine, as if everyone else didn't exist.

"That must be such a fun job," I said, clearing my throat.

"It is for now. I can see myself tiring of it."

I licked wine from my lips. "Why do you say that?"

"Someday when I have kids, I don't want to be working."

How nice to have that option. I inwardly rolled my eyes. "I'm guessing you were raised by a stay-at-home mother," I said.

"That's correct."

"That's nice. But not everyone has the luxury of choosing not to work. My mother certainly didn't." I bit my lip, unsure whether that came across as rude. Maybe I *meant* it to be rude, since there was something about Meena I didn't like. Perhaps it was the fact that she'd very possibly get to sleep with Dorian tonight? That was likely it.

"What type of art do you make?" Meena asked me after a moment.

"Well, I draw mostly wildlife, scenes of nature, and some humans. I don't have a specific name for my specialty. I guess you could say I like taking things found in nature and giving them a bit of a bizarre twist."

Dorian smiled. "Surrealism, maybe?"

"I like that." Our eyes locked until Brandon interrupted.

"Can I give you a bit of advice, Prim?"

Prim? I'd never liked when anyone shortened my name that way.

"Of course."

"Your technique is obviously excellent. There is no doubt about your talent. But don't be afraid to challenge yourself, to take risks, to use the opportunity to tell a story, make a point, change the world with your art. The animals are cute and all. But I feel like you might not be living up to your potential."

My chest tightened.

Cute?

Fucking cute?

It had taken me days to perfect each of those monkey portraits.

I'd never been great at accepting criticism. But when it came to my art, I was even more sensitive. Who the hell said art needs to always make a statement? Why can't it just be beautiful or open to interpretation?

"I'm not sure I understand what you're getting at," I finally said, feeling deflated.

"Okay...like, for example, the monkeys..." He chuckled. "Again, your talent is obvious. They're extremely realistic. And while there's clearly a theme...it's hard to see the point of putting a bunch of monkeys in various costumes."

I'd gone from feeling offended to wanting to cry. He thought my art was meaningless?

"Who died and made you the authority on art?" Dorian seethed.

I looked up suddenly.

Brandon shook his head. "No one. I've just...been around the art world a bit longer than Prim has. From a career perspective, I know what sells. People are looking for art that makes a statement."

"And you think some depressing image with a contrived agenda is going to be what brings someone joy?"

Brandon held his palms out. "Relax, I was just trying to give her gentle constructive criticism."

"By shitting all over something she worked her ass off on? That's not very gentle."

My head moved between them as if I were watching a tennis match. I could've said something. But I was enjoying this too much. I'd gone from the verge of tears to something else entirely.

"I absolutely did not mean to shit all over anything." Brandon turned to me, looking a little panicked. "And if I in any way implied that—"

"Sure," Dorian interrupted. "When I first saw her monkey paintings, I laughed like you did just a moment ago. And I've regretted it every day since. Because while funny on the surface, if you stop to actually think about the many possible interpretations, it opens up a cornucopia of discussion prompts. We as humans think we're the superior species. But we don't even fully understand where we came from. A world with primates at the helm is probably one of the greatest existential fantasies I could ever imagine. So, perhaps you should ask yourself if *you're* the one being short-sighted here, to suggest that in order to be meaningful art has to shove some loud message down people's throats. There's something to be said for subtlety." His chest rose and fell in anger.

The table went quiet.

I wanted to reach across the table and kiss Dorian—that was *one* of the things I wanted. The other was to smack Brandon in the face. Even if he was coming from a good place in offering what he felt was an honest opinion, critiquing my art on the first date was not a way to win me over.

The whole experience gave me a burst of confidence mixed with a dash of *fuck it all*.

"You know what? I'm kind of tired all of a sudden," I announced, standing from my seat as the chair skidded against the wooden floor. "I'm gonna head home."

Brandon stood. "Prim, I didn't mean any offense."

I placed my hand on his chest. "I know you didn't. But I have to go. I'm sorry." My eyes narrowed. "Also, I don't like to be called Prim."

Dorian flashed me a proud smile.

I walked over to Janelle, who was now at the next table. "Do you think we could leave?" I asked.

"Actually, I need to sober up before I drive." She leaned across to speak into my ear. "But also, I'm really enjoying Michael's company and am not ready to go."

"No problem." I hugged her. "I'll call a ride. You have fun. You deserve it. Don't have anything else to drink, though, if you're gonna be driving yourself home. And please just call a ride if there's any doubt."

She winked. "Maybe I'll ditch my car here and let Michael take me home."

"Be careful," I mouthed.

Feeling feisty, I snuck out a side door. I didn't want to return to the table in the event Dorian felt obligated to give me a ride.

I regretted not saying goodbye to him. But more than that, I didn't want to spend another second sitting across from him and his date. Not sure why I'd ever thought going on a double date with a man I was practically obsessed with was a good idea. Every second that I had to look across at them had pissed me off more than the last. I clearly wasn't ready for that.

The ride I'd called never showed, so I walked a couple of blocks to a nearby pharmacy to pick up a few things. Then I called another car to take me back to the mansion.

When I finally made it home, I turned the key and froze at the sight of Dorian standing in the entryway—alone.

What the hell?

CHAPTER 14

"What are you doing here?" I placed my hand over my chest.

"I drove home as soon as I figured out that you'd left the bar. I didn't think I'd beat you. You should've let me take you back."

"You left your date?"

"I apologized and excused myself. Left her sitting there with your date, actually."

"That's so wrong." I chuckled.

He shrugged. "Barely met her, and I wasn't feeling it. Better not to waste her time."

"You really didn't need to follow me home."

"Technically you followed me. What took you so damn long?"

"First car I called ghosted me. Then I stopped at the store." I sighed. "Anyway, I still don't understand why you're here."

"I was the reason you left. I upset you when I argued with Art Boy."

"Are you kidding? That was the best part of the night."

"Thought maybe I overstepped and ruined your date."

"Well, I ruined yours last time, so I guess we're even."

"Technically, you've ruined *two* of my dates." He wriggled his brows. "Not that I'm counting."

"I think I'm addicted to stealing you away from people," I admitted.

He moved toward me. "Are you stealing me, or am I unable to see anything else when you're around?"

"You tell me." My breaths quickened. "Although I find that hard to believe. That chick was the prettiest one so far. Surprised you didn't want to hook up with her."

He inched closer. "The only woman I want to take home and fuck is the one I live with."

My heart nearly leaped out of my chest. *Holy shit.*

He placed the back of his hand against my cheek. "I couldn't even tell you what color her eyes were."

Without warning, I closed my eyes, turned away from him, and panted, "What color are *my* eyes?"

His breath danced over my cheek as he answered, "Neither blue nor green...aquamarine."

I opened my eyes as I remembered what he'd written on that restaurant bill. "Oh my God. The note."

"Now you get it." His mouth curved into a smile. "Your eyes are the most beautiful I've ever looked into. Aquamarine with the tiniest speckles of gold, actually, in a certain light. I've been transfixed from the very beginning. You've *owned* me from day one, whether you knew it or not." Dorian shook his head. "I've tried so hard not to cross the line with you. But seeing another man so much as brush up against you tonight made me feral."

I swallowed. "I felt the same way seeing you with someone."

"I should've broken his fucking neck for disrespecting you." He looked down at my body. "Why did you have to look so sexy tonight? These fucking leather pants. You had me *really* wanting a tequila shot."

When I realized what he meant, my body tingled. I could practically feel his tongue on me all over again. "If I'd known you liked leather, I would've pulled these out a long time ago."

Silence filled the air as he looked at me. You could cut the sexual tension with a knife.

"Fuck it..." He closed the space between us, taking my mouth with his. He groaned, low and deep, vibrating down my throat.

Oh. My. God. His lips felt better than I could've imagined. He *tasted* better than I could've imagined. This *night* was better than I could've imagined.

"You've wanted me to lose control for a long time, haven't you?" As his hands cradled my face, he nudged my mouth open with his eager tongue. "Well, this is me losing it."

I could practically taste the desperation. Raking my fingers through the shiny black hair I'd always longed to touch, I closed my eyes and wondered if I was dreaming.

Dorian's hands lowered to my ass. He squeezed and muttered over my lips, "These fucking leather pants. They make me want to fuck you so hard."

He circled his tongue around mine as I felt the heat of his rock-hard cock at my groin.

Then he stepped back. His chest heaved.

Please don't stop.

He looked at me hazily as he reached for my hand and pulled me toward the stairway. I'd never climbed so fast. It felt like we flew upstairs. I followed him to his room, realizing the dogs were nowhere to be found.

When the door shut behind us, Dorian lifted me up as I wrapped my legs around his torso. Our mouths met again, brought together by what felt like magnetic force as his erection throbbed beneath me. Dorian spun around and moved us closer to the bed. A second later, I felt my back bounce against the mattress. Then Dorian was on top of me, ravaging my neck. An unintelligible sound escaped me as I relished the feel of his mouth on my skin.

I stretched my legs wide to make room for him. Dorian kissed down the length of my body before reaching to unsnap my pants.

"Is this okay?" he murmured.

I nodded eagerly and uttered an incoherent sound.

The next several seconds were a blur. Clothes flew everywhere as our bodies rubbed desperately against one another until we were skin to skin. When he knelt over me, I got the first look at his beautiful, hard cock. He lowered himself as the tip dripped precum on my stomach. I grew wetter than I could ever remember.

As the muscles between my legs throbbed, I clawed at his back, and he spread my legs apart. A moment later, Dorian stilled as he looked down at me and caressed my face.

"Do you want me inside of you, Primrose?"

I had to smile at that direct question, paired with the vulnerability in his eyes. *As if there's any doubt.* I answered by reaching up and pulling his lips against mine. That was almost immediately followed by the burn of him entering me.

Fuck.

His body shuddered. Dorian moved his thick shaft in and out of me. When he pushed harder, I gasped, unable to fathom how sex had never felt like this before, so raw and powerful. That tender question he'd asked to request permission was the last gentle part. Much to my thrill, Dorian fucked me relentlessly, his low groans matching the rhythm of his thrusts. I lifted my hips, wanting him deeper inside me. There was no such thing as deep enough, given how long I'd waited for this.

He wrapped his hand around my neck as he moved his hips, a delicate possessiveness I absolutely loved. The bed rocked as Dorian ravaged me, and every movement in and out felt tight as he filled me completely.

The muscles between my legs pulsed as I fought the urge to climax. It wasn't until I felt his body shake over me that I let myself go.

Dorian made a guttural sound that vibrated through my body as I felt the sweet heat of his cum filling me.

No matter what happened between us, I would never get over this man.

After, we were both breathless as we came down from the high of our orgasms. I would likely be in shock for days. Not only had Dorian fucked me, but he'd fucked me the way no one ever had.

Blissfully sated, we turned to each other. I rested my chin on my hand as I stared into his eyes. "Well, that was an interesting homecoming."

"Emphasis on the *coming*..." He panted. "You're fucking exquisite."

"What the hell changed?" I asked.

"Nothing changed in terms of my feelings. I've always been this crazy about you. I just happened to lose my mind after seeing you with another man. I came home expecting to talk to you, not attack you. But I lost control the moment I laid eyes on you again. The truth is, I've wanted this for a long time. I just needed a straw to break the camel's back. Tonight was fucking it."

"And now here we are."

"Here we are," he repeated softly.

"What's next?"

"I have no clue. This is all against my better judgment. I'm scared shitless to ruin things with you. You're all I fucking have that's good in life. But rather than waste time worrying about why something that feels so right has to be wrong, why don't I cook for you tomorrow night, and we'll take it from there?"

My eyes widened. "I thought you didn't make anything besides apple crisp."

"I don't. But I think it would be a nice gesture and a way for me to say thank you for putting up with me."

"Putting *out* for you or putting up with you?" I teased, running my finger over his chin.

"Both." He winked. "But please don't stop putting out for me. Because now I'm addicted, and I'm most definitely going to need to fuck you again, multiple times."

"You're not the only one."

His expression turned serious. "I'm actually a bit freaked out by my lack of control. I didn't wear a condom."

"I'm quite aware of that. The evidence is between my legs."

"That's not a precaution I normally forget. This is a conversation we probably should've had *before* we had sex, but I want you to know I'm clean. I had a full checkup before I left Boston, and I haven't been with anyone since I got here."

"Me, too. And I have an IUD. So we're good. I wouldn't have let you do it if I wasn't protected."

"Well, at least one of us was thinking with their brain. All I was able to think about was getting inside of you."

"I wouldn't mind an encore." I batted my lashes.

"You think I'm gonna let you out of this bed without an encore?"

Smiling blissfully, I looked around. "Where are the dogs, by the way?"

"When I got home tonight, they were jumping all over me, wanting to play. Practically took my balls off for real this time. I didn't want you to walk into that ruckus—I really did think we were just gonna talk, believe it or not—so I asked Benjamin if he'd keep them next door."

"The dogs are not gonna be happy about sleeping in the guest house tonight."

"There's only room for one woman in my bed tonight, not three."

"You really haven't been with anyone since Boston?"

"I haven't. And you wanna know something else?"

"What?"

"You're the first woman I've ever slept with in this house."

My eyes widened. "Get outta here. How is that possible?"

"Very easy. I never brought women home when I lived with my father. And there hasn't been anyone since I've been back."

"Who's the last person you were with?"

"I was seeing someone casually, but regularly, back in Boston."

"Casually, meaning she was desperately hoping for more, and you strung her along?"

"I never made promises."

I stiffened. "That's why I have to be careful with you."

"*You're* the one who has to be careful? You told me yourself that you've broken up with every guy you've dated before he had a chance to end things. I fear I'm the one on the chopping block here."

He had a point. Only time would tell which of us would break the other's heart.

CHAPTER 15

The following day, Dorian texted me to meet him downstairs for dinner at seven, with no peeking beforehand. He'd gone to the office today but came home earlier than he normally did. He'd sent Patsy and Benjamin home for the day, so it was just the two of us in the house.

I'd been walking around the mansion all day in a haze of happiness after last night, alternating between giddy smiling and inwardly warning myself to be careful about falling for Dorian to the point of no return. I could already feel that happening. For now, though, I was willing to get burned if it meant getting to experience more of what we'd had last night. Falling for Dorian was like the worst drug imaginable—you know it's bad, but you're already planning your next hit.

And he wanted to make me dinner. No man had ever cooked for me before, and given that Dorian didn't cook in general, this was bound to be interesting.

Rummaging through my closet, I wanted to make sure I wore the sexiest outfit I could find. He liked leather, so I laid out the only other leather item I had, a black leather corset. It was a departure from my usual crop tops, but I was excited to see his reaction. I decided to pair it with dark jeans and black leather boots.

I retreated into the bath to take a shower, still not feeling worthy of Christina and Remington's luxurious bathroom. But considering no one else would be enjoying it in my place, I supposed my undeserving ass was better than some stranger in this beautiful space.

Just as I rinsed the conditioner out of my hair, I froze at the sound of the fire alarm. A shot of panic sliced through me as I jumped out of the shower, grabbing a towel.

I practically flew out the bedroom door and ran down the hall.

Dorian raced up the stairs. "It's okay." He panted, holding out his hands. "It's not a fire."

"It's not?"

"Just smoke. I fucking burned dinner. Everything is okay, though."

"Oh no." I held my hand over my mouth, trying to hold back laughter as relief coursed through me.

"I knew you'd be scared, so I came up as fast as I could." He ran his hand over my hair. "You're dripping. Go back and get dried. I just didn't want you to worry. I'm sorry about this."

He looked even more frazzled than I felt after the alarm.

"Are you okay?" I asked.

"So much for YouTube tutorials on how to charbroil steak."

"Oh, man." I shook my head. "I'm sorry. It's the thought that counts."

"Actually, please do your best to erase this from your memory." He laughed. "Go back and finish your shower."

"I'll meet you downstairs in a bit," I said.

"Take your time. I've got the windows open to air out the kitchen." He brushed his fingertips down my arm, sending a shiver through me. My body buzzed with excitement.

I ran my hand through his hair. "Thank you." Burning dinner was even more adorable than his attempt at making it.

After completing my shower, getting dressed, and blowing my hair out, I went down to the kitchen, where the aftermath of Dorian's attempt at dinner remained.

A pile of uncooked asparagus sat on a tray next to a frying pan of something unidentifiable.

"You were gonna make asparagus, too?"

"It would've paired well with the steak." He sighed. "I was trying to recreate the meal you recommended to me the night I ate at your restaurant. It was the one thing I was sure you'd like. See those lumps of charcoal? That's the steak, by the way. Turns out there's a fine line between charbroiling and burning."

I covered my mouth. "I bet it would've tasted delicious."

"Speaking of tasting delicious…" He gave me a once-over. "You're trying to kill me again with this outfit, aren't you?"

Shrugging, I grinned impishly. "Well, you said you liked leather."

"On you? Yeah. The fire alarm may very well go off again."

"Sorry to say, but if it goes off again, it's from this lingering smoke." I coughed.

"That's what I get for trying to expand my horizons. I need to stick to apple crisp."

"No one expects you to be a gorgeous, brilliant innovator *and* also be able to cook."

"Yeah, but shouldn't you be suspicious of someone who allegedly designs things, yet can't even cook a steak properly? Ask yourself that."

I wrapped my arms around his neck. "How about we order pizza and forget it?"

"I wouldn't have suggested something so basic, but pizza sounds good, if that's what you're up for."

"I'm in the mood for pizza and a movie."

"A girl after my own heart." He slid his hand down my back. "What do you like on your pizza?"

"Bacon and black olives."

Dorian squeezed my ass. "You didn't even have to think about it."

"Nope. My mom and I always used to order that. It's our favorite."

His smile faded. "Remington used to like pizza, too."

"What was his favorite?" I asked softly.

"Dad liked it plain. We'd order half pepperoni for me and the other half just cheese."

"Then you should order half pepperoni now."

"You sure? Will one pizza even be enough?"

"I'm not gonna eat more than a few slices. This corset doesn't leave much wiggle room."

"It's causing my pants to fit tighter, too…" He winked.

After Dorian ordered the pizza, he opened a bottle of red. "This was supposed to be for our steak. According to the sommelier at the wine shop, it paired well with what I was making—which was apparently charcoal."

I burst out laughing. "The fact that you even wanted to cook for me warms my heart."

Dorian leaned in to kiss my forehead. "So, while you were in the shower, Benjamin came over after he heard the fire alarm. I had to admit I'd been cooking."

"What did he think?"

"He couldn't believe it. He busted my balls and said the next time I wanted to *play* in the kitchen, I should let him know, and he'd help me make sure I didn't burn the house down."

"That's funny."

"He asked if you were home, and I told him the dinner was for us. He seemed pretty amused by that, too."

"Surprised or amused?"

"Oh, not surprised. He seemed to see this coming from a mile away."

"What is *this* exactly?"

"Not sure I have a name for it." He brought me close and leaned his forehead against mine. "Whatever it is, it feels good, though."

A moment of pure contentment washed over me. "I agree."

Dorian kissed my nose before taking my mouth. As he bent me back into a passionate kiss, I realized I would've been fine with skipping dinner and going upstairs for the rest of the night.

While we waited for the pizza to arrive, I helped Dorian clear out the mess he'd made. When I dropped a couple of pieces of asparagus on the floor, the dogs came racing to fetch the scraps. Tallulah and Tess were so comfortable around Dorian now that I hadn't noticed they'd been quietly sitting in the corner.

We'd just finished our glasses of wine when the pizza arrived. The smoke smell had finally dissipated somewhat.

"We should watch a movie *with* our pizza," I suggested when he returned with the box.

"That sounds fantastic," he agreed.

We headed downstairs to the basement, Dorian carrying the pizza box and some plates while I'd taken the bottle of wine and glasses. I couldn't think of a better way to spend the evening than a casual dinner in the coziness of home. Well, if a mansion could be considered *cozy*.

"This isn't the impressive first official date I had in mind," Dorian noted as we settled in the theater.

"Is this really our first date, or have we been inadvertently dating since our first night together in this very room?"

He smiled. "Something has definitely been growing between us since that night. Every moment with you has made my life better—a feeling I never imagined after everything that's happened."

His words touched me as I whispered, "Same."

Dorian's eyes lingered on mine for a moment before he switched his attention to the pizza, serving us a couple of slices each while I walked over to the laptop.

I scrolled through the choices. "We never did get to watch *Pulp Fiction* together. Wanna watch it now?"

"Sure, yeah." He poured us each another glass of wine.

We ate in comfortable silence as the movie began.

I looked over at his handsome profile from time to time in the flickering lights of the movie.

During the scene where Mia is talking to Vincent about uncomfortable silences, I turned to Dorian and whispered, "One thing we do very well is enjoy each other's company without having to make small talk."

He nodded. "I'm comfortable with you whether we're talking or not."

"The only time I wasn't comfortable around you was when I felt like I had to hide my feelings. That was really hard to control," I added.

Ignoring the movie, he turned to me. "Control is an illusion. Because if you have to try to control something, are you really in control or are you just putting off the inevitable?" He leaned in. "In fact, I'm feeling pretty *out of control* at this moment."

Dorian reached out, urging me onto his lap. We fell into a kiss as I straddled him on the theater chair.

The sounds from the film faded into the background.

Threading my fingers through his hair, I looked into his gorgeous eyes as he leaned his head back against the seat.

Dorian cupped my breasts. "You wore this leather top to torture me, didn't you?"

"Maybe," I said, enveloping his mouth with mine once again.

His fingers scratched at my back before I felt him lower my zipper. Dorian loosened the ties of my corset before lifting it over my head, exposing my bare chest. My nipples tingled, begging to be sucked. Thankfully, he understood the assignment, licking his bottom lip before taking my breast into his mouth. He tugged gently on my nipple.

"You taste even sweeter than last night." He sucked harder, groaning under his breath.

My loins were on fire, and I'd completely forgotten any vow I'd made to take this slower. The feeling of need was too intense. I began to grind over his rigid cock.

"Don't do that unless you want to get fucked in this chair, Primrose."

I moved my hips faster, sending a clear message.

"I don't have the strength to push you away," he groaned. "So you'd better get off of me unless you want me inside you right now."

I lowered my mouth, kissing him on the neck. Sliding my hand down his chest, I landed on his crotch, cupping his cock. Then I stood. His eyes looked pained at the prospect of me stopping. But I kicked off my boots and unzipped my jeans before slipping out of them. Wearing nothing now but a thong, I soaked in every moment of Dorian devouring me with his eyes.

"You are simply the most exquisite woman I've ever laid eyes on." His gaze darkened. "Tell me what you want right now."

"I want you, in any way you'll give it to me."

"Have you ever been fucked in a theater?" He smirked.

"Ask me tomorrow." I flashed a smile.

"Come here," he ordered.

Dorian straightened in his seat as I charged toward him. He ran a line down my abdomen with his tongue, stopping short of my underwear. Pushing the material aside, he lapped at my clit. My knees nearly gave out at the unexpected contact. He stopped for a moment only to slide the thong down.

Dorian then dropped to his knees, burying his mouth between my legs. He circled his tongue in hard, swift motions as the sound of gunshots from the movie rang out.

I tugged on his hair, forcing him to stop. "I almost came."

He flashed a mischievous grin as he looked up at me. "Good."

I pushed him back into his seat and straddled him. Unfastening his pants, I took his cock out and placed it at my opening.

He smiled. "That's it, baby. Ride me."

This was heaven. Dorian looked up at me with hazy eyes as I swayed my hips over him, riding his cock like there was no tomorrow as a vague awareness of Vincent accidentally shooting Marvin in the face played on the screen behind me.

CHAPTER 16

Three weeks later, I woke up on Saturday morning feeling a panic attack coming on. That made no sense considering that things in my life were going better than ever.

The weeks since Dorian and I first slept together had been the absolute best of my life. Each day my connection to him seemed to grow. Almost a month into our relationship, I should've been on top of the world.

Dorian had been coming home earlier from the office at night. The house we shared felt more like a home each day instead of the ghost town it had been after Christina and Remington passed. Dorian and I had started learning to cook together, making dinners by following video tutorials. He'd actually made a pretty mean lasagna one night, and breaded chicken cutlets and roasted broccoli were apparently my jam.

On the weekends, we'd stroll around Orion Coast or go into L.A. He'd come with me to a couple of art exhibitions and had taken me on a tour of the Vanderbilt Technologies offices after hours.

After that first night we were together in Dorian's bed, he and I hadn't spent a night apart. We'd now migrated to my bedroom; although thankfully Tallulah and Tess still preferred Dorian's bed. At first, he'd felt a little strange sleeping where his father once had, but that made the most sense, as it was the biggest room. He'd gotten used to it after the first few times, and my room quickly became *our* room.

We hadn't defined our relationship, yet it felt like we'd evolved from lovers to partners—a true couple, doing coupley things. Case in point, Chandler and Candace were coming over to have dinner with us tonight. We'd been gearing up for the perfect evening with friends.

So then why the rapid heartbeat this morning?

Why the feeling of absolute dread?

Sadly, deep down, I knew *exactly* what it was: everything was going *so* well that I now worried I had to break up with him. This was my MO, a self-protective mechanism that had ruined every relationship I'd ever been in. But the stakes were higher this time because I wasn't just in a relationship with Dorian. I had fallen in love.

I started to shake, praying Dorian didn't wake up and find me freaking out. But soon enough, he turned over and noticed me trembling.

He sat up. "What's wrong, baby?"

"I'm having a bit of a...panic attack."

"What brought it on?"

I stuttered, "I, um..."

How do you tell someone you have the urge to break up with him because things are going so well that there's nowhere to go but down?

"I…"

I couldn't do it.

"What is it, Primrose?" he asked, worry in his eyes.

I finally let the words out. "I think I'm about to break up with you."

His eyes narrowed. "You're scared," he finally said.

"Very…"

"Because there's a lot to lose here, isn't there?"

My breath shook as I exhaled. "I feel like I should be moving out and ending this before it's too late. I've never felt this way about anyone, Dorian. So the urge to end it is worse than usual."

He placed his hand behind my head and stared into my eyes. "You can't break up with me."

"Why?" I whispered.

"Because I love you."

The world stopped spinning for a moment. Hope filled me. "You do?"

"I do." He nodded. "I love you so much. And I don't want to live in a world where you're not my girlfriend."

Girlfriend.

Love.

My heart had gone from breaking to aching—in a good way. "You've never called me your girlfriend before."

"Did you need a definition? Can't you *feel* it? Can't you feel how crazy about you I am?"

I smiled. "I can."

"Believe what I'm showing you, not just what I'm telling you. You're more than a girlfriend to me. You're the reason I want to get up every morning. Before you came along, I wished I could sleep all day. You're the reason for every smile. Every laugh. Every good thing in my life. You're the first thing I think about in the morning and the last thing I want to see before I drift off at night." He leaned in and spoke over my lips. "You're the love of my life, Primrose." Dorian kissed my forehead gently. "I know how distrusting you are of men because of your dad. I know I have to work a hundred times harder to prove you're safe with me. I am totally up for the challenge. I'll do whatever it takes to make sure you understand that I'm not going anywhere. And neither are you—I think. Because you love me, too, don't you?"

Jesus. Did I not say it back?

"I do. I love you, Dorian. So much it hurts." I wiped my eyes. "God, I'm such a disaster."

"You're *my* disaster, Rosebud."

I blinked. "Rosebud?"

Dorian's cheeks reddened. "It's what I've called you in my head for some time. I guess this is the first time I've said it aloud."

"Well, I love it." My cheeks hurt from smiling.

He held me close for a moment before he got up from bed.

"Well, good. I'm glad we got that settled." He brushed off his hands. "So now, what do you want for breakfast?"

I clutched the sheets. "What do you eat to celebrate being a hot mess?"

"Pancakes?" He grinned.

"Sounds good to me."

Dorian went downstairs, leaving me sitting in bed, a pile of mush from the love fog he'd put me in. I'd gone from panicked to euphoric. I'd broken up with several men in my life, yet not a single one had fought me on it. Not a single one had told me they loved me in response. Every single one of them had let me go without a fight.

I shook my head and got myself moving. This was nothing like those other relationships.

• • •

After a nice breakfast of pancakes that Dorian managed not to burn and a day of working in my art room, I felt like a new woman. By the time Chandler and Candace arrived, I was ready to see friends and celebrate my happiness—our happiness.

When the doorbell rang, I went to the door while Dorian set out some drinks. It was a cooler night, so we'd opted to have dinner inside rather than an evening barbecue out by the pool.

They were all smiles when I opened the door. Candace wore a long, blonde wig and looked totally different from the first and only other time I'd met her. She had such a pretty face that it didn't matter what she had on her head, but the wig definitely complemented her.

"Your hair. I love it!"

"I *wish* it were mine." She shrugged. "You really like it?"

"It looks so good. For some reason, I pictured you as a brunette, but the blonde really suits you."

"I asked Chandler who he felt like fucking later. He said Daisy."

"We have names for all the wigs," he added, rubbing his wife's back. "They're now her different personas. The blonde is Daisy. Short brunette is Lorelei. And the redhead is Gia."

Candace chuckled. "Gotta find some enjoyment in this situation, right?"

I ran a hand over her tresses. "I can't wait to meet them all."

"Hey!" Dorian wrapped his arms around me from behind. "Who brought blondie?"

Dorian told me he'd filled Chandler in on the evolution of our relationship, but I wasn't entirely sure *what* they knew. They didn't seem too surprised to see Dorian hanging all over me. But I had a feeling I'd be explaining a lot to Candace tonight.

The four of us migrated to the kitchen where Dorian had set out wine and glasses, along with the snack plate of crackers, cheese, and fruit that I'd prepared earlier.

"So, by the way, thank you both," Candace said as she munched on a cracker.

I looked over at Dorian then back at her. "Thank us, why?"

Candace smacked her hand on the counter. "I won a hundred bucks because of you two."

"What did we do?" Dorian asked as he poured some wine.

"I bet Chandler that you two would get together before the end of the year. It happened even faster than I'd anticipated."

"I wasn't lying to you that day, by the way," I told her. "There really wasn't anything happening between us the first time we met."

Dorian took a sip and laughed. "Those were actually the final hours before everything blew up."

"The sex game, you mean?" I chuckled.

Candace stopped mid-chew. "Oh my God. What are you talking about? I need to know."

"Remember that card game you found in the pile?" I asked. "After you guys left, Dorian and I sort of played it."

Dorian nuzzled my neck. "It's all innocent until you do a body shot off of the woman you've been trying to resist for weeks."

Chandler and Candace both had their mouths hanging open.

"Let's just say if Dorian hadn't been a Boy Scout the rest of that night, we would've gotten together *a lot* sooner," I added.

"What did he do…or not do?" Candace asked, looking all too amused.

"He actually turned me down that night," I confessed.

Chandler's eyes practically popped as he turned to his friend. "Are you out of your mind?"

"We both were a little out of our minds that night," Dorian replied. "A little too drunk. So, yeah, I forced myself to be good. But it was hard."

"I bet it was," Chandler chided as we all cracked up.

Candace smiled. "I'm so happy for the two of you."

"Thank you." Dorian kissed the side of my forehead.

"How are things going with you guys?" I asked them.

Candace's smile faded as they looked at each other.

I tensed. *Maybe I shouldn't have asked.*

"We've been better," she answered.

"Her treatment wasn't as effective as they'd hoped," Chandler explained. "So, we have to try something different."

"We thought I'd be done and able to celebrate tonight. But the doctor called this morning after my latest scan this week and...not so lucky."

I felt sick as Dorian looked over at me, seemingly at a loss for words. Remembering she didn't like when people said "I'm sorry," I scrambled to find something comforting to say. "I'll continue to think positive thoughts, Candace."

"Thank you," she murmured.

"We'll never give up." Chandler kissed his wife on the cheek and offered a strained smile. "Anyway, tonight is much needed after a not-so-great week."

Dorian forced a smile as well. "We've got dinner on the way."

I nodded. "Dorian and I have been learning to cook, but we've spared you as our guinea pigs tonight. We ordered from that new Moroccan restaurant, and it should be delivered soon."

Chandler raised his eyebrows. "Dorian has been cooking?"

Dorian shrugged. "Getting there. Almost burned the house down the first time I tried. But you know, practice makes perfect."

Candace gasped. "Are you serious?"

"I had to jump out of the shower when the fire alarm went off." I laughed.

"It was just an excuse to get her to come out naked," he joked. "I'm slick like that."

It made me happy to see Candace laughing and escaping a bit from the bad news she'd received earlier today. *You can have a dozen problems until you have a health problem,* I'd heard someone say. *Then you only have one problem.*

After a minute, Dorian and Chandler took their drinks into the living room while Candace and I stayed behind, chatting around the kitchen island. The food soon arrived, and we were just waiting for the guys to rejoin us after their chat.

"I can't tell you how relieved I am that you're so nice," she said to me. "Dorian has never been known for picking women. But you're a gem."

"I've met a few of his dates, so I know what you mean." I took a sip of my wine.

She ran a finger along her glass. "I feel like he always chose a certain closed-off type because he was afraid of getting too close to someone. He stuck with people he couldn't necessarily fall in love with. But I'm glad he seems happy now, especially after everything that happened with his dad. I was worried about him after Remington passed. I'm thrilled you guys found each other."

"Everything does seem perfect, doesn't it?" I looked away for a moment. "Despite that, I still have my fears."

She cocked her head. "Fears about what?"

"Monogamy is not normally his thing. I worry he'll wake up one day and remember that. Everything is new and fresh now, you know? It's always bliss during the honeymoon stage. But what happens when it's over?"

"Well, if there's one thing I know," she said, "it's that you can't live in fear. It will steal the joy from this amazing thing you and he are experiencing. So, try not to overthink it."

I nodded. Gosh, if she could live day to day with her situation, I sure as hell could learn to manage my fears surrounding Dorian.

Candace looked over her shoulder, lowered her voice, and continued, "But even as I stand here giving that advice, I still struggle with fear. Like for example, want to know what scares me even more than death?" She shut her eyes tightly and shook her head. "Never mind."

"It's okay," I said softly. "Tell me what's on your mind, Candace."

She nodded and let out a long breath. "Whenever I look at my husband, I wonder if someone else will get to love him someday…if someone else will have his babies." She shut her eyes. "That one kills me. It scares me and makes me profoundly sad. It's not that I wouldn't want him to be happy if I weren't around. Of course, I'd want that. But I want a life with him so badly. To grow old with him." Her eyes watered. "I love him so much."

I opened my arms and pulled her into an embrace. Sniffling, I felt a tear roll down my cheek. "I know I'm not supposed to cry, but I felt your love for him in my soul just now. I will pray so hard that you get everything you want and deserve."

"Thank you." She wiped a tear, too, and then shook off her mood, bravely feigning a smile. "Where the hell are those two anyway? I'm starving."

"I'll go fetch them," I said, still feeling like I could cry.

When I approached Dorian and Chandler in the living room, they were mid conversation. Rather than interrupt, I stepped back behind a wall for a moment.

"Anyway, you've listened to me ramble on enough..." Chandler said.

"Talk as long as you need to, man. You know I'll always listen. Never feel bad about talking to me about this. You need to let it out."

"Thanks. It's definitely better to vent to you than make her feel worse than she already does." He sighed. "I just love her so much. I can't let her see me scared."

I closed my eyes as I felt tears well up again. *Shit.* I couldn't let them see me crying. I waited and continued listening for a few moments.

Then Chandler asked, "Anyway, are you as happy as you seem, lover boy?"

"Honestly?" Dorian said.

"Yeah..."

"I'm probably even *happier* than I seem. I'm happier than I've been in my entire life. And to say that so soon after the hell I've been through the past few months is amazingly unexpected."

"Well, damn. It makes me happy to see you happy."

"I truly am. And that's even after she tried to break up with me this morning."

"Say what?" Chandler chuckled. "I think you need to back up."

I cringed. There was no way Dorian could spin the story so I didn't sound like a complete lunatic.

"It's a long story. But she freaked out a little because of how fast things have moved. She says she loves me, yet

I think she's afraid to fully trust me. That's partly my fault because I told her I wasn't into monogamous relationships when we first met. So I can't blame her. But she's changed how I feel about that. I just have to accept that trust takes time. It can only be earned."

"Well, I hope you told her how you feel."

"I told her I loved her. And I do."

"Wow."

"I know, right?"

"And she said it back?"

"Yeah." Dorian paused. "You know, I always thought when I found someone, I'd have this worry in the back of my mind, wondering if she loved me for me, or whether somehow she was after my money. But with Primrose? I know it's not about that. We have this natural connection that leaves no doubt. She looks at me, and my feelings for her are reflected back. Like we're both on the same page. I've never had that synchronicity with anyone before. I never imagined I'd fall in love this fast. But here I am."

I pulled in a breath. My heart was beyond full. Between the tears I'd shed over Candace and Chandler's love and now this, I felt ready to burst.

I waited for another pause in their conversation to pretend I was just entering the room.

When it finally came, I cleared my throat as I came around the corner, trying to seem nonchalant. "Your ladies are hungry."

They both turned.

Dorian stood. "Sorry, Rosebud. We've been yapping."

Chandler arched a brow. "Rosebud?"

Dorian shrugged.

Chandler punched him playfully in the arm. "You got it bad, dude."

"That I do." Dorian put his hand at the small of my back as we headed to the kitchen.

I felt like I was walking on air. He had no idea how much peace that conversation had given me. There was something so endearing about overhearing someone talking about you. No ulterior motives, nothing to prove. Just pure honesty. Though I had believed him when he'd poured his heart out this morning, any remaining doubt had been removed after hearing him tell his closest friend he was in love with me.

For the rest of that evening, I was on cloud nine. And with each passing day for the next couple of months, I fell more deeply in love with Dorian Vanderbilt—until the day my worst fears started to come true.

CHAPTER 17

Finally, my paranoia had gotten the best of me. After Dorian took off for a business trip to London, I'd invited Janelle over one Saturday evening for an emergency analysis of the situation. As I waited for her to arrive, I ruminated about everything all over again.

I could pinpoint the day Dorian had started acting strange. It was about two weeks ago, a little over three months after he and I had made a commitment to each other.

He'd gone to work that morning without saying goodbye. Normally, he'd kiss me and whisper something in my ear. Then, with a smile, I'd roll over and go back to sleep. But that morning two weeks ago was the first time Dorian didn't wake me up.

I would've thought nothing of it if the rest of the day hadn't also been strange. He didn't respond to my texts the way he usually did, and that night he told me he had to work late and didn't come home until almost midnight. Every day since had been more ominous than the last.

A few days into his change in attitude, I'd confronted him about whether something was wrong. He said he'd encountered some unexpected hiccups at work and apologized in advance that he might not be able to give me the attention I deserved for a while. That night, we'd made love, but it had felt different—like Dorian's mind was somewhere else. He hadn't looked me in the eyes once or said anything.

I tried to chalk it up to stress, which certainly can impede someone's ability to fully immerse themselves in a sexual experience. I went to sleep that night praying it was just one bad day.

But the next day had been almost exactly the same. While he'd kissed me before he left for work that morning, he'd once again worked so late that I didn't get to see him until we lay in bed together. Things got progressively worse over the week that followed.

Then a few days ago, Dorian had announced that he was going to have to travel to London for business. This was the first time he'd left me alone in this house since the day he arrived after his father's death.

As much as I hadn't wanted to be alone and had dreaded his leaving, I had no choice but to accept it. I'd just wished I hadn't had the weird feeling that something was off before he had to go. It made me worry that perhaps he wasn't being forthright about the reason for the trip.

Once Janelle arrived, she sat across from me in the kitchen, leaning her elbows on the table. I could tell by her face that I'd alarmed her.

"Have you asked him directly if he's lying to you?"

I shook my head. "I've been afraid to confront him about his change in behavior because I don't want him to think I don't trust him."

"But clearly you don't."

"I *did* trust him—until he changed."

"Well, the sooner you bring it up with him, the better. You can't continue to live like this."

"I know you're right. But I don't want to make things more difficult for him if he's going through a lot at work. I feel like I shouldn't start the conversation until he gets back."

"That's your prerogative, if you can wait that long. It doesn't sound like you're handling the unknown very well."

"Clearly not, but I don't think any serious conversation should happen while he's away. You can tell a lot by looking into someone's eyes."

She nodded. "I agree with you there. When does he come home?"

"He didn't give me an exact day, but I'm hoping by the end of this coming week."

Janelle sighed. "For your sake, I hope so, too."

I felt sick. Sometimes you don't need to be told when something is wrong.

You just know.

• • •

With each day that passed, I felt worse about my impending reunion with Dorian. I'd made up my mind to confront him the moment he got home.

In the meantime, I'd decided to test the waters and see what would happen if I stopped initiating communication with him. After two days went by that he didn't call, my nervousness transformed into anger. On top of that, he'd yet to give me a clear answer on when he was returning from London.

So the last thing I expected was for him to walk in the door before the end of the week.

But that's what happened on Thursday evening. I'd just gotten out of the shower and jumped at the sight of Dorian standing in our bedroom.

Hand on my chest, I gasped. "You scared the shit out of me."

He looked down at his feet. "I'm sorry."

Alarm bells sounded in my head. He hadn't initiated a hug or kiss. After such a long time away, you'd think he would've been more affectionate.

"Why didn't you tell me you were coming home?"

"I only realized this morning that I was booking a flight."

"So you wanted to...surprise me? You nearly killed me from a heart attack."

As I could now look in his eyes again, I was absolutely certain something had changed in him. Dread filled me, and every wall I could build around me went straight up. He hadn't spoken yet, but the worst had already been confirmed, even if I didn't understand it.

This was not the Dorian I knew. The look in his eyes was hard to describe—a mix of despair and sheer blankness. Empty. Devoid of all emotion, but almost in a forced way. Like he wasn't allowing himself to feel anything for fear that if he did, he'd break.

My *heart* felt like it was breaking. "I need you to tell me what's going on."

His face reddened. His eyes became glassy. As Dorian Vanderbilt stood before me on the verge of tears, I sensed my world as I knew it was ending.

His voice shook. "I'm so sorry, Rosebud."

The only word I could conjure was, "Explain…"

He looked down, then met my eyes again. "I can't do this anymore. I can't be in a relationship with you."

The room swayed. I'd known in my gut that this might've been coming, but there was no way to prepare for those words. No way to prepare for the end of the only love I'd ever known.

As I stood there in shocked silence, he continued. "It has nothing to do with you. You're amazing. I—"

"Fuck you, with the it's-not-you-it's-me bullshit," I screamed, as my shock transformed suddenly to rage. "Fuck you for making me believe you loved me."

"I'm not the right man for you," he said shakily. "I'm not built for this."

"Built? What are you, a fucking robot?"

A tear fell from his eye. "I need to end things now before they get more serious."

"You're breaking up with me, and you don't have the decency to explain it in a way that makes sense? I need answers, Dorian. How long have you known? Because *I* remember the exact morning you changed. And you had sex with me *that* night. You knew you were going to end things, and you had sex with me anyway?"

He shook his head as his voice trembled. "I didn't know anything for sure until I went away."

My voice grew louder. "So your London trip had nothing to do with work, then? You just wanted to get away from me so you could figure out how to end it?"

When he didn't answer, I felt something rising in my stomach. "I'm gonna be sick." When he took a step toward me, I whipped my hand out. "Don't touch me! Stay the fuck away from me!"

With that, he began to sob. None of this made any sense. How could someone so callous also be crying at this moment? He didn't care about me, yet he was visibly upset?

He raised his voice. "I know you don't want to hear this, but you have to let me say it."

I closed my eyes and let him speak.

"The last thing I want to do is hurt you," he said. "I would rather die. But continuing to be your boyfriend will mean hurting you even worse later. I know you were blindsided by this. And I won't ever forgive myself for it. But I only want what's best for you. And what's *truly* best for you is a life apart from me. I'll never be the man you deserve." He shook his head. "I do love you, Primrose."

"You love me?" I screamed. "You *love* me?"

"Yes," he muttered as he closed his eyes, tears falling down his cheeks. "As much as you might not be able to see it now, I'm breaking up with you *because* I love you. It's very possible to love someone but know you're not the right person for them. I'm setting you free *because* I love you."

"How exactly does someone wake up one day and realize he's not the man for someone he claims to love?"

"I can't explain it in a way you'll understand. *I* don't even fully understand it."

I paced. "What happened from one day to the next?" I whirled on him. "You don't love me. You couldn't *possibly* love me." But then a wave of grief washed over me. "Oh my God. I can't believe this is happening...with you. I can't believe you're doing this. I really thought you were it for me." I felt a panic attack coming on. "I need to get out of here."

He followed. "I'll give you whatever you need—"

"Fuck you!" I spewed, eyes blurry with tears. "I'm not taking shit from you!" I began throwing random things into a bag.

"You *need* to let me help you," he insisted.

I whipped around and pointed my finger at him. "I'd rather die than let you pay for me to leave. I'll be fine. I'll stay with Janelle until I can find a place. I don't need you or your filthy money."

He continued to walk behind me. "Where are you going? You can't leave upset. Please. You need to let me—"

I turned around one last time. "I don't *need* to do anything with you anymore. I just ask that you not be here during the day this weekend. I'll be coming back to get my stuff in shifts."

Dorian hung his head and muttered, "Whatever you need."

After going outside to get some air, I returned about ten minutes later and finished packing an overnight bag as fast as I could. Thankfully, Dorian had left my room, and I didn't find him to say goodbye before I ran to my car.

But before I could start the engine, I laid my head on the steering wheel and sobbed one final time.

By Sunday, Janelle's brothers had just about transported all of my belongings into a truck and carted them off. Thank God for her and her family; they were all I had at this point.

I'd texted Benjamin to let him know I'd be stopping to say goodbye to him and Patsy, if they wanted to meet me in the guest house. Dorian had left multiple messages asking if he could help in any way, and I'd ignored them all.

The guest house door opened before I had a chance to knock. Patsy and Benjamin had apparently seen me coming. I could only imagine the pity they felt. Patsy must've been thinking, *I told you so.*

Benjamin held out his arms, and I fell into his embrace. Patsy then hugged me from behind. The three of us had become a team in those weeks after Remington and Christina died. It made me so sad to leave them.

When they let me go, I asked, "Have either of you spoken to him?"

"I won't be speaking to him." Patsy grimaced. "I have nothing good to say to Dorian after he hurt you."

"He came by to see me last night," Benjamin said.

I looked down at the floor and let him continue.

"He seemed very distraught. I'm not happy about the fact that he misled you. But I do care about his well-being. I can't help that, since I've known him for so long. It was very sad to see him in that state. Hurting you has definitely had a profound effect on him. But I'm happy he didn't waste any more of your time."

"That's for damn sure," Patsy muttered.

"Does Janelle have room for all of your things?" Benjamin asked. "You're welcome to keep some items here."

"Thankfully they do seem to have the space. Her dad is letting me keep most of my stuff in his garage until I can find a place. I'll be crashing with them for now."

Benjamin nodded. "If you need anything at all, please let me know."

"Thank you."

I didn't have the heart to tell them I never planned to set foot anywhere near this mansion again. But I could always meet them somewhere. I promised to keep in touch with them, so long as they never mentioned Dorian. I didn't want to know if he eventually met someone. I didn't want to know anything. Before I left, they agreed.

As I drove off of the property that day, with Janelle's brother in his truck behind me, I felt a heaviness in my chest at the finality of it all.

And soon after moving in with Janelle's family, I realized it would take more than leaving the mansion to heal me. Being here in Orion Coast, so close to Dorian, with the threat of running into him at any given moment, was too much to handle. I'd lost focus at school and was only wasting money as my ability to create art became stifled in the wake of my broken heart.

After finishing the semester, I made the difficult decision to move back to Cincinnati. I'd drive my car to Ohio and pray it made it there in one piece. At least in Ohio I had some extended family. It made more sense to move back home than to start fresh in an entirely foreign place.

The day I drove out of Orion Coast for the final time, I decided to take a route past the mansion—one final goodbye from afar. I wouldn't stop in, of course. Just drive by.

While I was thankful not to see Dorian as I passed, something else unexpected met my eyes: a for-sale sign.

PART TWO

Five Years Later

CHAPTER 18

Staring at myself in the mirror, I moved my gaze from head to toe. The fitted bodice was nice, but the tulle ballgown wasn't my style.

"I'm not sure about this one." I pouted.

Lucy moved her finger in a circular motion. "Turn around." When I did, she added, "The back is gorgeous."

Holding out the sides of the skirt, I grimaced. "I think it's a bit...much."

"Let's face it. You're gonna be a beautiful bride no matter what you're wearing, but if you have any doubt, it's not the one. Simple as that."

I looked over at the smiling store attendant. "This isn't the one. I think it looked better on the rack than it does on me." I shrugged. "Sorry."

"No need to apologize," she said. "Helping you find the perfect dress is what I'm here for. Any idea which direction you want to go?"

"I feel like I want something a little less conventional. Do you have anything with feathers or maybe in a blush color, not stark white?"

To my surprise, she didn't hesitate. "Actually, we do have a couple of dresses embellished with feathers. They are white, though. Let me find them. Be right back."

After she left, Lucy chuckled. "Feathers? What, are you hoping to escape the wedding and fly the coop?"

She had no idea the nerve she'd hit with that comment. There was, indeed, a part of me that sometimes felt like flying away when I thought about the wedding.

It wasn't that I didn't love Casey. But from the moment he'd proposed, I'd been unsure if marriage itself was the right decision. Yet perhaps the biggest reason that all of this *did* make sense was the two little eyes looking up at me right now.

"Mommy, you look like a princess."

I lifted my daughter. "I figured you'd like this one. It makes me look like a Disney character, doesn't it?"

I wasn't originally going to bring my three-year-old daughter, Rosie, dress shopping, but since her father had to work, and the one person who could babysit was here alongside me as part of the bridal party, I didn't have much choice. Having her here now, though, and seeing the way she looked up at me, so proud, I had no regrets. Most kids don't get to see their mother marry their father. That was one plus about having gotten pregnant at the start of a relationship and doing everything in reverse order.

"I have to go potty," my daughter announced.

Lucy stood. "I'll take her."

"Thanks, Luce."

Lucy was my best friend here in Cincinnati. We'd met in a children's clothing shop while pregnant with our kids and had been inseparable ever since.

I continued to look at myself in the ballgown as I reflected on how far I'd come in five years. After I'd moved back to Ohio from California, I'd been in a rough place for about a year, feeling really lost and alone. I never went back to art school and mainly just waited tables to pay the rent for my small apartment.

Then I'd met Casey, a software engineer who owned the single-family house across from my apartment. One night we were both taking the trash out at the same time, and we got to talking. That was the first time since Dorian that I'd felt a connection with someone. Casey was smart, kind, and came from a big, warm family who lived in town. They took me in and made me feel like part of a tribe. It was a sense of safety I'd badly needed.

Was it insta-love between Casey and me? Definitely not. Our relationship had grown over time. I did love Casey, but it wasn't the frenzied kind of love I'd felt for Dorian. But experience had shown me that kind of love couldn't be trusted as real—at least not in the way it was returned.

About a year into my relationship with Casey, I got pregnant after a condom broke at the most inopportune time. I'd gone off birth control after the Dorian breakup, vowing that I was done with men and done with the side effects of my IUD. So Casey and I had used condoms from the start. All it took was one breaking to change my life and bind me to Casey. He hadn't forced the relationship with me, but it made sense to work on things for the sake of our child.

Rosie was my reason for getting up every morning. I was eternally grateful to have been given what I never knew I needed. If I'd had a choice, I might never have become a mom for fear that I couldn't provide enough for my child. But sometimes the universe knows what you need before you do. I certainly never imagined I'd love being a mom as much as I did. And I thought I'd done a pretty good job of it thus far.

Lucy and Rosie returned from the bathroom, and shortly after, the attendant brought out two more dresses, one of which immediately caught my eye. It was strapless and fitted until just below the knees and had strategically placed feathers throughout. This *definitely* seemed more my style.

I pointed to it. "I'd love to try that one."

After I put it on, I knew it was the one. "This is it," I said as I looked in the mirror.

Lucy tilted her head. "Really?"

"You don't like it?" I asked, immediately deflated.

"I think it looks gorgeous on you. I just feel like you haven't tried on that many to make a decision."

I shrugged. "When you know, you know."

If only I felt that secure about the marriage itself. Was a piece of paper really necessary to prove a commitment? Casey and I had our daughter to link us forever. To me, that was greater than any legal document. But marriage and family meant so much to Casey. I also knew how much it would mean to Rosie when she was old enough to understand. Right now, she just knew there was going to be a big party to celebrate her mommy and daddy, and she'd get to wear a pretty dress.

"I'm sure," I said. "I love it. There's not one thing about this dress that I would change."

"Okay, then." Lucy smiled. "I'm so happy for you. And Casey is going to die when he sees you in it."

"I don't want Daddy to die," my daughter cried.

"Oh no, honey. It's just a saying. Don't worry," Lucy assured her, flashing me an apologetic look.

I looked down at my daughter. "Do you like this dress?"

She scrunched her nose, shook her head, and giggled.

"Not sure if I can trust that reaction, silly girl."

After the woman took my measurements and some photos, she poured Lucy and me each a glass of champagne to celebrate saying yes to the dress. Orange juice for Rosie.

She put the champagne bottle on a side table. "Shall we go over to the bridesmaid selections now?"

I looked over at my friend. "Definitely."

"How many in your wedding party?" she asked.

"Just Lucy and my daughter."

"Did you want your daughter to wear a white dress?"

"I was thinking something like a mini bridal dress, yeah. Rosie will want something with a flowy skirt. And Lucy can select whatever color and style she likes."

The attendant flashed me a skeptical look. "Shouldn't *you* be choosing the color of the wedding?"

My ambivalence was probably becoming obvious. Maybe a red flag, even. Why hadn't I cared about the flowers when Casey's mother asked me? I guess this just didn't feel like a significant way to prove anything. I didn't have the energy to delve into whether there was any deeper meaning to my attitude.

"I'm open," I said. "Details like this sometimes make me flustered, so it's easier to let someone else choose. If I could afford a wedding planner, I would've let them make all the decisions. I can work around whatever Lucy chooses for her dress."

"Okay, then." She smiled. "Follow me. We have lots of choices."

I held my daughter's hand as Lucy and the woman walked ahead of us. She brought us into another room that had a rainbow of dresses tightly sandwiched along a rack. The idea of having to choose among them made my head spin.

"We're gonna be here all day." Lucy laughed.

"You must have some idea what color you like," the attendant said. "That way, I can narrow some choices, since not all dresses come in all colors."

Lucy ran her hand along the gowns. "I was thinking maybe a blue. But not quite blue. A hint of green."

"Like an aquamarine," the woman added.

My chest tightened. *"Neither blue, nor green. Aquamarine."*

My mind fell into a haze as an unwanted feeling of sadness and longing overtook me. *Dorian.* I'd tried so hard to keep my unresolved feelings for the man who'd shattered me at bay, but when they came up unexpectedly, as they sometimes did, it was always painful. How could I still have these feelings for a man who'd thrown me away? And it wasn't just that he'd discarded me; he'd made me trust him fully before doing so. That had forever ruined my faith.

Trying to forget Dorian over the past five years had been a skill I'd practiced, a muscle I had to exercise. And it was a technique I'd nearly perfected. But occasionally, something would smack me in the face and remind me of him. It wasn't that I missed him—how could you miss someone who broke your heart? But I did miss the experiences I'd had with him before he ended things. I missed the innocence I'd never get back. And I missed the connection I'd felt with him, even if it had been an illusion. I'd never been able to replicate that with anyone.

I missed the way I'd felt during those months. I missed waking up and looking forward to each day. I missed the passion I'd thought we shared. I missed the girl I'd been before the fantasy was destroyed.

Lucy snapped me out of my thoughts. "Are you okay, Primrose?"

"Hmm?"

"Are you all right? You look like you're about to cry."

"I do?"

"Yeah..." Lucy said. "You've been staring into space, and you look sad."

My inability to hide it made me so damn angry. My daughter was here, for heaven's sake. And I was thinking about another man while dress shopping for my wedding to her father. There had to be a place in hell reserved for that kind of behavior. If only I could control it.

"I'm fine," I insisted.

I'm so not. Well, at least not when I think about Dorian.

"But I don't like aquamarine," I added. "So *any* color but that, okay?"

• • •

That evening at dinner, I gave Casey the rundown on our bridal shop trip—minus the aquamarine freakout, of course.

He wiped his mouth. "I'm so happy you found a dress you like."

"Well, *some of us* liked it." I glared teasingly at Rosie, who was playing with her pasta.

Casey laughed. "What do you mean?"

"Your daughter didn't appreciate my style."

He chuckled and tickled her side. "You didn't like Mommy's dress?"

She scrunched her nose and shook her head.

"You don't mean that," he said.

She giggled.

"Oh, I think she does. She wanted me in a conventional ballgown to match her Disney princesses."

Casey smiled. "That's *so* not your taste."

"It's not."

"Did Lucy get a dress?"

"Yup. She picked yellow, actually."

He made a face. "Interesting. Not sure how I feel about that."

"I know. But I told her she could pick the color." I sighed. "I'll get used to it. We also got a dress for Peanut."

"Oh, that's right. I forgot she was getting a dress today, too." He turned to our daughter. "Tell me about your dress, baby girl."

She shook her head.

I wiped some spaghetti sauce off her mouth. "You're being silly."

"It's so pretty," she finally said.

"It is." I nodded. "It's white with sparkles."

"Sparkles!" Casey beamed with exaggerated amazement. "I should've known. Can't wait to see how you dirty that up by the end of the night."

"Oh, you can count on that." I laughed.

After I washed Rosie's hands and face, she played in the living room while I returned to the kitchen. As I was stacking the dishwasher, Casey came up behind me and rubbed my back. "Everything okay with you?"

I froze. "Why do you ask?"

"Well, for someone who went dress shopping today, you seem a bit…down. Shouldn't that have put you in a good mood?"

How could I look my fiancé in the eyes and tell him I was down because the mere mention of a color had sent me into a tailspin over an old boyfriend?

Casey didn't know too many details about the Dorian Vanderbilt heartbreak. When I met Casey, I told him I'd had a boyfriend back in California and things had ended badly. I never mentioned Dorian's name; although Casey knew the man I'd dated was Christina's stepson. Whenever he'd pry, I'd shy away from the details. There were no words to properly describe the betrayal I'd felt when I moved out of the mansion. What happened with Dorian had made me forever doubt my judgment. The one time I'd decided to trust someone had backfired.

The situation with Casey, though, was different than anything that had come before it. Since my pregnancy with Rosie was accidental, at first he and I might've been together out of a sense of obligation. But over time, he'd proven trustworthy. If the situation had been different, I might've broken up with Casey before I had the chance to learn what a stand-up guy he really was. While I'd always be scarred by Dorian, I *was* truly working on not taking out my fears and bad experiences on a good man who didn't deserve it.

If my relationship with Dorian had been like a fast-moving luxury boat that wound up on stormy seas, my time with Casey was a smooth tugboat ride on a sunny day, slow and steady. Casey was dependable, loving, and a damn good father. I had no regrets, even if the level of passion I'd once experienced with the man who broke me was something I didn't have with my current partner. But you know what? That kind of fire only gets you burned. Casey was a warm breeze that kept me comfortable and safe. That's what I needed in my life.

"Do you not feel fulfilled?" he suddenly asked.

Feeling ashamed and, sadly, also somewhat seen, I said, "Why would you ask that?"

"I know you're not really practicing your art, and we don't have the space for a studio."

Relief washed over me as I realized he wasn't referring to our relationship.

"What, you don't think drawing animals to order for kids is my life's dream?" I teased.

About a year ago, I'd decided I needed to do something for myself. I was a stay-at-home mom with a two-year-old and going a bit stir crazy. So, I'd started a business called Paint with Primrose. I'd travel to kids' birthday parties, paint their faces, paint animals to order, and do caricatures of people. Turns out there was a real market for it. I'd put up fliers around the city and often found myself booked at least two Saturdays a month. The extra money was helpful, but mostly it saved my sanity. It certainly wasn't perfecting my talent, but it was a way to make some extra cash and keep my creative well from running completely dry.

"I'm sorry if I seem a little sad today. There's no good reason for it," I assured him. "Just one of those days." I shook my head. "I suppose sometimes I think back to my life in California and the amount of free time I had to explore my art and miss it. But the truth is, nothing is stopping me from picking it back up again."

Well, nothing besides the artistic drive I seemed to have lost. Dorian had taken my creativity with him. Something had died inside me the day he broke my heart, and I hadn't been able to get it back.

"Well, if you ever want to go out back and do your thing in the sunroom on Sundays, I'll take Rosie to one of those indoor kids' gyms so you can work in peace."

I smiled. Casey was so thoughtful. He worked hard during the week but was eager to spend time with his daughter any chance he got. It would've been smart of me to take him up on his offer of some alone time on Sundays. That room was at the back of the house and mostly used for storage. It was surrounded by windows that let the sun in beautifully, and I'd often toyed with the idea of turning it into an art space. Maybe this was my chance to see that through.

"I really appreciate that." I reached up on my tippy toes to kiss him. "And I appreciate you. Thank you."

"I love you, baby," he said before walking away to join our daughter in the living room.

After he left, guilt settled in my stomach. I hated not being a hundred-percent honest with him. At the same time, some things were better kept inside, weren't they? Especially when my inner thoughts and feelings didn't always make sense. Like still being affected by a man who'd treated me like dirt.

Thankfully, moments like the one I'd experienced in the bridal shop today were rare. Overall, I'd done a good job of burying thoughts of Dorian. However, when those moments did arise, I sometimes found myself tempted to search for him online, something I'd forbidden myself to do to protect my mental health. Like all the other times, I let the urge pass tonight, not giving in, and once again ensuring that I stayed focused on my future, not the past.

CHAPTER 19

A few days later, I woke up in a sweat, my body buzzing from head to toe. This wasn't the first sex dream I'd had involving Dorian. But it was the first one in a year—probably triggered by the incident at the bridal shop.

We'd been back at the mansion pool, and Dorian had done a body shot off of me. But unlike real life, this version had morphed into something altogether different. His head had been between my legs after he'd poured tequila over my clit, licking it off. My brain was incredibly cruel for creating these dream sequences when I'd been working so hard to block him from my mind. These vivid sexual dreams felt like setbacks, even if they shouldn't have meant anything. Why couldn't I have had these dreams about Casey, or literally *anyone* else in the world but Dorian Vanderbilt? Maybe because the more you try to bury things that remain unresolved, the more your subconscious works to bring them out. And there was nothing I'd tried to bury deeper than Dorian.

"Are you okay?" Casey asked.

Shit. "I'm okay," I answered as I caught my breath.

"You were breathing heavily in your sleep. You should maybe get checked for sleep apnea."

Trust me, that's not the problem. "Was I?"

"Yeah. Moving around a lot, too. Your legs were wiggling."

No surprise there. "I think I was just having a bad dream." *About my ex-boyfriend's head between my legs.*

"I'm sorry you had a nightmare."

"Me, too. Thank you." I sighed as I rolled over. "Maybe I should try…taping my mouth or something."

Casey wrapped his arms around me from behind. As he held me, I felt both guilt and relief. Somewhere in my subconscious I was still lusting for Dorian Vanderbilt, but in reality, I had Casey, someone unlike Dorian whom I could trust and who truly loved me. Someone I was pretty sure would never leave me or our daughter.

And someone who most definitely deserved better than a woman who had more emotional baggage than he knew about.

・・・

Later that afternoon, I was feeling restless, so I called Lucy to see if she and her son, who was around Rosie's age, were up for a playdate. Luckily, she, too, was feeling a bit bored today and encouraged us to come by.

Playdates were as much about mental sanity for the moms as they were socialization for the kids. I loved my daughter, but some days it felt impossible to come up with enough ways to entertain her while she wasn't in preschool. When the weather outside was crappy, like it was today, that made it even harder.

A little while later, as Rosie and Sebastian played in the living room, Lucy and I sat with the coffees I'd picked up on the way here. The sun had finally come out and filtered through the window, casting a glow on Lucy's blonde hair. It was amazing what a little patch of sunshine, good coffee, and pleasant company could do for one's mood.

Then Lucy had to go and ruin it.

"Can we talk about what happened when we were dress shopping?" she asked.

My heart beat faster. I'd thought I'd dodged a bullet, but Lucy was more perceptive than I'd given her credit for.

"What do you mean?" I made one last attempt at playing dumb.

"I don't know. Your mood took a pretty big turn. I couldn't help but wonder if maybe you were having doubts about going through with the wedding..."

Ugh. "That wasn't what the mood switch was about."

Silence descended upon the room as she waited for me to elaborate.

"We don't have to talk about it if you don't want to," she said.

But now I knew I couldn't let it go. Burying it was clearly not working. I hadn't spoken about Dorian to anyone, not even a therapist, which I probably should've done a long time ago. Lucy was my best friend. I'd lost touch with Janelle after moving from California, which I'd always regretted. I'd seen from social media that she was married now with a baby on the way. Thank goodness I'd found Lucy. She and I hadn't known each other more than a few years, but it sometimes felt like we had. If I couldn't talk to her, who could I talk to?

I sighed. "When you made a comment about the color of one of the dresses, it threw me into a bit of PTSD."

"Oh my gosh. How is that possible? A color?"

"It's a long story." I looked down at my phone. "Not sure we have time for it today."

Lucy looked over at the kids and sipped her coffee. "They seem to be playing well. And I ain't going anywhere. So, I'm listening."

I took a deep breath and began the story of my heartbreak, starting with when I'd moved to the mansion to live with my aunt and ending with my leaving Orion Coast after the devastation of Dorian's one-eighty. I also explained the aquamarine thing. She listened intently—the story unfolded like some kind of television drama, complete with handsome billionaire, tragedy, and picturesque California scenery.

When I finished, she cocked her head. "You haven't googled him all this time?"

"No. I don't want to know anything. I know that might seem hard to believe, but there's nothing I could find out that would make me feel better about the situation. I don't want to see that he's moved on with someone. I don't want to see his face. I was supposed to have kept in touch with Patsy and Benjamin, but I lost touch with them as well. Reaching out to them could mean learning something that would upset me. I need to move on."

She sighed. "Wow, I can't believe you and I have known each other all this time, and you never told me this story. Your time there clearly had a major impact on your life, and it all makes so much sense now."

"What makes sense?"

"Why I sometimes catch you deep in thought, like something is on your mind, and yet you always claim to be fine. You have this air of mystery around you, something I could never put my finger on. And certainly this explains why you acted strangely at the dress shop."

"When you truly believe you love someone with all of your heart and soul and they betray you, your trust in everything dies. I trust Casey as much as I possibly can. But also it's..." I hesitated.

"What?" she prodded.

"It's as if..." I thought a moment. "It's as if I don't care anymore. Like the worst has already happened. And now, I just do what's best for my daughter, regardless of whether Casey or anyone else might end up hurting me." I shook my head. "I don't think I'm capable of being hurt anymore."

Lucy nodded. "That's sad, but sort of reasonable."

"I love Casey, but it's different than what I experienced in California. I'm not sure if I'd ever be able to love someone the way I loved Dorian."

"Hmm..." Her eyes narrowed. "Did you say his name is Dorian?"

"Yeah, why?" I tried to avoid saying it out loud as much as possible.

She stared into space for a moment. "Dorian... I feel like I heard that name somewhere recently. What's his last name?"

"Vanderbilt."

Her eyes widened.

"What?"

"I could swear I heard that *exact* name recently. Dorian Vanderbilt. I shit you not. I just can't remember where."

A surge of adrenaline rushed through me. Hopefully, she was just imagining this. Dorian Vanderbilt wasn't exactly a common name, though. If she thought she'd heard it, maybe she had.

Lucy rubbed her temples. "It's gonna drive me nuts until I figure it out."

As the minutes passed, I tried to calm myself. This probably meant nothing. People confused names all the time.

Rosie and I stayed another hour at Lucy's before I had to round my daughter up so we could get home to prepare dinner. Just as I was gathering our things, Lucy snapped her fingers. "I know where I heard that name."

I froze. "Where?"

"It was someone who rented a car recently."

Lucy worked part time at the car rental place at the airport. Blood pounded in my ears.

Then she laughed. "But you know what? I get client names wrong all the time. I remember thinking what a strong name that was, but for all I know, it could've been Damien or Darren Vanderbilt." She shook her head. "Maybe it was Van der Beek."

The tension in my neck relaxed a bit. I could totally see Lucy screwing up the name. She likely ran across all kinds of similar-sounding names with the volume of business at that car rental place. I laughed it off. "Well, thanks a lot for the scare, but I'm gonna choose to ignore it."

"As you should with my scatterbrain." She chuckled.

We said goodbye, and I vowed to let it go. Just wasn't sure that I could.

• • •

Later that evening, I wished my guardian angel would drop something on my head to knock some sense into me. I knew I'd regret what I was about to do. And yet I couldn't seem to stop myself.

After both Casey and Rosie were asleep, I snuck out of bed into the living room with my laptop.

Rather than freeing me, my obsession with Dorian had grown worse after recounting my story to Lucy earlier. It made me wonder if the reason I hadn't been able to let go of him was because I was still hanging on to the Dorian of the past. It was easy to do that when I hadn't googled him to see who he was now, what sort of life he was living. If I could see with my own eyes that he was married or was still playing the field, maybe that would help me to move on.

Otherwise, it was as if Dorian, or at least the memory of him, had been frozen in time—as if the Dorian I knew was still out there somewhere, regretting his decision to hurt me. My mind kept giving me conflicting messages, one second warning me against searching his name, the next encouraging me to get it over with.

What are you doing?
This is a mistake.
Just do it!

My pulse raced as my fingers hovered over the keys. A minute later, I typed his name.

D-O-R-I-A-N V-A-N-D-E-R-B-I-L-T.

After I hit the search button, I closed my eyes. I didn't really want to know. A wave of nausea came over me as I forced my eyes open. Then the title of the news article I saw rocked me to my core.

Orion Coast Tech Mogul Dorian Vanderbilt Missing at Sea

I'd been through a lot of shocking moments in my life—the day Christina died, the moment Dorian broke up with me, the day I'd learned I was pregnant—but never in my life had I felt the weight of something so heavy, so profoundly soul-crushing.

I'd prepared myself for a number of potentially upsetting scenarios: finding out he was married, finding out he had a child, confirming that he looked more beautiful and happier than ever. But never had I considered a scenario like this.

Gulping, I clicked on the article.

> *Authorities in Turkey are searching the Aegean Sea for the bodies of tech billionaire Dorian Vanderbilt and a business associate after the luxury boat they were traveling in was found empty and unmanned about thirty miles from shore. Local authorities, along with the Turkish Coast Guard Command, have been searching the waters for the past forty-eight hours after a member of Van-*

derbilt's staff reported him missing. According to Vanderbilt associates, while on vacation, the tech mogul went out on a leisurely ride, accompanied by longtime family friend Benjamin Crane. Neither Crane nor Vanderbilt have been seen nor heard from since. It's feared that the men may have gone swimming off of the boat and drowned. At this time, there are no indications of foul play.

I felt the walls closing in as tears rolled down my cheeks. I looked at the date of the California newspaper article, and my stomach sank. It had been published a year or so after I'd left California. *Years* had gone by, and I'd been worrying about all the wrong things. All of this time Dorian had been dead? Or missing? I didn't know which. But I didn't want to keep looking. I couldn't bear to see that he and Benjamin had died. I wasn't ready for that.

Oh my God. Poor Dorian.

I didn't care what he'd done to me. He didn't deserve to drown. And *Benjamin*.

Feeling a violent churning in my stomach, I ran to the bathroom off the kitchen and vomited into the toilet.

Presumed dead.
Presumed dead.
Presumed dead.

I vomited again.

When there was nothing left, I sat in a corner of the bathroom, huddled on the floor. All I felt in that moment was love—love for a man I'd vilified for being honest about his feelings. Love for a man who'd been through so much after the loss of his father, only to be...presumed dead. Drowned. *How could this have happened?*

Maybe I could find the courage to keep searching for information. But not today. Today I wasn't ready to hear that the love of my life had died. And yes, it was now clear to me that the love of my life could also be the greatest heartbreak of my life. Dorian Vanderbilt was one and the same.

CHAPTER 20

There was only one time of day when I could get things done: the three hours in the morning that Rosie was at preschool, and she only went three days a week. I'd drop her off shortly before eight and pick her up at eleven. The time always flew by. Usually, since I was already out, after dropping her at school, I'd treat myself to a latte from the café, bring it home, and enjoy twenty minutes of me time before tackling whatever household things were on my long to-do list—anything from bills to laundry to cleaning up the mess my daughter had made the previous night. But those twenty minutes sitting in the sunroom with my latte, closing my eyes occasionally and letting the sun from the windows beat down on my face? Heavenly—and much needed. Although, as of the last six days, my breaks hadn't been as relaxing as they once were. My time alone was now consumed by an urgency to go online.

It was a constant battle to stop myself from seeking the information I wasn't ready to handle. I knew eventually I'd give in. It was only a matter of time. But I wasn't ready to face the truth. As long as I was ignorant, there was a chance Dorian was alive. And I needed him to be alive, even if it was just an illusion.

This particular Wednesday morning after my relaxation time, I'd turned the living room upside down, vacuuming under the couches and washing the windows. Anything to keep from going online.

When I looked at the time and saw that I only had a half hour before I needed to go get Rosie, I started to move faster. Once she came home, I'd make her lunch. We'd do some activities together, and then before I knew it, I'd need to start preparing dinner so it would be ready when Casey got home. Whoever said being a mom wasn't a full-time job needed their head checked.

The doorbell rang, prompting me to shut off the vacuum. Sometimes the mailman would ring the bell if he left a package at the door. No one else came by at this time of the day, so I assumed it was him.

But when I opened the door, the predictable day I'd imagined before me no longer existed.

Time no longer existed.

If I hadn't felt my heart pounding, I might've doubted I was still alive—perhaps I'd died and gone to some twisted version of the afterlife. A place where everything you've suppressed suddenly meets you on the other side, forcing you to face it.

Am I dreaming?
Hallucinating?
"Hi, Primrose..."
I managed to utter his name. "Dorian..."

"Hi," he said again.

"You're...alive..." My lip trembled.

"Yes." He reached out to cup my face, a look of wonder in his eyes as if he were also in a dreamlike state.

I willed my foolish heart to stop beating so fast for him. But I'd thought he was dead. Regardless of what he'd put me through, I was ecstatic to find out Dorian was alive.

But then fear took over, and my protective instincts shut everything down. I pulled away. "You shouldn't be here."

"I know this is a shock."

"*Shock* is not a strong-enough word." I shook my head. "How. *Why*...are you here?"

"It's hard to explain."

"How did you know where I live?"

"It's not that hard to find someone these days. Simple internet search."

Of course. Not everyone specifically avoided Google like I had for the past five years.

It was a miracle I remembered the time. "I have to go pick up my daughter from preschool. I can't be late." I paused. "I...have a daughter now."

"I know," he said softly.

"You do?" My eyes widened. "How would you know that?"

"I was hoping we could talk." He looked down for a moment. "I'm sorry I chose a bad time to come by."

I shook my head. "I don't know..." Silence filled the air.

"Primrose, look me in the eyes, please."

I realized I had been looking at the floor. I was afraid of what looking into his eyes would do to me, what it would cause me to remember.

And sure enough, when my gaze met his, a feeling of torturous nostalgia came over me. The same deep sadness that had been in his eyes the last time I'd seen him was there now.

"Please..." he breathed. "I know you don't owe me anything. But I *need* to talk to you." He reached into his pocket and handed me a sticky note. "I wrote down where I'm staying here in town, along with my number. It's not the same one I used to have. Not that you'd still have the old one. I wouldn't blame you if you'd completely erased me in every possible way." He exhaled. "I'm not leaving Cincinnati, though, until I've had a chance to speak with you. I'll wait as long as necessary until you have a moment to talk to me."

What the hell is this about? "I'll see what I can do," I finally said.

"Thank you." He nodded and took a few steps back. "I'll let you go get your daughter."

I watched blankly as he got into his car and drove away.

After he was no longer in sight, I closed the door and leaned my back against it, attempting to catch the breath that felt like it had been sucked out of my body. I was confused and scared about what he could possibly have to say to me. The list of questions I had for him was certainly long.

The alarm on my phone went off, scaring the crap out of me. I always set a ten-minute warning in case I lost track of time, never wanting to be late for preschool pickup.

I quickly entered Dorian's number into my phone, along with the address on the sticky note, before heading out to my car. I took in some of the cool September air, hoping it might calm the turmoil inside me.

The tree-lined ride to the preschool felt like a blur, as my thoughts spun out of control. When I got to the pickup line, I didn't even know how the hell I'd gotten there.

Today was Wednesday. I decided the only time I'd be able to meet with Dorian was two days from now, on Friday. That was the next time Rosie had preschool. Curiosity might kill me before then, but I didn't have the kind of life where I could just leave the house whenever I wanted to on a whim. Not to mention, Dorian didn't deserve to have me jump at the chance to meet him. He wasn't dead after all. Therefore, I could go back to being angry, since I no longer had to mourn him. I almost laughed at that. *You're ridiculous.*

As I sat in the pickup line, waiting for Rosie to appear with her teacher, my mind continued to race. Dorian had looked so handsome. Perhaps my memory of him had faded just enough to make me forget exactly how stunning he was. He had the same gorgeous mane of black hair, the same beautiful face, and the same amazing smell. And he also had the same ability to make me feel things I knew I should be forgetting.

The back door of my car opened, and I forced a huge smile as Rosie arrived.

"She had a great day," her teacher said.

"That's awesome!"

Rosie handed me a picture she'd drawn. It looked like a colorful fish.

"So nice, honey. You're really getting good at drawing. Good job."

"She's on her way to becoming an artist like her mom." Mrs. Harrington winked.

After the teacher shut the car door, I looked in the rearview mirror at Rosie's little face. Her cheeks were red. She loved school, but she also looked forward to coming home each day. Such a happy girl. My daughter was an absolute joy.

"Are you hungry?" I asked.

She jumped in her seat. "Yes!"

I put the car in drive and drove off. "What do you feel like for lunch today?"

"Peanut butter and fluff!"

"That's very sugary. How about peanut butter and banana?"

She pouted. "Fluff!"

"I'll give you a little fluff and some banana on a peanut butter sandwich, okay?"

"Okay, Mommy." She smiled.

My sweet baby, oblivious to the emotional dilemma pummeling her mother right now. She deserved better than to be in the middle of this.

After we got to the house and parked, I looked around my quiet neighborhood street, feeling paranoid. Dorian knew where I lived. Had he been here before today? It freaked me out that he'd been staying nearby, and I hadn't known. How long had he been here? I supposed these were all questions I needed to ask him on Friday.

I put on a TV show for Rosie in the living room, and I realized I'd left the vacuum out, since Dorian showing up at my door had distracted me from putting it away. I returned it to the utility closet and went to the kitchen to make her sandwich.

As I spread peanut butter on two slices of whole wheat bread, my mind wandered. Before I knew it, I'd been spreading the peanut butter around for three minutes, and I'd nearly ruined the bread. I added a little marshmallow fluff and layered it with half a banana, thinly sliced.

I washed a small bunch of red grapes and cut each one in half, since I worried Rosie could choke if I left them whole. I could be so responsible in some aspects of my life, yet so very irresponsible in others, like—I don't know—planning to visit an ex-boyfriend while my daughter was at school on Friday. I cringed at the thought.

After carrying the food over to Rosie, I sat and watched her eat as she enjoyed her video. If I was physically present right now, that might make up for the fact that my mind was still on Dorian.

I gently patted her hair as she devoured the sandwich.

"What should we have for dinner tonight?" I asked.

She answered the way she always did.

"Spaghetti."

"Will you eat little trees with it if I make you spaghetti?"

Little trees was what we called broccoli around here. She nodded.

"Deal, then."

Spaghetti was likely all I could manage tonight anyway. If tasked with cooking anything that required me to follow directions, I'd ruin the whole thing. I needed to give myself grace for now. Maybe tomorrow night, too. Or as long as whatever the hell was going on with Dorian lasted.

As I took Rosie's plate back to the sink, I realized I hadn't formally committed to meeting him. So there was still a chance I could back out. But that wasn't what I wanted. I reached for my phone and pulled up his name before I could change my mind.

> **Would you be available to meet with me Friday around 8:15 in the morning?**

His response was almost immediate.

> **Dorian: Absolutely. Thank you for making time for me. Where would you like to meet?**
>
> **Primrose: I can come to the address where you're staying.**

Going to his place felt even more forbidden, but there was really no other choice; being in public with him would be too risky.

> **Dorian: Great.**
>
> **Primrose: See you then.**
>
> **Dorian: See you Friday.**

Letting out a long exhale, I pushed the phone away, forcing myself to return to life at hand. I called to Rosie. "Wanna go play outside?"

"Okay!"

I grabbed our jackets, vowing not to think about Dorian again until I had to.

CHAPTER 21

Guilt and dread twisted in my stomach as I dropped Rosie off at preschool Friday morning. When the teacher came out to get her, I waved to my daughter, feeling like a fraud. I hadn't told Casey what I was doing this morning. I'd decided not to mention anything until I understood what was going on. I didn't want to alarm him, and this felt like something I had to do without any outside voices complicating the matter. Also, Casey was under a lot of work stress lately, and this would only compound that. Keeping business as usual on the homefront seemed like the best idea.

My stomach churned as I pulled up in front of Dorian's rental property in a residential neighborhood, tucked away at the end of a cul-de-sac. The beautiful two-story brick house was huge. Not sure why this surprised me. It made perfect sense.

I'd planned to sit in my car and find my bearings for a few minutes, but I didn't have the chance. Before I could even take my seatbelt off, the front door opened and Dorian appeared. He held a hand up in a wave, then slipped his hands in his pockets, seeming anxious. The beauty of the house paled next to the man standing at the doorway.

I got out of my car and walked toward the door. I stopped a few feet away, keeping my distance. I looked up at the house. "This place is nice." Though as lovely as it was, it was a drop in the bucket compared to the Vanderbilt mansion.

"Thanks. It was the only thing I could find that didn't require a minimum stay." He moved aside. "Come in."

The inside was even more impressive than the flawless exterior. The entry opened to a huge living room with a large wraparound couch the color of sand. Everything coordinated perfectly, and large windows let in an abundance of light. This place was meant for a large, wholesome family, not some mysterious meeting between ex-lovers.

Dorian had a roaring fire going.

"Let's sit," he said, leading me to the couch in front of the fireplace.

The flames crackled. It was a scene way too intense for eight fifteen in the morning.

"You're nervous," he said.

"I can't help it." I licked my lips. "I don't understand any of this."

He sat across from me on the far end of the couch, rubbing his palms along his thighs. "Believe me. I'm nervous, too. Can I get you some coffee?"

I shook my head. "No, thank you."

He nodded and exhaled. "I don't even know where to begin."

"Why don't you start with why you showed up at my doorstep after five years? Why did you wait so long if you have things to say to me?"

"I didn't have much of a choice."

"I don't understand."

"You're not supposed to understand, but do you know anything at all?"

"What am I supposed to know about?"

"Have you googled me?"

"Only very recently. Like literally a week ago. That's part of why it was such a shock to see you. I came across an article about you having gone missing, and I was afraid to keep searching because I thought you were…" My voice trembled. *Shit. Why am I crying? He's fine.*

"Oh, baby. I'm so sorry." He moved to sit next to me and took my hand in his. "I'm sorry to have worried you like that." He sighed. "You'd never searched my name before that?"

Sniffling, I shook my head. "Not even once. I chose to erase you from my life like you did me. It wasn't going to make anything easier to keep tabs on you. It would've been painful to see your face." My confusion worsened by the second. "Why? What would I have found if I'd kept searching?"

"Just some things that wouldn't have made sense without me explaining—like the real reason I went missing, why I eventually walked away from my father's company. Nothing you would've found told the full story, though. You would've probably just been more confused."

"I did know you put the mansion up for sale."

"A while back, yeah. How did you know that?"

"I drove by on my way out of Orion Coast. One final goodbye. Saw the realtor sign. I was shocked but figured you had your reasons."

He stared at me a few moments.

"What?" I asked.

"You're so fucking beautiful. It hurts to look at you, Rosebud." He shook his head. "I'm sorry. I knew it was gonna be tough seeing you. But it's even harder than I thought."

I cleared my throat, hardly able to breathe. "This is hard for me, too."

"I know it is. Thank you for putting aside your fears and coming. It means a lot to me."

My body stiffened as my protective instinct kicked in. "Well, I don't have all morning. I've got to be back at the school by eleven, so…"

"So I should cut to the chase." He licked his lips.

"Yeah."

Dorian took a deep breath. "Nothing is what it seemed, Primrose. When I ended things with you, it wasn't because I wanted to. It was because I *had* to." He paused. "Your life was on the line. You just didn't know it."

My stomach dropped. "What are you talking about?"

"I need to back up a bit. Please bear with me because… it's a lot to take in."

Shifting in my seat, I nodded.

"I have to start by going back to the time right after my father and Christina died. Something about their deaths never sat right with me. It was a feeling I had even before I moved to California from Boston. My father had been working on a number of inventions at the time of his death that, for various reasons, could've been motivation for someone to kill him."

My eyes widened.

"Soon after I came home to Orion Coast, I hired a team of investigators to look into what really happened at that private villa where my father and Christina had been staying. The local authorities had deemed it an accident, but I wasn't convinced."

"How come you didn't mention any of this to me at the time?"

"I didn't want to burden you with it, especially since I was never sure there was any validity to my concerns. I didn't want to scare you. I never imagined what the investigation would spiral into. Every day that you and I lived at the mansion, though, the investigators I hired were working tirelessly to get to the bottom of what really happened to my dad and Christina."

A sinking feeling grew in my stomach. "What did they find?"

He sighed. "It was worse than anything I could have imagined. Vanderbilt Technologies had been working on a new type of solar panel that would've garnered a huge government contract. It would've been the most lucrative product they'd ever created. For a long time, Remington was credited as the sole creator. But in reality, the technology was originally designed by a man named Alfred Mills. Unbeknownst to anyone until years later, Mills had pitched the idea for the panel to my father in the hopes of partnering with Vanderbilt to get it patented and sold. But unfortunately, my father wasn't as honorable a business partner as I'd always assumed him to be."

"Remington was crooked?"

Dorian nodded. "My father modified Mills's design somewhat and filed the patent solely under his own name, leaving Mills off of it. Mills filed a lawsuit, but it was eventually thrown out due to lack of evidence. He was never able to prove he was the original designer. I'd known about that but had always assumed Mills was lying."

"But Remington was the liar..."

He nodded. "Right before my father and Christina died, Vanderbilt was about to launch the stolen solar panel product. Their deaths stalled the release and distribution, and the potential buyers, including the government, lost confidence with Remington gone. One of the first things I was tasked with when I took over was getting the solar panel release back on track. Little did I know that Mills and the people working for him were planning my demise as well. I wondered if Mills might have been behind the carbon monoxide incident, but it wasn't until I started noticing that I was being followed that I realized my suspicions were right. The guys I'd hired to look into things discovered that people had been taking photos of the house. Photos of us." He paused. "Photos of you."

Holy shit. "That's when you started to pull away."

Dorian looked into my eyes and nodded. "I was terrified. I knew I needed to get you away from all of it. I would've never forgiven myself if something happened to you. But I also knew how loyal and dedicated you were. I knew if I told you what was going on, you wouldn't leave my side. I couldn't risk you getting hurt. The company I'd hired to investigate was based in London, which was why I went out there before I broke up with you. During my trip, they presented me with all the evidence they'd gathered. It became clear that I needed to develop a safety plan. So I lied to you to get you away from me, though that was the last thing I ever wanted. I didn't want to scare you or drag you into it. I wanted you to live your life, even if it killed me to let you go."

My heart had never felt heavier, and my mind swirled. Yet there was still so much he hadn't yet explained. "What happened after we broke up?"

"I kept tabs on you, to make sure you were okay while you were living at Janelle's. I had someone looking out for your safety that entire time. You just didn't know it. And when I found out you were leaving California, I was relieved, even though I was already pretty sure that after moving out of the mansion and out of my life, you were no longer a target. Once you left California, I felt more at peace with planning my eventual disappearance."

My head hurt. "Where have you been all this time, Dorian?"

"First, I flew to Turkey. That's where we staged the boat incident to make it look like Benjamin and I were lost at sea."

"How were you able to manage that?"

He scrubbed his hand over his face. "There's nothing the right amount of money can't buy. I paid these guys to smuggle us on their yacht into Greece. That's where I was before returning to California recently. I had a few trusted confidantes at the company who knew my whereabouts. For a while, I was still running Vanderbilt as best I could remotely."

"What happened to allow you to come out of hiding?"

"A couple of things. One, in the midst of numerous production delays on our end, a bigger and better solar panel product was developed by a competitor, which essentially took away demand for Vanderbilt's. But the biggest thing was, while we were finally able to gather enough evidence to prove Mills was responsible for the carbon monoxide attack, before he could be arrested, Mills died."

My eyes went wide. "He was murdered?"

"No. He died of natural causes, believe it or not, about six months ago."

"So...back up. The carbon monoxide. How did Mills make that happen?"

Dorian shook his head. "Sorry. I got ahead of myself. Mills hired a mole who befriended my father. That guy, Philip Steele, was on the trip with them. He was actually the person who invited them to Hawaii. Steele was the one who manipulated the vent at the place where they were staying, and he eventually took a plea deal after confessing what he'd done. But because Mills is dead now, there's no further action to take. It wasn't until his death that I felt safe enough to come back to the States. There's no indication of an active threat now, but even so, I'd had enough. A few months ago, I sold my shares of Vanderbilt to a new owner. I'm no longer a part of the company, aside from doing some remote consulting work for them."

I felt numb, unable to fully process everything. "I can't believe this..."

"Primrose, I've thought about you every day. I never wanted to let you go, never wanted to go down the nightmarish path I've been navigating these past several years. It killed me that you thought I chose to end what we had.

You were the best thing that ever happened to me. But at the time, I didn't see another choice. I couldn't let them use you as collateral to get to me."

"I wish you had told me the truth."

"You say that, but that wouldn't have been the right choice if it meant you could've been harmed." He paused. "Would you have left me if I told you everything?"

"Absolutely not."

He nodded. "I knew that. Even when I was overseas and presumed missing, I didn't trust that I was fully safe because I was still investigating the man responsible for my father's death. I never quite knew whom I could trust. But when Mills died, I got my life back."

Closing my eyes, I took a moment to let everything register. "Holy shit." I shook my head. "I'm sorry for being rude to you when you showed up at my house on Wednesday. I obviously had no idea that—"

"Don't you dare apologize, Rosebud. I'm the one who's sorry for the pain I put you through. After everything was lost, the most I could hope for was an opportunity to finally explain everything. Thank you so much for giving that to me today."

A part of me wanted to pull him close and tell him how much I'd missed him. But I had to remind myself that despite hearing the truth, I was no longer the woman I'd been when he left me. Nothing about my life was the same.

"That was really the short of it," he said. "There's so much more I could tell you about my time away. I mostly lived modestly in Greece to stay under the radar. I used an alias and tried to immerse myself in the culture, tried to find some enjoyment in life, even when things felt like they were falling apart."

The door opened behind us, causing me to jump.

Dorian stood, and I turned to find an old familiar face smiling back at me.

"Primrose..."

"Benjamin?" I got up from the couch and ran to him. "What are you doing here?" I asked as we embraced.

"That's the other thing," Dorian said from behind me. "Benjamin's been with me this whole time."

I looked between them. "He has?"

"Back when everything was first coming to light, I confided in him. Benjamin knew everything from the beginning. When I told him of my plans to flee and disappear for a while, he wouldn't let me go it alone. He's been my partner in crime ever since."

I covered my mouth. "Wow."

Benjamin patted my back. "I felt terrible lying to you the last time we saw each other, the day you moved out. I knew I'd likely not see you for a very long time, but I couldn't tell you anything for your own safety. Patsy was in the dark, too. I hope you'll forgive me."

I reached out to hug him again. "I'm just glad to know Dorian wasn't alone. And that both of you are okay."

Benjamin turned to Dorian. "I also have to apologize. It wasn't my intent to come back so soon and interrupt your conversation. I went to the market but realized I left my wallet here."

"I'm glad you came back." I smiled. "It's so good to see you."

"Oh, I wasn't gonna leave town without seeing you. I just wanted you and Dorian to have privacy today so he could talk to you before I intruded."

"It warms my heart that you two have been together all this time."

"I had to look out for him." He winked. "Now, if you'll excuse me, I'll get out of your hair." He turned to me. "Don't worry. I won't leave town until you and I have had a proper catch-up, Primrose."

"You better not."

After he left, I turned to face Dorian again. Benjamin's presence had allowed for a brief reprieve from the tension. Now that he was gone, it returned in full force.

"He's amazing," I said.

"That he is," Dorian agreed. "I don't know what I would've done without him."

"I always wondered why he'd never reached out to me. I mean, I know why I didn't reach out to *him*..."

"Because you didn't want to find out I'd moved on?"

I nodded. "Yeah. I always felt guilty about not initiating contact with him, but I also thought Benjamin would check on me eventually. When he never did, I assumed it was because he knew something and didn't want to hurt me. So I never pushed it."

"He certainly knew some things. Just not what you likely envisioned. I'm sorry you were led to believe he didn't care—that *I* didn't care."

We returned to our seats and continued our conversation. Dorian had done enough digging into my life to know I was with Casey and had a child, but he didn't know the circumstances in which I'd met my fiancé or gotten pregnant. I spent a good deal of time catching him up on how my current situation had come to be. I shied away from going into too much detail about my feelings for Casey, though. Not sure if that was because I didn't want Dorian to sense my hesitancy about the wedding, or because I didn't want to assume Dorian was ready to talk about Casey.

"I'm proud of you, Rosebud," he finally said.

"Why?"

"You're a good mother. It wasn't a situation you asked for, but you rolled with it. It seems like you've dedicated your life to your daughter."

"Why wouldn't I? That's what you're supposed to do, right?"

His stare was piercing. "Are you happy?"

"I'm happy being a mom."

"What about everything else?"

"Are you asking if I'm happy in my relationship?"

"Yes," he answered immediately.

I swallowed. "I love Casey. He's an amazing father and a hard worker."

"You're *in love* with him?"

"I just said I loved him."

His gaze was unwavering. "I asked if you're *in love* with him."

"What's the difference?"

"You can love people for many different reasons." He paused and held out his palms. "I swear to you, Primrose, I'm not here to stir up trouble. I'm just curious. Because I know how you felt about me. I also know the pain I caused you. For you to have fallen in love with someone else a year later seems..."

"I didn't fall in love with Casey a year later. I accidentally got pregnant a year later. I've *learned* to love him over time in the years since Rosie was born."

Dorian nodded. "I understand. Thank you. It's none of my business. I just want to know you're happy and fulfilled."

My cheeks flushed. "I feel like I'm on the hotseat."

"I don't mean to pressure you."

"I never imagined I'd be sitting across from you again."

"I know. It's surreal. As much as I've imagined this moment, it still feels like an out-of-body experience. Of course, my biggest wish when everything resolved was that somehow I could work things out and come back to you. But since I discovered your situation, I've been working to accept that the happily ever after I wanted isn't gonna happen." He stared into the fire. "I debated not coming at all. I don't want to disrupt your life. But ultimately, I couldn't stand the idea of you believing I'd fallen out of love with you."

"I'm not the same person anymore," I confessed.

"Really? Or are you just saying that because it's the safest thing to hide behind?" He turned to look at me. "And don't get me wrong, I wouldn't blame you for that."

After several seconds of quiet, he hit me with another question that was hard to answer.

"What's going on with your art?"

"I haven't painted for *me* in years," I admitted. "I have a business, though. I paint for kids. Faces. Animals. Caricatures. It does well."

"That's cool. But why aren't you painting for *you* anymore?"

How could I admit that every ounce of true creativity had been sucked out of me the day he ended things? That would be like pouring salt in his wounds.

"I lost my way, I guess."

"That's sad to hear. I'm sorry if I had anything to do with it."

He knew. I couldn't deny it. So I said nothing.

When I checked my phone, it was five minutes past the time I should've left to get Rosie. I jumped up. "I have to go."

A look of panic bloomed on his face. "Already?"

"I don't have much free time these days."

He followed me toward the door. "I'd like to talk more."

I looked away, unsure whether that was a good idea.

"Rosebud, look at me." He reached his hand out and gently lifted my chin.

That simple touch nearly undid me.

"I'm not going anywhere until you tell me to," he said, removing his hand. "I promise I'm not here to make trouble for you. I just need closure. I need to know there's nothing left unsaid between us. And more than anything, I need to know you're truly okay and happy."

I nodded. Even though I hated keeping secrets from my family, I wasn't ready to let him leave town just yet. "I can come back on Monday at the same time, so we can finish talking," I said before I could think better of it.

Dorian let out a relieved breath. "That would be amazing, but only if you want to. I don't want you to feel obligated."

I opened the door. "I have to go."

"Yeah. Of course. You shouldn't be late to get her."

Stalling for one more moment, I realized this doorway separated my old life from my new one, both equally precious to me for different reasons.

"Bye, Dorian."

He followed me out to my car and stood at the edge of the driveway as I backed out.

I offered a wave, and he returned it, a slight but sad smile on his face.

As I drove off, I wondered how I could possibly get through the next few days without giving myself away to Casey. Surely he'd know something was wrong. I wondered if I should tell him what was going on, but it still didn't seem like the appropriate time. There was more I needed to learn, not only about Dorian's life, but about my own feelings on the matter, before communicating anything to Casey. Nothing I'd known before today was real. It was going to take me more than a day to absorb the truth.

My mind raced as I drove, and just like the day Dorian had shown up at my door, I didn't know how I'd gotten from point A to point B when I arrived at the preschool. When Rosie's teacher opened the car door, I put on my best smile to greet my daughter. Rosie grinned proudly as she handed me a picture. It was mostly scribbles with some cotton balls and glitter glued to it. To her, this was just like any other day, while my world had been turned upside down yet again.

"So pretty, honey," I managed.

The teacher buckled Rosie in. "Have a great weekend, Primrose."

Weekend? Gosh, I barely knew what day it was.

"You, too, Sharon," I told her.

When she closed the door, a pang of guilt returned. This little girl assumed I'd been home while she was at school. Meanwhile I'd snuck off to see a man who wasn't her father. I'd done nothing wrong, yet I couldn't help feeling deceitful.

So naturally, I did what any guilty mom would do: I took Rosie for a treat.

"Do you want an ice cream cone from McDonald's?"

Rosie bounced up and down. "Yay! Yay! Yay!"

I chuckled. "Okay, then."

I passed the turn that would normally take us to our house and drove instead to the drive-thru. After getting her a cone and myself an iced coffee, we went home.

Back at the house, I cleaned sticky ice cream off of my daughter at the kitchen sink and then set her up at the small table in the living room with a coloring book and some crayons. I promised to join her in a few minutes—right after I escaped to the bathroom and sobbed like never before.

CHAPTER 22

Dorian

I'd been sitting in the living room rubbing my temples when Benjamin returned from the market.

"How did it go?" He shut the door behind him.

I ran a hand through my hair. "I don't know. It wasn't enough time. I basically threw a bunch of information at her and watched how overwhelmed she got."

"Will you see her again?"

"She's gonna come back on Monday at the same time."

He offered a hopeful smile. "That's good, right?"

God love him for trying to remain optimistic when all odds were clearly against me. The idea that Primrose would leave her family for me seemed even more improbable after seeing her face to face. The time we'd spent apart had changed both of us. And while my feelings for her hadn't wavered, I couldn't get a sense of how she felt at this point. She hadn't had enough time to even digest everything I'd unloaded on her.

"I don't know," I muttered. "It was surreal seeing her again. The same beautiful Primrose, but at the same time, worlds away."

"Well, you'll have another opportunity to connect."

I stared into the fireplace. "Maybe this was a mistake."

"Don't you think it's a little too soon to throw in the towel?"

"I needed her to know the truth. But can I really expect her to leave her family to be with me?"

"She has a daughter—and a *boyfriend*. She's not married."

"She's *getting* married," I countered.

"Every decision she made was because she thought you'd abandoned her."

"Right. But that doesn't change her current reality. Doesn't matter how she got here." I shook my head. "I didn't come here to fuck things up for her."

"I'm sure she understands that."

"Seriously, though, what am I hoping to achieve here, Benjamin? Get her to leave him? That's her daughter's father. That's breaking up a family."

"You want to go back to California after Monday? Is that what you're saying?"

"No." I slowly breathed out, trying to calm myself. "I can't leave until she tells me to. I need to see this through until the day she looks me in the eye and tells me there's no hope."

"Okay, so what does seeing this through mean?"

"For one, it means figuring out if she's truly happy. And if she is, in her current situation, figuring out a way to accept that there'll never be another chance for her and me."

"And if you determine she's *not* happy?"

"Figuring out a way to get her back."

His mouth curved into a smile. "Gosh, it was nice to see her."

"At least you got a hug." I chuckled. "She wouldn't dare come near me."

"That alone tells you that you still have an effect on her."

Desperate for reassurance, I hoped he was right. The vibe I'd gotten from her was definitely a cold one. I'd had fantasies for the past five years about the day I might be reunited with Primrose. None of them had included her sitting across from me, seeming scared by every word coming out of my mouth. I'd had recurring dreams about her running toward me in an open field. But the reality was nothing like that.

"Hearing myself tell her the full story out loud..." I shook my head. "It all sounded so crazy, like something out of the kind of movies she and I used to watch. It's hard to believe that was actually my life for five years."

"*Your* life? How about *my* life?"

I couldn't help but smile at that. "You're right. Sorry. When my dad hired you, I'm sure you never imagined you'd be my partner in crime for life..."

Benjamin punched me in the arm. "We're family. You're stuck with me."

"I couldn't have survived without you. You risked your life."

"What can I say? I like to live on the edge." He winked. "And you pay well. So there's that."

I grinned. "What's the plan for tonight?" I asked as I followed him into the kitchen.

"I'm making tostones and arroz con pollo. Although no one makes it like my Puerto Rican grandmother. When I'm stressed, I like to make comfort food."

"What are *you* stressed about?"

"I was a bit nervous for you today when I planned dinner. I guess I wondered if things wouldn't go as well as they did."

I stepped back in surprise. "You think it went well? I didn't feel like that at all."

"She agreed to come back and talk more. I'd say that's as much as you could hope for."

"Aside from the fact that she probably thinks I'm a fucking stalker."

"Well, aren't you?" He arched his brow.

"Keeping tabs on someone over the years just to make sure she's okay is not stalking. Plus, I paid others to do it. So technically, it was only indirect stalking."

"I'm just kidding, my friend." Benjamin chuckled.

"Can you tell I'm extra fucking sensitive today?"

"You have every right to be."

I leaned against the counter. "I'd longed for this day and also dreaded it."

"Why dread?" he asked.

"I worried that I'd look in her eyes and be able to tell she'd fallen out of love with me."

"What *did* you see when you looked into her eyes?"

"Nothing but fear."

"Hmm…" He scratched his chin. "I would take fear over apathy." He began putting away his groceries. "I think she's afraid of her own reaction to you, perhaps."

"I'm not sure, but I won't be able to explore it any more until Monday."

Benjamin started singing that old song, "Monday Monday," as he finished putting everything away.

Monday couldn't come soon enough.

• • •

The following day, I decided I needed to make myself useful to get my mind off things. So I joined Benjamin on his grocery store run.

As we strolled the aisles, I made an announcement. "You made dinner last night. It's my turn tonight."

Benjamin stopped the shopping cart. "We could go out, you know."

"Are you trying to hint that you're afraid of my cooking?"

"You don't have the best track record, Dorian. I think we're going on three times now that we've almost had to call the fire department when you cooked. There was that time you tried to cook for Primrose at the mansion, then breakfast at the apartment in Turkey, and dinner at the rental house in Santorini."

"Three seems pretty low in the overall big picture of life."

We continued our way through the aisles for a while. Then I stopped short when I noticed a flash of familiar, long brown hair with golden streaks.

Primrose had been looking at the ingredients on the back of a box. My chest constricted at the sight of her angelic little daughter sitting in the cart. I'd never seen her face before. With her big, wonder-filled eyes, she looked just like her mom.

I'd wanted to turn around and head in the other direction, but Primrose noticed us before I could. She let out an audible gasp.

I couldn't avoid her now.

My throat felt ready to close. "Hey."

"Hi." She looked over her shoulder.

"Uh, we were just—"

Before I could get another word in, a man appeared by her side.

"Did you say we needed almond milk?" he asked her, glancing in my direction.

This was my first up-close look at Primrose's man. Casey. He was tall with sandy-colored hair and definitely gave me a run for my money in the looks department. I wished he were a lot less handsome. Then again, why would I have expected someone as gorgeous as Primrose to be with an unattractive guy?

"Uh...no. We don't need it," she stammered. "We have a full half-gallon at home that I picked up recently."

When he turned to look at me again, I made a split-second decision.

"I'm sorry, you said they don't sell wine here?"

Her mouth opened and closed before she said, "No. I don't believe they do."

"Thank you."

Benjamin nodded at them and followed me down the aisle.

That was close, but I was pretty sure Casey didn't suspect anything. I couldn't help but look back. Casey wasn't looking at me, and neither was Primrose. But Primrose's sweet little girl had turned around to watch us walk away. She waved at me. I waved back. "*Bye*," I mouthed with a smile. She smiled back.

Then I felt Benjamin's hand on my shoulder.

"You okay?" he asked.

Letting out a long breath, I nodded. We'd somehow ended up in the meat aisle. No way I could think straight enough to plan a dinner now. "Takeout is sounding better by the minute," I told him.

"Good decision."

As we left the supermarket, a hopeless feeling developed in my heart after my glimpse into the routine of Primrose's current life—a life I had no real part in anymore.

Benjamin and I had a late dinner of Chinese takeout, and after he retreated to his room, I sat alone in the living room, staring into the fire.

That beautiful little girl had smiled and waved at me with trusting eyes. *Rosie*. What a pretty name and perfect for her. Little Primrose. Rosie's innocent acknowledgement made me feel warm inside—and like a piece of shit for deceiving her, too. She'd assumed I was just a friendly stranger, not some man who'd come to town to seize her mother.

Not to mention, I'd forced Primrose into lying. If I hadn't freaked out and had just kept my mouth shut, maybe she would've introduced me properly to him. Although, I couldn't imagine what she would've said. I hadn't given her the chance to react, though. My instinct was to protect her. It would *always* be to protect her, even if I lost out in the end.

My phone buzzed, and I was surprised to see a text from her.

Primrose: Are you okay?

I immediately typed back.

Dorian: I'm okay. But I should be asking you that.

Primrose: I'm sorry about today. I can imagine it was a shock running into us.

I closed my eyes, speechless that she was concerned for *me*.

Dorian: I spoke before you had a chance to. I'm sorry. I should've let you make the call on how to handle it. I just didn't want to get you in trouble.

Primrose: You did the right thing. I wouldn't have known how to explain you. And I didn't want to have to lie to Casey. You sort of took that option from me, which was helpful.

Dorian: I'm glad you feel that way, because I've been sitting here doubting myself. Did he suspect something?

Primrose: Not at all.

Dorian: Your daughter's adorable. What a little sweetheart. She looks just like you.

Primrose: Yeah. Everyone says that.

Dorian: You saved Benjamin from having to eat one of my charred dinners.

Primrose: How's that?

Dorian: It was my turn to cook. But after we ran into you, I figured it was best if we got out of there before we could cause more trouble. So we got takeout instead. He thanks you for sparing him.

Primrose: You're not still trying to cook, are you?

I smiled.

Dorian: There have been two additional fire alarms after the one I set off trying to cook for you.

Primrose: I guess some things don't change.

Dorian: Nope. Still burning stuff, despite those lessons we took together.

Primrose: I've gotten better at it. I guess that's what happens when you're responsible for keeping another human alive and you don't want her eating crap all the time.

Dorian: Makes total sense, yeah.

After a few moments, I typed again.

Dorian: She turned around and waved at me.

Primrose: Rosie?

> Dorian: Yeah. It was cute. She obviously has no idea what a troublemaker I really am.
>
> Primrose: She's very trusting. It's something I have to keep an eye on.

Right. Definitely no reason to trust me. Especially since the sole purpose of my being in town is to see if I can steal you away for my own happiness. And fuck everyone else. God, I'm despicable.

> Primrose: Anyway, I just wanted to check in. I felt bad that I couldn't say hello to you and Benjamin.
>
> Dorian: Please don't worry about that. Despite the surprise, it was nice to see you and informally meet your daughter.

Your boyfriend, not so much.

> Dorian: I'll see you Monday?

I prayed she still planned to come back.

> Primrose: Yes. See you then.

I let out a sigh of relief and forced myself not to write back. *Leave her be.*

Putting my phone aside, I closed my eyes, hoping the heat from the fire would calm my foolish heart. She'd been thinking about me tonight, though I couldn't let that go to my head. Any false hope at this point could very well wreck me in the end.

But the more I tried to think about something neutral, the more my mind kept returning to what happened today and her daughter's angelic face.

Rosie, you should've been mine.

CHAPTER 23

Primrose

Casey stopped in the kitchen before he left for work Monday morning.

"Any plans today?"

The spoon I'd reached for to stir my coffee slipped out of my hand. I couldn't bear to lie to him, so instead I asked, "Didn't you say you have something after work today?"

"Yeah. A staff meeting. They'll be providing dinner. So I'll be home late. You girls eat without me."

"Okay. Sounds good. I'll make something for Rosie and me that I know you don't like." I smiled. "Have a good day."

He narrowed his eyes. "You okay?"

God, he's always so perceptive. "Yeah." I forced a smile. "Of course."

He stared at me a few moments before his mouth slowly spread into a smile. "Okay."

And trusting.

Casey poured his coffee into a travel mug and grabbed the backpack he always took to work. He bent to kiss Rosie on the head. "See you later, baby girl."

"Bye, Daddy."

Her sweet little voice was like a knife through my heart.

Casey came over and gave me a kiss on the cheek. "Bye, babe."

"Bye. Have a good day."

The moment the door shut behind him, I exhaled. Today *had* to be the last time. I needed to figure out whatever unresolved stuff I had going on with Dorian and move on. Not only was it making me incapable of focusing on anything else, but keeping it from Casey was wearing on me.

I got Rosie ready for school, and before I knew it, we were headed down the road as my heart pitter-pattered in anticipation for what lay ahead.

When we got to the preschool, I gave my daughter an extra-tight hug, a silent apology. It felt like I had a scarlet letter A on my chest.

By the time I pulled up at Dorian's rental home, I was certain I'd let him know that today would be the last time I could meet him.

But the moment he opened the door to greet me, and I looked into his eyes, I knew I couldn't let him go back to California that easily. Today couldn't possibly be the last time I'd ever see his face.

Dorian flashed a hesitant smile. "Thank you for coming back."

"Hi," I said as I stepped inside the warm house. I looked around. "Where's Benjamin?"

"He went out to explore. He wanted to give us some privacy."

I nodded, unsure how I felt about that. It might've felt less dangerous if Benjamin were here. It wasn't that I didn't trust myself. Of course I'd never cheat on Casey. But I didn't trust my feelings, and the more distractions the better.

The smell of cinnamon registered. "Did you make something?" I asked.

"I made an apple crisp." He flashed a crooked grin.

I couldn't help but smile. "You didn't have to do that."

"Well, I'm like Benjamin that way, I guess. I cook when I'm stressed. Or in my case, bake, since it's all I know how to do well. Needless to say, I've made a lot of apple crisps over the past five years. I tend not to burn them like everything else."

"Why are you stressed today?" I followed him into the kitchen. "Or should I say, which of the many reasons you have to be stressed is topping the list?"

"Just the unknown," he answered. "There's a lot you and I still need to catch up on." He gestured toward the kitchen table. "Sit. I'll get you a piece."

Dorian headed over to the stove and prepared me a slice of his dessert. As he handed it to me, his hand brushed against mine, making me all too aware of my unwavering physical attraction to him. A wave of nostalgia came over me as I thought back to a much simpler time when he'd first made me apple crisp. I remembered the giddy excitement of that night and also felt sad for that smitten girl who had no idea of the heartbreak to come.

"You fell into a trance just now," Dorian said as he sat across from me. "What's on your mind?"

"Just thinking back to the good old days at the mansion."

"Those months with you were the best of my life, Primrose."

Rather than reciprocate that sentiment, I looked down at my plate and cut into the apple crisp with my fork, grateful for an excuse to look away from him. All my eyes wanted to do, however, was explore his face, every beautiful angle that I'd missed so much.

"Can I get you some coffee? Water?" he asked.

"No. I'm good," I said with my mouth full. "This is great. Thank you."

"You're welcome." He smiled as he watched me chew.

We ate in silence for a bit until he finally put his fork down. "I know we don't have that much time. So I'd like to ask you some questions, if that's okay?"

Moving my plate aside, I licked the corner of my mouth and cleared my throat. "Okay."

Dorian took a deep breath. "Will you tell me more about your relationship with Casey?"

I swallowed. "What do you want to know?"

"I want to know how he turned out to be someone you didn't end things with out of fear, like all the other guys before him, except me. Is it more than just your daughter? Or is she the main reason you've stayed with him?"

He definitely wasn't wasting time. These were questions I didn't have clear answers to, questions I'd been battling internally for some time, especially with the impending wedding. How was I supposed to admit things to Dorian I hadn't been able to admit to myself?

Suddenly feeling a bit reckless, I decided to be as honest as possible. "I can't say whether he and I would still be together if I hadn't gotten pregnant. But I've never felt stuck with him. If I were unhappy, I wouldn't have stayed. At the same time, I no longer have anxiety over getting hurt because the worst has already happened to me. In a weird way, you broke the pattern. After you left, it wasn't possible for anyone to break me any more—I was already broken. And I guess losing that fear allowed me to stop sabotaging things."

Dorian lowered his gaze to the table. "Wow." He scratched his chin. "That's very interesting." He exhaled and stared up at the ceiling for several seconds before he looked at me again. "You alluded to the fact that you're not *unhappy*, but I don't understand what that means. *Not* unhappy. Not being in a state of unhappiness isn't exactly a state of joy."

Fidgeting a bit, I felt myself getting flustered. "What are you needing to hear from me? I gave you my honest answer, even if it's not black and white."

"I guess what I *need* to hear in order to leave Ohio in peace...is that you're truly happy. So happy that you don't have regrets about anything, and nothing I could ever say or do would change that. But I need you to mean it and not just say it to get me to leave because you're scared."

He'd hit the nail on the head. It would've been much easier to downplay my feelings for him in order to get him to leave. But was that what I wanted?

After a moment, he crossed his arms. "This situation is hard for me, Primrose. Because I don't even know what my goal is. I don't want to break up a family. But I've never stopped loving you. I need you to at least know that so that whatever you do with your life, you make an informed decision. I can't help how I feel, how I've felt this entire time. There wasn't one day when I wasn't in love with you. Not one day when I didn't hope that by some miracle I could find my way back to you and have another chance. But…" He paused. "When I found out you had a child with Casey, I realized I had to be prepared to lose you forever. I debated for a long time whether I should even come to you. But ultimately, I knew I couldn't live with myself if I didn't tell you the truth. I'm sorry if my decision has turned your life upside down."

I shook my head. "I don't fault you for coming. There's no reason to apologize."

Dorian let out a frustrated breath. "Fuck, Rosebud. I just need the truth." He looked around. "No one else is here. It's just you and me. Nothing you say to me right now will ever leave this room. I want to know what's going on in your head and how you were doing before you knew I was here. Rewind to last week before I showed up. Pretend I'm a fly on the wall. Tell me what your life is *really* like." He lowered his voice to a whisper. "Please."

The look of pain in his eyes gave me no choice but radical honesty. "My life…is that I've pretty much dived headfirst into being a mother. It makes it easier not to deal with the things I haven't wanted to."

"Like?"

"Like the fact that things aren't perfect in my relationship. I love him, but it's different from what you and I had."

Dorian tilted his head. "Different in what way?"

"Less passionate. But I trust what I have with him more than I've trusted anything. My feelings for Casey have grown authentically and gradually over time. So has my trust. Sometimes things that grow fast end just as fast."

Dorian nodded. "You believed that I'd abandoned you. So safety was what you were looking for. I understand."

"Yes, of course."

"Why have you waited so long to get married?"

"I wasn't sure marriage was really necessary."

"But you ultimately decided it was?"

"I ultimately decided it would be best for my daughter if her parents were married."

"What about what's best for *you*?"

"I had no plans to leave him, so I figured there was no reason to keep putting it off."

I cringed. *Had* no plans? I needed to be more careful with my word choice.

"But you're not sure you want to be married?"

"I'm not a hundred-percent sure it's the right decision." I swallowed. "But that could also just be fear of failure. A marriage can't fail if it never happens."

Dorian searched my eyes. "Would you have said yes if I'd asked you to marry me before things changed with us?"

I'd been so hopelessly in love with Dorian that I would've said yes in a heartbeat. Yet, I responded with, "The answer to that question is complex."

"How so?"

"Because while I would've said yes to you, I'm not sure that matters. I'm older now, more mature, and don't think it's a good idea for someone to agree to marry that fast. So, in retrospect it wouldn't have been wise to say yes, even if that's what the person I was back then would've done."

He kept nodding and looked like he wanted to say something.

"What?" I asked.

"I want to give you advice, but I also recognize that I'm biased. I don't want to steer you in the wrong direction to suit my own needs. Even so, I think you need to hear this."

I straightened in my seat. "What advice do you want to give me?"

"Making a decision out of fear won't ever suit you. Doing anything but following your heart will catch up with you eventually."

"What if my heart isn't sure of the right thing?"

"The *right* thing is irrelevant. The heart always knows what it wants, wrong or right." His stare burned into mine. "What do you want in your heart of hearts, if hurting others wasn't a factor?"

Adrenaline rushed through me. Because any answer besides "*you*" would be a lie. But I didn't feel right admitting the truth. I felt myself shutting down. "I can't come here again."

His brows drew in. "Okay...but why? Because you don't want to or because you feel like you shouldn't?"

"I don't want to lie to Casey when he asks how my day was. I'm not a liar. It's not in my nature."

"So why can't you tell him the truth? We're not doing anything except talking."

"It would still hurt him." My voice shook. "I don't want to hurt him."

"Why would he be hurt if I'm not a threat to your relationship?"

My mind didn't want to go there at all, so my walls just grew taller.

When I stopped answering him, Dorian posed the question a bit differently. "If what you want is to go back to the way things were before I showed up, what does he have to worry about?" He paused. "Then you just explain that an ex-boyfriend came back to town to clear his conscience over something that happened in the past. Any man who's confident in his relationship shouldn't have a problem with that."

Maybe I *was* underestimating what Casey could handle. Or maybe I didn't trust myself, didn't trust that my feelings for Dorian *were* a thing of the past. They sure as hell felt very much like a thing of the present.

Rather than address Dorian's very fair question, I turned the tables on him. "What is your next move here? How long are you planning on staying in Ohio?"

"I'm staying until you tell me to leave," he said matter-of-factly. "I told you that."

"Don't you have a life to get back to?"

"I have a lot of things I could be getting back to." He shook his head. "But none of them is more important than you."

Oh my. If I'd thought coming here today was going to resolve my feelings, I was sorely mistaken. All I felt right now was sheer turmoil. "I'm sorry. I'm not handling this well," I said, feeling my eyes water.

"Who said you needed to handle this any certain way? There's no playbook for this situation. It's fucked up. I know that."

My voice cracked. "When you're not right in front of me, it's easier to go on with my life. But when you're right here...everything feels so familiar. There are moments when I feel like my old self. I thought she didn't exist anymore. But I feel her when I'm with you," I confessed. "At the same time, I don't know how that girl fits into my life now."

"When was the last time you created art—not for kids or for hire, but for you?"

"A long time," I murmured.

"That makes me sad."

I shrugged. "I'll find my way back to it. This is a season of my life where it's been more important to focus on my daughter. I don't regret that."

Dorian nodded. "I'm proud of you." He let out a long breath. "I wish I could just let you go, Primrose. Not come here. It would've made your life easier. But I can't give up hope until *you* tell me there's none left."

"And if I say there will *never* be hope for us... You go back to California and what?"

"I try to move on. My life has been on hold for too long. I need to figure out a new normal."

"What do you want out of life now?"

He shrugged. "I want to be happy. I would like to have a family, but not with the wrong person. I'm not sure how I move on with someone else if I'm still in love with you, but maybe I do what you're doing."

"What *I'm* doing?" I blinked.

"Yeah. Go through the motions. Have a kid. Devote my life to them so I don't need to feel anything else that's missing."

His words were like a knife to my heart. Because they were true.

Dorian tilted his head to look at me. "That *is* what you're doing, isn't it? You're not fulfilled in your relationship."

"I didn't say that."

"You didn't have to."

The tension grew thick between us. After several seconds of quiet, Dorian stood. "Let's move to the living room. We'll be more comfortable."

Grateful for the momentary reprieve, I followed him and took a seat next to the blazing fire.

The heat was no match for the intensity I felt in Dorian's presence today, though.

CHAPTER 24

Dorian

It was hard to look at her. Primrose had only gotten more beautiful over the years. Even harder than that, though, was knowing in my soul that she still had feelings for me. Knowing that if she didn't believe her daughter bound her to Casey, we might've stood a chance. But that wasn't reality. That sweet little girl did deserve a happy home, one with both of her parents. At the same time, Primrose deserved to live her happiest life. It seemed like an insoluble conundrum, the only certainty being that someone would get hurt.

The fire lit up her beautiful eyes. *Neither blue, nor green. Aquamarine.* I could see the flames from the fire reflected in them.

Looking over at my phone, I realized we didn't have much time left. "When is the wedding?" I asked.

"Six months."

I nodded, relieved that it wasn't any sooner, and yet stressed that I only had six months to correct five years' worth of damage that I'd caused.

I thought about how beautiful she'd look walking down the aisle, about their daughter scattering rose petals. *Rosebud* petals. *My* Rosebud—who wasn't mine anymore.

I also thought about the ring I'd bought, the one I'd tucked away in the family safe five years ago while I figured out the right time to give it to her. That had been just a couple of weeks before everything went to hell. I'd likely never get the chance to give it to her now. She'd never know exactly how committed to her I was.

Primrose snapped me out of my thoughts. "Where are you living now, Dorian?"

"Funny you should ask." I grinned. "I actually repurchased the mansion. I just haven't made it a home again yet."

Her jaw dropped. "I'm surprised you'd want to do that."

"Why?"

"There are so many negative memories associated with it."

"But more positive ones." *Like almost every memory I have with you. Being there makes me feel closer to you when I can't be.* "I gave up my dad's company, everything he built. It felt like the right thing to at least get the family home back, so not all was lost."

"Okay, that makes sense." Primrose bit her bottom lip. "There's something I want to ask you, but I'm afraid."

"Ask me anything, please. It's what I'm here for."

"Whatever happened with Candace?"

Now, *that* was a question I was more than happy to answer. My mouth curved into a smile. "You mean, Candace, Chandler, and their two beautiful babies?"

"Really?" Primrose covered her mouth. "Oh, thank God."

When she lowered her hands, I could see tears in her eyes. She hadn't shed a tear until now, even if at times she'd looked like she was about to cry.

"I'd been so worried that things didn't work out. I was always afraid to look her up, not only because I didn't want to inadvertently get information on you, but because I preferred to imagine her happy and healthy."

"Well, it seems you manifested that."

"She's in remission?"

"Yes. She finished all of her treatments and adopted a very Zen lifestyle. She runs a yoga studio now. She and Chandler had frozen her eggs before she started cancer treatments, and they were able to use the embryos and a surrogate to have two kids."

"What do they have?"

"A girl and a boy. Maya and Mitchell."

She beamed. "I'm so happy for them."

"Me, too."

"Did they know the truth about you all this time?"

"I did eventually let them know. They were the only friends besides Benjamin who knew what was going on."

"Gosh, I'd love to see Candace."

"I'm sure she'd love to see you, too."

"Do they know you're here in Ohio?"

"Oh, yeah." I laughed.

"Why do you say it like that?"

"They've been texting me for updates. They're driving me crazy."

"That sounds like them." Primrose closed her eyes and leaned back into the sofa.

Making myself more comfortable, I used the opportunity to stare at her beautiful features. "What are you thinking about?"

She opened her eyes and spoke softly, "I'm thinking that despite the fact that I should be tense around you, I feel pretty at peace right now."

"I'm surprised you can feel that way in my presence."

"I'm slowly getting used to you again."

I grinned, and she returned it.

Her smile faded. "Have there been a lot of women in your life in the years you were away?"

"Is that what you imagine?" I asked. "That I've been out there all this time fucking away my sorrows?"

"I have no idea."

"There was only one woman, actually."

Her eyes widened. "One?"

"Yes. Those first two years, I couldn't fathom being with anyone who wasn't you. And I actually hadn't planned to."

"How would that even be possible?"

"It was simple. I didn't want anyone else and had it in my head that when I was out of danger, I would come find you and tell you I'd waited for you, even if you hadn't waited for me. I was still committed to you, even though you didn't realize it."

She frowned. "What changed?"

"I found out you had moved on and had a child. I thought it was over for us. And I met a woman in Greece. Annabella eventually became my girlfriend. She was a really good person, but..." I shook my head. "She wasn't you. I couldn't replicate what I'd felt for you with anyone else."

"So you broke her heart like you broke mine?"

"It wasn't the same thing, but yeah, I broke up with her before I left."

"I'm sorry." She looked down. "My comment was rude. And uncalled for. My emotions are all over the place right now. I'm engaged with a child, and I'm getting jealous over some woman you dated in Greece. It's like I'm one person when I go home and another person altogether when I'm in front of you."

My chest filled with hope at the prospect of her jealousy. I warned myself not to get my hopes up, though. "From the get-go, I knew the thing with Annabella wasn't going anywhere. She lived in Greece. All of her family did. She was close to her mother and sisters, and I knew she'd never leave them. It was probably one of the reasons I gravitated to her. Because I knew it would end, and I didn't want a true commitment. I never hid the fact that I planned to go back to the States. I always made that clear."

"Did she know *why* you were in Greece?"

"That was the other thing. I was still using an alias. She knew bits and pieces of my actual life, but no, she didn't know everything. Not even my legal name."

"That's crazy." She stared into the fire, deep in thought.

"Talk to me," I finally said.

"I'm sorry. I still don't know what to say. To understand that everything I believed for the past five years was a lie... I just don't think I can process it that quickly."

"I don't want to make you sad, nor do I want to make your life difficult. I just needed to get this load off my chest. I couldn't live with it anymore. If somehow getting another chance with you was part of the equation, that would've been a dream. But I also know that this situation is very complicated and that expecting that dream to come true could be a delusion. I'd settle for your forgiveness and your friendship. I don't want to live in a world where you pretend I don't exist because the thought of me causes you pain. I want to see you happy and know that you understand that I love you, not just as your former lover, but as your friend."

As I looked at her conflicted face, I made an executive decision that seemed like the right thing to do, even if it killed me. "Originally, I thought I wouldn't leave until you told me to go. But I actually think it might be better if I put some space between us. You shouldn't have to lie about your whereabouts just to appease my need to talk to you. Nor do I want you to feel pressured. So, I think I'll go back to California."

Her brows furrowed. "Really?"

"Yes. I think that's best. Don't you? I don't want to be some secret that's stressing you out."

An alarm went off on her phone.

She looked down at it. "Shit. I lost track of time. I have to go."

"Go get your daughter," I said, feeling choked up and a bit depressed.

"When will you be leaving?" she asked, her voice shaking.

"Probably tomorrow."

The look of alarm on her face told me she didn't want me to go. But I knew her hands were tied right now. My gut told me to remove myself from the equation to allow her to draw whatever conclusion was best for her.

"It won't be the last time you see me unless you want it to be. All you ever have to do is tell me you need me, and I'll be on the next plane back. Primrose, I need you to know I will always be here for you."

To my shock, she reached for me, wrapping her arms around my neck and pulling me into a tight embrace. I felt her heart beating against my chest and closed my eyes, relishing the feel of what I knew to be true: Primrose still loved me.

Maybe that love was different now, maybe it would have to remain unrequited. But there was solace in knowing it hadn't totally disappeared. I'd take that over nothing. I'd take that over her believing I was the heartless prick she'd lived the past five years thinking I was. But I also wondered if this hug was goodbye. That wrecked me.

She pulled back and wiped her eyes. *Fuck.* I was really messing with her mind. That only validated the fact that I needed to give her space.

"You have my number. You know where I live. I'm not going anywhere, Primrose."

"Okay," she whispered.

A moment later, she disappeared out the door.

As she drove away, I tried not to think about the fact that I might never see her again. Instead, I had to believe.

When Benjamin walked in a few minutes later, he found me staring blankly into the fire.

"What happened, Dorian?"

My gaze stayed fixed on the flames. "I decided we should go back to California."

"Why?"

"It's too much for her. I've said what I needed to. Now I need to give her breathing room. She needs time to digest all this."

"When are we leaving?"

I finally turned to him. "Tomorrow."

"I'm sorry."

"For what?"

"That this isn't the outcome you were hoping for."

"It's not over yet. I feel it in my heart. I just don't know if I'm gonna have to wait three years or thirty. But I'll wait—at least until she tells me it's over and decides to marry him."

"Is that being fair to yourself? If she remains unsure, you just stop your life for the next six months or whatever? What does that even look like?"

I shrugged. Any life outside of one with Primrose seemed remarkably unimportant right now. "I don't know. I haven't thought that far. But one thing about growing up and maturing is realizing that it's not all about me. Her little girl needs to come first. Whatever Primrose needs to do for her daughter is what she's gonna choose. And I'm okay with that. Because I love her. And I also love her daughter because she's a direct extension of her mother. I need to follow my gut here. And my gut is telling me to physically walk away, even if my heart is still with her."

Benjamin placed a hand on my shoulder. "Okay, then. I'll start gathering our things."

CHAPTER 25

Primrose

An all-consuming energy followed me around the rest of that afternoon. Rosie colored in the living room after I picked her up from school, and I went into the adjacent sunroom and picked up my brush for the first time in forever. I'd had all of the equipment set up for a while now but rarely touched it. Yet today, I *really* felt like painting. It seemed so natural once I started the first strokes.

When I began, I wasn't sure where I was going with it. But gradually the canvas transformed into a scene from my past. It was the pool at the mansion, lit up at night with multicolored lights. It wasn't clearly identifiable as the pool, as it was more abstract, but the colors were exactly as I remembered them. The image embodied the nostalgia I felt as I thought about Dorian returning to California tomorrow. This wasn't my best work, but it reminded me why I'd always created art: to express myself. I realized it had been hard to do that after my breakup with Dorian because I'd felt dead inside. Being around him again had lit the fire that had been missing—in a different way even than my daughter being born. Dorian had come all the way out here, risking his own heart to make sure I knew I mattered to him. Yet I'd given him nothing back because I was too afraid to feel anything. The cornucopia of colors I'd just created reflected the chaos inside of me.

I stood back and looked at the painting. In the process of creating it, I'd gotten some clarity. Before Dorian left, I owed him honesty. I had no choice but to catch him before he flew to L.A. if I wanted to make sure I didn't leave anything unsaid. I certainly hadn't been able to express myself this morning.

Casey was working late tonight, so I asked Lucy if she'd be willing to watch Rosie for me. Thankfully, she said yes without inquisition, although she had to be at work for her evening shift pretty soon, so I didn't have much time. I told her I had some personal business to take care of and would fill her in later.

After I dropped Rosie at Lucy's, I sat in my car and texted Dorian.

My hands shook as I typed.

Are you still here?

He responded almost immediately.

Dorian: Yes. Our flight isn't until early afternoon tomorrow.

Primrose: There are a few more things I need to say before you leave. I just dropped Rosie at my friend's. Can I come over?

Dorian: Of course.

Primrose: Okay. Heading there now.

I drove to Dorian's house as fast as I could.

When I arrived, per usual, he opened the door for me before I could even ring the bell.

"This is a surprise," he said as I entered.

"I know." I walked past him into the living room.

"What's going on?"

Turning to face him, I rubbed my palms together. "I realized this afternoon that I couldn't let you go without saying some things."

"All right." He looked a little wary.

"First…" I paused. "I'm sorry."

"Sorry?"

"You came to Ohio and poured your heart out, and I gave you nothing in return. I've been too scared to say what I truly feel. I've been paralyzed by the battle inside me—a battle between what I want to say and what I feel is appropriate."

"It's okay," he said softly. "I understand."

"No, it's not okay." I exhaled. "You know what I did when I got home today?"

"What?"

"I painted. I painted for the first time in a long time because just being in your presence breathed new life into me."

His eyes filled with emotion. "That's wonderful, Rosebud."

"The truth is, I feel so much every second we're in the same room. I don't know how to process it, but it's every bit as powerful as it was before everything happened."

Dorian moved closer. "You once told me that you wished people would be direct, that they'd just say what's on their mind. So I'm gonna be direct right now, even if I'm making a fool of myself." His eyes locked with mine. "I want you to leave him. I want you for myself. Yes, looking into your little girl's eyes gave me pause. Because I realize now that not everything is about me." He shook his head slowly. "But I can't help how I feel. I know there are certain things you can't say out of guilt, even if you're thinking them. But I *can* fucking say them. I don't have anyone or anything holding me back, no one to answer to. I would give anything to make love to you, Primrose. I can't tell you how many times over the years I've closed my eyes and tried to remember what it was like to sink inside you and lose myself. It never felt like that with anyone else."

His lip trembled. "And I fucking miss you. I miss us. I miss the life I had with you. It was short, but it was the only time I felt like my true self. Even if we never get to be together again, Rosebud, I want you to know that you've left a greater impression on me than anyone else. You taught me how to love. And you were the first woman since my mother who loved me for me and nothing more. I owe you so much for that."

My heart swelled inside me, impossible to contain. "You leaving me...it never felt real. Now I know why. Thank you for risking your heart to make sure I knew the truth. I can't imagine how hard this has been for you."

"The pain is worth every second of getting to see you again. To see what an amazing woman you've become, even more amazing with time. Rosie is so lucky to have you as her mother. She has no idea just how much she hit the jackpot. I don't know your little girl, but I love her because she's a part of you."

Before I could respond, the alarm I'd set on my phone went off.

"You have to leave already?"

I nodded somberly. "I have to get back. My friend is watching Rosie, but she has to leave for work. It's almost Rosie's bedtime, too."

"Thank you for giving me one more opportunity. I wasn't sure I'd ever see you again."

Despite knowing I had to go, I couldn't move. I didn't want to leave him.

Before I could force my legs toward the door, Dorian inched closer. My heartbeat accelerated because I thought he was going to try to kiss me. But instead, he placed his forehead on mine. We breathed together for several seconds. The feel of his breath on my face comforted and aroused me all at once. He was respectful of my boundaries, but I never wanted to leave this spot.

When he pulled back, cold air replaced the warmth of his body. If I didn't put one foot in front of the other now, I might never go. So I did just that and walked out, more unsure of my life than ever.

CHAPTER 26

Dorian

A week after I returned to Orion Coast, I invited Chandler and Candace over to tell them about my trip.

I opened the door to their smiling faces. "Hey!"

"I'm surprised you're back so soon," Candace said as she stepped inside.

"Yeah. Leaving when I did felt right." I looked down, expecting to find their little ones, but they'd come alone. "Where are the kids?"

"With my mother," she said.

"You should've brought them. They could've gone swimming."

Candace shrugged. "We wanted to get the full scoop in peace. They don't give me a moment to think straight."

"You love that, though," Chandler told her.

"I do." She smiled. "So...we've been dying to know what happened with Primrose."

"She cried when she found out you were okay."

"Really? Oh my God. That makes *me* want to cry." Candace sighed. "She was always so nice. From the moment I met her, I loved her."

I spent the next hour rehashing my trip. But it wasn't the fairy tale they'd hoped for. Certainly wasn't what I'd hoped for, either, though I had more peace now than before I went. Bittersweet was the best way to describe the experience.

Candace squeezed my shoulder. "I'm proud of you for knowing when it was time to go. But please tell me you haven't given up hope."

"He can't just sit and wait forever for her to come around," Chandler countered before turning to me. "She may very well decide to stay with this guy, and then where does that leave you?"

"I have a lot to think about. But I feel at peace with her knowing the truth about what happened. I said what I needed to say, even if I didn't exactly get closure."

Candace grimaced. "I couldn't imagine being in her position, finding out that everything you thought was true about the love of your life simply wasn't. But now you've already moved on and have a child. As a mother, I can totally relate to her deciding not to break up her family."

Chandler wrapped his arm around her. "You're supposed to be on Dorian's side, babe."

I sighed. "I don't even know if *I'm* on Dorian's side." I thought of Rosie's sweet little face and how she'd waved at me. "Haven't I disrupted Primrose's life enough? And that's without the guy or the little girl knowing I exist. Although, we had a near-miss with that. Almost accidentally met them."

"What do you mean?" Candace leaned in.

"Benjamin and I went to the supermarket, and the three of them were there. At first, it was just Primrose and her daughter, but before I could say anything, he appeared, too."

Chandler's eyes widened. "No freaking way. What did you do?"

"I pretended to be a stranger asking her whether the store sold wine." I shook my head. "Then Benjamin and I got the hell out of there before he suspected anything. But not before I turned around and saw her little girl looking back at me. Practically staring through my soul."

Candace clutched her chest. "Oh, my heart."

"Yeah. It messed me up inside."

"What are you gonna do now?" Chandler asked.

Throw myself into the mansion so I don't have to feel anything else. "I'm gonna try to breathe life into this place again. I have a gardener coming tomorrow to help me replicate my mother's rose garden."

"That's amazing." Candace beamed. "I could totally help with that. I'm so glad you were able to buy this place back."

"It's what my father would've wanted. More than that, it's what *I* wanted. It's bad enough that I gave up the company. The house is the last shred of what once was. It's a legacy I can handle, unlike the business, which was eating away at my soul."

Chandler nodded. "Well, not for nothing, but you don't need the money. You made the right decision in unloading those problems onto someone else."

"Not sure Remington would agree…"

"Your father died because of his job," Chandler pointed out. "You nearly did. Pretty sure he'd be good with your decisions now."

"You don't know my father very well, then." I laughed angrily.

Candace pointed her finger at me. "I say good riddance to all the stress that came with running Vanderbilt. You deserve to have the life you dream of. You've sacrificed enough. I know what it's like to stare death in the face, and there's no substitute for peace of mind. Our time on Earth is too short to devote to something that doesn't speak to your soul. And life is also too short to live alone and not let love in. My kids have brought me more love than I could ever imagine. I hope someday you can experience having a child of your own."

Pain moved through my chest. "I don't know if that's in the cards for me."

"Primrose moved on because she thought you had broken up with her," Candace said. "But I guarantee you, she doesn't regret having her daughter, despite everything."

"Of course she doesn't," I agreed.

"You don't need to be hopelessly in love with someone to start a life and have children." She looked around. "Imagine being able to create a new story for this place."

"I thought you were hoping for a miracle with Primrose. Now you think I should knock someone else up?" I challenged.

"Well, of course I'm hoping for a miracle. But the reality is, you can't wait your entire life for her to come to her senses. There's always the chance that she'll just love you in secret and marry her daughter's father. I think if she goes through with this wedding, that should be your sign to move on."

I nodded.

"When is the wedding?" Chandler asked.

"A little over five months away."

He sighed. "Well, then, you'll know fairly soon, right?"

"Right."

Candace frowned. "Well, like I said, if she marries him, you *do* need to find a way to move on, even if you fake it 'til you make it."

I'd done a lot of faking it in my lifetime but never when it came to my feelings. Not sure how I'd pretend to be in love when my heart belonged to someone else.

• • •

Later that evening, the phone rang. When I saw Primrose's name on the screen, I couldn't pick it up fast enough.

"Hey."

She let out a breath. "Hi."

"I wasn't expecting to hear from you."

"I know."

I wiped sweat from my forehead. "What's up?"

"How have you been doing since returning to California?"

"Things are okay. Trying to acclimate to the mansion again. Spent the day with Chandler and Candace, actually. They stopped by."

"Ah." She paused. "That's great that you have them nearby again."

There was something off about her tone. Dread filled me, and I tightened every muscle in my body in preparation for the worst. "What's going on, Primrose? I sense something in your voice."

When she didn't immediately say anything, I realized what was happening here before she managed to get it out. Trying to sound strong, I said, "I've got all night...take your time. But I have a feeling I know what's coming."

"You do?"

"You're marrying him. You're trying to figure out a way to let me down easy. Am I right?"

Rather than dispute it, she remained silent. That was all the confirmation I needed.

"There's no such thing as making this easy for me, Primrose. I'm never going to want a life without you. But I have to accept whatever you decide is best for you."

Acceptance was one thing. But it would be a while before the devastation wore off. The feeling of having been punched in the gut made me realize just how much I *had* been hanging on to the dream of getting to be with her again. I certainly hadn't expected her to come to this conclusion so soon.

She finally spoke, her voice shaky. "I want to give my daughter the life I never had. That's what's most important right now. And you don't deserve to be strung along. You've been through enough. I didn't want to waste any more of your time."

I closed my eyes, reluctant to speak. She'd hear the pain and sheer devastation in my voice.

"I'll always cherish you, Dorian. I...just need to do what's best for my family."

I'd somehow thought *I* was still her family. But I wasn't. The trauma from my abandonment had influenced this decision, too. She'd never be able to trust me the way she trusted him, a man who had no history of letting her down. And she'd never be able to give Rosie the life she felt her daughter deserved if she were to choose me.

I understood it. Even if it killed me.

I'd prepared for this moment, yet I didn't know what to say now that it was finally here. I hadn't realized how much it would hurt to be rejected by the only woman I'd ever loved. I felt foolish for having fantasized about her showing up at my door, telling me she couldn't live without me and that despite everything, we could make it work if we loved each other.

Someone else would get to see her walking down the aisle toward him. Someone else would get to love her. Primrose and I were done.

We're really done.

"You need to do what you need to do, Primrose," I managed to mutter.

"I feel terrible for doing this to you after everything we've been through, but I didn't want to put it off."

"I'll be fine," I told her. The last thing I wanted was to make her feel guilty for putting her child first. It was hard to argue with that decision. "You're not doing anything *to* me. Don't look at it that way. You're just choosing to continue living the life I interrupted when I came to Ohio. Everything that transpired has been my fault, my doing."

I fell silent, just breathing into the phone for several seconds. *I can't believe this.*

"Are you okay?" she whispered.

"I will be." My voice shook as I wiped a tear from my eye.

"Are you crying?"

I didn't want to admit it, but clearly it was obvious. I didn't answer.

She sobbed into the phone. "I'm so sorry, Dorian."

"Stop apologizing. You did nothing wrong, and I'll be okay." My tone was stern as I desperately tried to stifle my tears.

Primrose sniffled. "I hate myself right now. I hate myself for hurting you like this after everything you've been through."

"Sometimes we have to make tough decisions. Boy, do I know about that. I made one when I pretended not to love you anymore. And you're making one right now, pretending not to love me."

CHAPTER 27

Primrose

It had been two months since the night I'd called Dorian. The back-and-forth debate I'd endured for a week before making that decision had nearly killed me, and I'd needed to put myself out of my misery. The only way I knew to do that was to force myself to choose.

My decision, though, had brought me very little peace. I'd thought about Dorian every hour of every day since. I'd hoped that setting him free would somehow squelch the longing inside of me, but it had only made it worse. The hurt in his voice when I'd called him still haunted me. So did his words—that I was *pretending* not to love him. That was the truth.

After I told Dorian I was going forward with the wedding, I'd decided to keep everything that had happened to myself and not upset Casey. And I couldn't bear the thought of going through it all again. Did I love Casey? Yes. But I loved him for different reasons than I loved Dorian. Reasons that weren't as authentically pure and unconditional. I'd never dreamed *I* would be the one to ultimately hurt Dorian after I'd felt so hurt by him for so many years. But my hurting *him* was ultimately what ended us.

You did it for Rosie, I kept telling myself.

It was mid-morning, and I had an hour before it was time to get Rosie from preschool. This was always the time of day when I was tempted to search Dorian's name online or even pick up the phone and call to see how he was doing. But nothing good could come from reopening wounds still in the process of healing. So I resisted.

The doorbell rang, and I opened the door to find a delivery man holding a small package.

"I'm gonna need your signature for this, ma'am."

"Sure." I signed his electronic pad and took the box. When I saw the name on the return label, my stomach dropped. *Dorian Vanderbilt.*

I took the box to the kitchen before rummaging through my junk drawer for scissors. My hands shook. After carefully slicing through the tape, I opened the package. Inside was a small box. When I lifted the cover, I nearly fell back at the sight of a sparkling engagement ring.

What?
Why?
Has he lost his mind?

The diamond had to be at least four carats.

There was a note inside.

> *Primrose, after my father passed away, his and Christina's personal belongings that had been with them at the time of their deaths were shipped to me in Bos-*

ton. One of the items was Christina's engagement ring. I'd kept it in a safe deposit box at my bank. Recently, I went back to Boston and cleared everything out. As you're Christina's next of kin, I believe you should keep this ring. I hope you're doing well. -Dorian

Now that I looked more closely at the ring, I did recognize it as Aunt Christina's. She didn't always wear it, but I had seen it a couple of times. My heart pounded. What the hell had I been thinking? That he was sending me a proposal in the mail? Begging me to change my mind?

I stared at the ring for several minutes, the sun in my kitchen sparkling off what I was sure was a flawless diamond—absolutely beautiful yet so bittersweet because this had been on Christina's hand when she died. This was my opportunity to have what might've been her most cherished item. It was an honor.

I reread the note a few times. So formal. No salutation at the end. He'd just signed it *Dorian*. I understood completely, even if I hated that after everything we'd been through, this was the only type of communication we had left.

I walked the box out to the recycle bin and almost discarded it before I noticed one other item inside with the tissue paper. My chest constricted at the sight of it.

A single red rosebud.

Oh, my heart.

My Dorian.

A week later, I was scrolling social media, once again fighting the urge to search Dorian's name online. Over the past week, I'd caved and searched more times than I could count.

He didn't have social media accounts that I could find. That made it easier for me. But his friend Candace did have social media. And if I checked *her* page daily, as I tended to do on my phone at night, one of these days I was going to see something that would upset me.

I'd first browsed Candace's page with genuine curiosity. Once Dorian had told me she was doing well and had two kids now, I had to see it for myself. I'd felt so much joy as I scrolled through the photos of her and Chandler playing with their beautiful kids. But months later, I knew my daily checking had everything to do with getting a glimpse of Dorian. To torture myself? Maybe. But also to see if he was okay, and to maybe catch a smile on his face so I didn't have to feel so terrible about my decision.

But today I got more than I'd bargained for.

Candace had posted a photo taken at what I recognized as the pool area at Dorian's mansion. Chandler lifted their beautiful little boy into the air from the water, but the background is what caught my attention. I used my thumb and index finger to zoom in on what looked to be Dorian sitting in one of the lounge chairs with a woman leaning against his chest. It was a little blurry, yet she seemed beautiful. No surprise there. She also seemed to have an amazing figure. My heart sank. Why did I have to have this reaction?

I wanted Dorian to move on, didn't I? That's what I'd told myself. But in all reality, *most* of what I'd told myself these past few months had been disingenuous. I was the only one who knew that every moment I'd spent away from Dorian since he came to Ohio had been agonizing. And I wasn't doing all that great a job being discreet about my online research, either. This past week, Casey had asked me more than once what I was doing on the computer while he sat on the other side of the living room watching TV. I'd blown it off and said I was just scrolling.

I was about to leave Instagram when I noticed that the photo I'd been looking at was actually the first in a slideshow of *multiple* photos. The temptation was real. Adrenaline coursed through me as I debated whether to slide my finger across to the left to look at the other images.

My finger hovered until I finally bit the bullet and swiped. The second image was Candace applying sunscreen to her little girl. The third was Dorian and Chandler holding up their beers. I lingered on that one because it was the first time I'd gotten a good look at Dorian's face since I last saw him. He looked so beautiful with his black hair slicked back from the water. How I missed a lazy day at the pool with him. My heart beat faster with every second. Had I made the right choice in keeping my family together? I wasn't sure. But my love for Dorian had never been up for debate. I'd always love him. A part of me had still loved him even when I thought he'd intentionally ended us.

I braced myself and finally swiped to the last photo. My heart sank, because it was exactly what I'd dreaded: a close-up and clearer version of Dorian's new girlfriend, sitting on his lap with her arm around him. As the blood rose to my face, I whispered to myself, "This is what you wanted. You need him to move on so you can move on with *your* life. This is good. You should be happy for him."

All lies.

Consumed by jealousy, I didn't realize my finger was still on the image until a giant heart appeared on the screen.

Oh no.

Shit. Shit. Shit!

I'd accidentally liked the photo. I immediately unliked it. But the damage had been done. People got notifications whenever someone liked one of their photos, even if the liker retracted it. It was too late to take back my mistake. Candace didn't have very many followers. It seemed to be just close family and friends, even if her photos were public. So she wouldn't likely miss the notification.

Fuck!

But it was time to pick Rosie up. So I swallowed my humiliation and put my phone away. Dread knotted in my stomach the entire way to the preschool. It lightened a bit as I saw my smiling daughter running toward the car. *Get back to reality, Primrose.*

The teacher opened the door and got her settled in the backseat.

"You look like you had a good day, honey."

My daughter squealed in delight. "We got to pet the animals!"

"We had the animal man come today," her teacher explained. "He brought all sorts of critters with him. The kids loved it."

"Which one was your favorite?" I asked her.

"The iguana. Can we get one, Mommy?"

"Maybe someday."

As we drove off, I tried my best to focus on the road and clear my mind so I could be present for my daughter for the rest of the afternoon.

When we got home, I made her a peanut butter and jelly sandwich and sat with her as we chatted more about the animals she'd encountered at school.

After, since the weather was decent today, I took her outside so she could play on the swing set Casey had recently assembled in the yard. I pulled up two chairs—one for sitting and one to kick my legs up on. My nerves activated again as I opened Instagram. This time, there was a new message request from Candace. My stomach dropped. *Oh no.*

This was my biggest nightmare. She had to know I was stalking Dorian. And if there was any doubt about it, I'd liked the *one* photo of him and his new girl to prove it.

I cringed.

Though I wished I could put off reading her message until after Rosie went to bed tonight, curiosity was killing me. So I clicked on it. Because we weren't following each other, I had the option to accept the message or not. Once I accepted, though, she'd see that I'd read it. So, I opted to read it first and then decide whether to accept.

> *Hey, Primrose. I hope it's okay that I'm messaging you. I saw that you'd liked one of my photos. I then clicked over to your account to make sure it was you. You look*

beautiful, and your daughter is absolutely adorable. It's so great to see you after all this time. Dorian told me a bit about his trip to Ohio. He said you got emotional when he told you about my remission. That really touched me. I've wanted to reach out to you for a long time now but didn't want to overstep. I know the situation between you and Dorian is complicated. I just wanted to say hello and let you know I was thinking of you. I also followed you. I hope that's okay. If you ever want to talk, I won't say anything to the guys.

I had to stop for a moment to process that. She'd also given me her phone number and encouraged me to call her. *What good could possibly come from that?* However, I did appreciate her saying she wouldn't discuss any conversations we had with Chandler or Dorian. I believed her, even if that might've been dumb. Candace had always struck me as a real girls' girl. I didn't take her to be a liar. Yet I couldn't accept the message yet. Would it be a good idea to engage? That was a slippery slope. If I never accepted the message, she could assume I never saw it. That might be one way to leave well enough alone, if I could curb my curiosity.

What Dorian was up to these days wasn't any of my business. Talking to her would tempt me to ask about him, and then I'd become privy to information I had no right to have—unless, of course, it was coming from Dorian himself.

A couple of days went by, and I hadn't responded to Candace's message. The more time that passed, the more I told myself it was better to let sleeping dogs lie. It wouldn't be good to obtain information I had no right to know. *Probably I should take it one step further and stop checking her damn page altogether.*

Monday when Rosie was at school, though, I had an abrupt change of heart. Or maybe I just stopped kidding myself. Either way, I accepted the message. Ultimately, that's what I wanted. And now that she could see I'd viewed it, I needed to respond.

> *Hey, Candace! It's so good to hear from you. I have to admit, I'm a bit embarrassed for being caught stalking your page. But if it gave me the opportunity to say hello, it was worth it. Your kids are gorgeous, and needless to say, I'm very happy to see you looking so vibrant and healthy. My Rosie is a handful but also a joy. I'm happy we're both getting to experience motherhood. It's truly a gift. Thank you for taking the time to reach out to me.*

I decided to leave it at that and not say anything about a phone call. I closed the app feeling relieved about putting the whole thing behind me.

But after making a quick snack, I checked my messages again and saw that Candace responded.

It's great to hear from you! Let me know when you have time to chat. If you're around in the next hour, my kids are out getting an early breakfast with Chandler. Might be a good time to talk.

She'd left her number again and clearly didn't want to drop the phone-call thing.

I looked at the time on the message, and she'd sent it five minutes ago. Wouldn't it be rude not to call her? If I was going to do this, better to get it over with and not miss the window.

I took a deep breath and dialed.

After a couple of rings, she picked up. "Primrose?"

"Yes! Hi. Wasn't sure you'd know it was me."

"Well, I don't have too many people other than Chandler calling me at this time. I'm glad you called."

"This is a good time for me, too. My daughter is in school for another couple of hours."

"Aren't these little breaks when they're out of the house like gold?"

"The only time I can think straight and get stuff done." I exhaled.

"I know." She paused. "I hope I wasn't being too forward in asking you to call me. I feel more comfortable talking than typing everything out, especially since Chandler sometimes uses my phone to scroll on social media. He doesn't have his own account."

"Ah. Well, I don't want you to have to hide anything from him."

"Oh, I know. I love my husband, but I don't trust that he wouldn't run to Dorian and tell him everything. I want you to be able to talk to me honestly, if you want to, without having to worry about that."

I smiled. It made me happy that we were on the same page. "I appreciate that," I said. "At the same time, I feel like I shouldn't be talking about Dorian behind his back, especially to one of his friends."

"You don't have to say anything you don't want to," Candace assured me. "I just wanted to say hello and acknowledge that I've thought of you, too, all these years. When I found out the real reason Dorian broke up with you, I felt horrible that you were out there somewhere with a broken heart, not knowing the full story."

"Yeah," I breathed. "Needless to say, the truth was a shock, but I'm grateful he came to find me to explain everything." Then I changed the subject, asking about her health. We spent the next several minutes discussing her remission and her fears of recurrence, especially now that she had children. She seemed to be in a good headspace overall, though—much better than mine, if I were being honest.

"So..." she said the moment there was a lull in our conversation. "I couldn't help but notice that you liked and then unliked the photo of Dorian and Liv. I'm sure it wasn't easy to see that."

She had a name. *Liv.*

"I don't know how to feel," I told her. "I do want him to be happy."

"She's an acquaintance of mine. That's how they met."

I felt unjustifiably betrayed by that news. "Really..."

"Yeah. I invited them over at the same time one day. I suspected she'd be a good fit for him, but I had my reservations because I knew he wasn't over you, despite knowing you were moving forward with your wedding."

I swallowed the lump in my throat. "It looks like it worked out."

"They've been dating ever since, and I know she's crazy about him. But..." She hesitated.

"What?" I urged, sitting at the edge of my seat.

"I've struggled with feeling like maybe I made the wrong decision in introducing them. I don't want her to get hurt."

"I'm getting married..." I said defensively.

"I know that." She went silent.

I got the impression she was digging for my true feelings on the matter, trying to see if there was still doubt on my end. She wouldn't have had to dig very far to figure it out. I was grateful she couldn't see my face. She'd probably see right through me.

"I'm not going to do anything to disrupt his life again," I eventually said.

"Not intentionally. But you're still breathing, right?" She chuckled. "I think you're always going to be in his heart. Anyone else comes second."

Her candor made me sweat. "I can't do anything about feelings Dorian still has for me. I'm not sure what you want me to say..."

"I'm sorry. You don't have to say anything. I'm just being honest about how I see the situation. I understand if you'd prefer not to know anything."

"I *would* prefer not to know. Because it's hard for me." My voice shook. "It was hard for me to see him with her." I shut my eyes, realizing I'd admitted more than I intended.

"I'm sure…" She sighed. "And I won't continue to bring this up. It's just… I think he's forcing himself to move on, and while that could be construed as a good thing, it also has the potential for disaster."

"How serious *are* they?"

"She told me she's falling in love with him. But he hasn't mentioned the L word to her. And while she hasn't moved in officially, she's at the mansion a lot of the time. I could see this getting serious."

That felt like a punch to the gut. *Liv* was living my former life.

"If there's any chance of you pulling a runaway bride, I wanted you to know that if you wait too long, things are gonna be a lot more complicated," Candace said. "I promise I'm not trying to stir up trouble. I just want to protect my friends. I still consider you one of them. To be clear, I'm not on anyone's side here. I wouldn't have dreamed of getting involved if I hadn't seen that you liked and unliked the photo of them. That made me wonder if you haven't fully gotten over him."

I'd *never* get over him.

She sighed. "I'm not gonna interfere anymore, and I'm not gonna tell anyone we had this conversation. What you do with this information is totally up to you."

"Thank you for reaching out to me, Candace," I said after a long pause. "I appreciate it."

"I hope I haven't overstepped."

"No. I respect you for sharing what you think is important for me to know."

"I also hope I haven't scared you off and that you'll want to keep in touch. I swear, we don't have to talk about Dorian next time."

"It's all good," I said, though if I knew what was good for me, I wouldn't initiate any additional communication with her, even if that made me sad. There was no real way to separate Candace from Dorian.

"Well, I'm sure you have things to do," she said. "So I'll let you go."

"It was good talking to you, Candace."

"You, too, Primrose. Truly."

After we hung up, I sat in a daze, the weight of the conversation heavy on my shoulders. I'd hoped to come out of that phone call feeling better, but it had only made me feel worse. Dorian was getting serious with that woman. What if he was falling in love? And more than that, why was I so invested if I wanted him to be happy? Why did this feel so utterly devastating? Did I expect to move on and marry Casey while Dorian pined for me alone at the mansion in perpetuity? Of course not. That would be the most selfish thing imaginable. I'd made my decision. I'd ended things with Dorian. And I had to come to terms with it.

The door opened. I jumped and turned to find Casey entering.

I sprang to my feet. "What are you doing home?"

"I decided to take the rest of the day off." He dropped his bag. "Surprise!"

"You never do that." I flashed my best fake smile.

"I know. It just hit me today how much I miss out on because of work. I got ahead on my to-do list and told Jim I needed the afternoon off. I want to surprise Rosie at pickup."

Running a shaky hand through my hair, I forced another smile. "She's gonna love that."

"Just her?" He wrapped his arms around me and kissed me on the cheek. "I was hoping you'd be happy, too."

"Of course I am." I stiffened. "What do you want to do after we pick her up?"

"I was thinking we could get sandwiches from the deli and take them to the park. After, we can hit the zoo. We don't use those season passes nearly enough."

"That sounds like an amazing plan."

Casey kissed me again. Immediately, I noticed his erection.

He whispered in my ear, "You think we can get a quick one in before we have to pick her up? I'm so freaking horny."

My first instinct was to lie. "I just got my period."

"So?"

"I'm not comfortable."

"Okay." He pouted. "I understand."

My heart sank. Lying to get out of having sex was a first for me. But I couldn't bear to do that right now. It didn't feel right when I'd spent the morning agonizing over Dorian. I added another notch to the long line of things I felt guilty about lately.

That afternoon, Casey, Rosie, and I had what by all appearances was a wholesome family outing. Inside my brain, though, was a tornado of inappropriate thoughts contaminating the entire experience. I felt like the worst mother and wife-to-be on Earth.

CHAPTER 28

Primrose

Lucy smiled from behind me in the mirror.

"It looks so much more beautiful now that it's perfectly fitted to your body, doesn't it?"

We were at my final dress fitting, and she was right. The dress was absolutely perfect and fit like a glove.

I should've been on top of the world. Yet for the last couple of weeks, since the phone call with Candace, instead of excitement over my wedding, I'd been preoccupied with the idea of losing Dorian forever. I was certain he and Liv were getting closer.

As the wedding date had grown closer, too, more than anything, I became more and more ashamed of my inner turmoil as it related to Casey. He had a right to know what was going on in my mind. I'd been so afraid to hurt him, yet wasn't I hurting him anyway by keeping him in the dark? Somehow I'd justified it.

As I looked at myself in the beautiful white dress, I imagined walking down the aisle, but all I could see at the far end waiting for me was Dorian. *His* beautiful face smiling back at me, tears in his eyes as I made my way toward him. *That* was my dream. As a tear rolled down my cheek, I doubted more than ever whether going through with the wedding was right. I couldn't continue to pretend I was happy. I wasn't.

It suddenly felt like the dress was squeezing me—choking me. I needed it off.

I turned to the attendant. "Can I get out of this?"

She rushed toward me. "Is everything okay?"

"Yes. I'm just having a...hot flash or something and don't want to ruin the dress."

"Of course."

I escaped into the dressing room and slipped out of the gown, eventually handing it to the attendant to hang. I looked at my red, blotchy face in the mirror and knew I'd reached my breaking point.

"Are you okay in there?" Lucy's voice came through the door.

I wiped my eyes. "I'm fine! I'll be right out."

I managed to pull myself together before returning to Lucy. Thankfully, she didn't pry, though she had to know something was off with me.

As I drove home, I felt horribly conflicted, dreading what needed to be done, but unable to ignore it anymore. I stopped at the one place I knew might give me peace and clarity before facing Casey.

It was a cloudy day, perfect for a trip to the cemetery where my mother was buried. I knew exactly how to get to her plot from the entrance, never needing a map. I was grateful to be back in Ohio so I could visit her again.

I knelt by Mom's gravestone. "Boy, Mama, I could sure use your advice right now." I looked up at the sky. "I wonder if you'd be disappointed in me. As you probably know, I have a wonderful man who loves me and our child—your sweet granddaughter. And I'm seriously considering throwing it all away. I don't want Rosie to have a broken family like I did. She deserves better. But doesn't she also deserve a mother who's true to herself?"

I brushed my fingers along the top of the headstone. "I've been lying to myself. I feel safe but not fulfilled. I'm struggling to accept the fact that my happiness should ever be more important than Rosie's. Wouldn't that be selfish? Doesn't your own happiness stop being a priority the day you have a child? I want to believe you'd tell me I'll be incapable of being the best mother to my daughter if I'm not happy myself. That's what I want to hear. But I can't put words in your mouth when you're not here." I exhaled deeply. "I really need you."

As birds chirped around me, I prayed for a sign. After a few minutes, when I felt some raindrops, I took that as my cue to leave. Before I walked away, though, I looked down and noticed that someone had left something at my mother's grave. *Holy wow*. What were the chances? It had to be a sign from Mom telling me following my heart wasn't just the best decision, it was the *only* choice.

I picked up the single rosebud and raised it toward the sky. "Thanks, Mama."

. . .

Back at home, I realized I had to get this over with before the stress killed me. Casey's mother had already been watching Rosie today, so I asked if she could take her for a few more hours tonight so I could talk to Casey as soon as he got home.

My stomach was upset. My legs were shaky. And more than that, I felt like the worst person ever. Like I deserved nothing but an angry, hateful reaction from him. Casey was going to be blindsided. I should've made this decision months ago when Dorian came to town. Even then I'd known what my heart desired, even if I refused to accept it. Instead, I'd sat on the inevitable. Now we were that much closer to the wedding, and everything would be so much harder. It wasn't just Casey's heart I was about to shatter. My daughter had been looking forward to wearing her princess dress, to seeing her parents united forever. I only hoped she was still young enough that she wouldn't clearly remember this time in her life when her mother turned her world upside down.

When the door opened, I felt ready to drop, like my legs might collapse under me.

A look of alarm crossed Casey's face. "Babe? What's going on? Did something happen?"

"No!" I wiped the sweat from my forehead. "Everything is fine. Rosie is with your mother for a few more hours."

"Why is she still there?"

"There's something we need to talk about. I needed to be alone with you." The room felt wobbly.

"Okay..." He put his hands on my arms and looked into my eyes. "Are you having doubts about the wedding?"

I was surprised that he'd immediately jumped to the correct conclusion. But I was downright shocked at the next question that came out of his mouth.

"Is this about Dorian Vanderbilt?" He let go of me suddenly.

I nearly fell back at the sound of Dorian's name exiting Casey's mouth. "How do you know his name?"

He paced. "You've been acting strangely for some time now. I'm sorry to say that after you've gone to sleep at night, I've occasionally checked your phone and computer. I can see your search history. Almost every day, you search that name." He stopped for a moment. "I looked him up and discovered he's from Orion Coast. I know you lived there with your aunt before we met. I put two and two together and realized *he* must have been the ex you've alluded to but would never speak about, the man you said broke your heart, yet you've given me almost no details about it over the years."

"Yes...that's him." I cleared my throat. "What else did you find?"

"I read an article that said he was presumed missing at one time, but later it was revealed he'd been in hiding. Pretty crazy story."

I felt entirely numb. "Why didn't you confront me about it?"

"Because I wanted to hear it from you first." He sighed. "And I didn't want to believe any of it meant anything. I'd hoped your searching was just innocent curiosity. But given the look on your face when I walked in just now, I have a bad feeling about this." He let out a long breath. "What were you about to tell me, Primrose?"

I closed my eyes a moment. There was no other way to explain it than to tell Casey the absolute truth from the very beginning. "Can we sit, please?" With a shaky hand, I gestured to the sofa.

I took a deep breath and went back to the time right after Aunt Christina died, explaining my time with Dorian at the mansion, his breaking up with me, and ending with Dorian's recent stay in Cincinnati. "I haven't been having an affair with him, Casey," I concluded.

"Just an emotional one," he countered.

I couldn't argue with that. "I promise that nothing physical happened while he was here. But I haven't been able to move past it."

"Because you still love him?" His eyes glistened. "Is that what you're trying to say?"

I took a deep breath and muttered the only answer that was true. "Yes."

"And you never loved me? Or you only loved me so long as he was dead to you…"

"I *do* love you," I insisted.

He crossed his arms. "But it's not the same kind of love as you have for him."

With tears in my eyes, I shook my head. "It's not." I'd come too far to deny anything anymore.

Casey dropped his head into his hands before looking up at me. "I knew something was wrong. I should've blown the lid off it earlier…but I needed *you* to tell me. I suppose, too, a part of me didn't want to know. But I'm not stupid. Things haven't been right with us for a long time. You stopped wanting to sleep with me…" He exhaled. "This explains so much."

Tears welled in my eyes. "Our daughter deserves better than me."

He met my gaze. "You're a damn good mother, Primrose. None of this changes that."

"How can you say that right now?" I sniffled.

"Because it's the truth. Regardless of what happens with us, you're a good mother. You give every bit of yourself to Rosie every day." He sighed. "You don't think I've known you had your doubts about us? I've just ignored it because I haven't wanted to believe I could lose you. But obviously, I can't ignore it anymore."

"I don't deserve you," I murmured.

"You deserve someone who fights for you." He placed his hands on my shoulders. "I love you—just as much, if not more, than this guy, whether you realize it or not, and regardless of whether you return the sentiment. I'm not letting you go that easily."

This wasn't the reaction I'd expected. Not sure how anyone could still have hope after what I'd just thrown at him.

"Don't get me wrong," he continued. "That doesn't mean I'm gonna make things difficult for you, if you want to be with him. It just means I'm not gonna give up without a fight. My family is on the line, but this isn't just about Rosie. I wouldn't try to save us if I didn't love you. I'll always love our daughter. That goes without saying. But even if she didn't exist, I love *you*, Primrose. I'd want to spend my life with you even if we didn't have a child together. I don't want to lose you." He suddenly stood. "That said, I'm letting you go."

Huh? I stared up at Casey.

He continued, "You were going to tell me the wedding is off. I'm not giving up hope when it comes to us, or our family, but I think you need to go live what you think is your dream. See if it's really what you want or if it's just an illusion."

I shook my head. "What are you saying?"

"I'm saying you should go to California."

"I can't just leave Rosie and go to California. I—"

"Rosie will be fine for a week. I'm not saying go indefinitely. But you should go." He looked at me for a long moment. "Maybe you need to see that the grass isn't actually greener."

"I'm not sure I can resolve anything in a week."

"Then take more time. I just don't think you're gonna be able to be away from Rosie for much longer, which is why I said a week."

"You're right. I won't be." I rubbed my temples. "I can't believe you're encouraging me to do this."

"Were you not going to end things with me today?"

I hesitated. "I was going to tell you the truth about what's been happening and call off the wedding."

"Well, then, I don't have much to lose, do I?" His stare was incendiary. "So, before you have a chance to break up with me, I'm breaking up with you. I'm making you a single woman again, giving you the space to figure out what you really want."

I narrowed my eyes. "There has to be a catch somewhere."

"No catch. I'm not playing games. I don't do that with my daughter's future. And yeah, maybe I'm also trying to come out of this with my damn pride intact." He ran a hand through his hair. "I've given this relationship my all. No matter what comes out of this, I have no regrets."

"Nor should you. You've been the best partner and father to Rosie."

Casey grabbed his jacket. "I'm gonna get out of here for a bit. Need some air. Let me know when you're leaving."

With that, he was out the door.

CHAPTER 29

Primrose

It took me a week after my conversation with Casey to make a firm decision. Once I'd committed, though, I had to break the news to my daughter.

On our way home from preschool, I announced, "Mommy has to go away for a little while, okay?" From the rearview mirror, I could see the look of concern on her sweet face.

"Where are you going?"

"California."

"Why?"

"I used to live there, and I have to go back for a visit. It's just for a week, and Grandma's gonna take good care of you while Daddy works."

"Can I go with you?"

That broke my heart. "No, sweetie. You have preschool, and Mommy has some things she needs to do by herself."

"Are you coming back?"

That question, along with the fear in her eyes, nearly made me cry. How could she think for one second that I would leave her?

"Of course. I told you, I'm only going for a week."

I didn't blame her one bit for being apprehensive. I was by her side every minute of every day except for when she was at school, and this would be my first time away from her. Mom guilt consumed me, even if I knew this trip was absolutely necessary. *You'll be a better person for her someday if you live with no regrets.*

"When are you leaving?" she asked.

"In two days."

"Are you going in an airplane?"

"Yes."

"Is it scary?"

"Not really." Nothing compared to my nerves about arriving at Dorian's door unannounced.

"Can we go in an airplane together sometime? You, me, and Daddy?"

You, me, and Daddy. Every word that came out of her mouth hurt me more than the last. "Maybe. I can talk to Daddy about it."

"Can we fly to see Mickey Mouse?"

"Maybe someday."

We were headed to Lucy's house after school today for a playdate. I pulled into the driveway and gathered our things. When I got my daughter out of the car, I hugged her tightly and murmured, "I'm sorry."

That afternoon, while Rosie was playing with Lucy's son, Sebastian, I told Lucy everything I'd been putting off. I had no idea how she was going to react.

Once I unloaded it all, Lucy seemed shocked.

"I don't even know what to say, Primrose. I usually have an opinion, but you've floored me here."

"I know," I assured her. "You're not expected to have the perfect reaction or give me advice at this point. That would be unfair to expect. This situation is really difficult to unpack, and I'm just happy you listened to it all."

"What are you gonna do with the wedding dress?" She chuckled. "I know that's the least of your problems, but for some reason it's the first question I have. Maybe I'm still in shock."

"The store said they'd buy it back—for a fraction of what I paid." I rolled my eyes. "That's better than nothing. They have that rack of mistake dresses they sell for a discount."

"You don't think there's any hope for you and Casey? It doesn't sound like he's giving up."

"I don't think marriage is in the cards for us, no matter what happens."

"Fair enough." She sighed and fell quiet for a bit.

"What are you thinking?" I asked. She had to be judging me. How could she not?

"I'm not sure you want to know."

"I do. Please just tell me what you think."

"Okay." She breathed. "Well, for starters... I feel bad for Casey."

Relief washed over me. "You *should* feel bad for Casey," I agreed. "He's the hero of this story, and I'm the villain."

"Don't say that. You can't help how you feel. The right answer is always to be true to yourself." She looked over at Rosie playing in the corner. "You'd give her the same advice if she were older and in your situation."

"Pretty sure my mother gave me that advice, too."

She tilted her head in confusion. "Your mother?"

I told her about the rosebud at the gravesite.

"Wow." She smiled. "See? That's amazing. You needed that."

"I sure did. It was the sign I asked her for."

"Okay..." She rubbed her palms together. "So what's the plan?"

"Which plan?" I asked.

"When you get to California."

Nervous butterflies came alive in my belly. "I have no idea."

"Are you calling him first?"

"I don't think so."

"Why not?"

"Something is telling me to just wing it." I thought for a moment. "Because I'm afraid he'll discourage me now that he's involved with someone. But I think he needs to see me either way. We need to look each other in the eyes and figure this out once and for all."

"Okay." She scratched her chin. "But that sounds risky to me."

"I don't want him setting up a scene for me or trying to protect my feelings, you know? I want to see things as they are. Even if it hurts. No better way to do that than just show up. If what we had is still there, nothing should stand in the way. And if he's moved on, I need to know that, too. Need to see it for myself."

"Well, I'll be crossing my fingers that you get the outcome you desire."

"What *is* the desired outcome in this mess?" I countered. "A custody arrangement? A long-distance relationship? I don't even know what the future would look like. I just know I need to see Dorian and tell him I made a mistake."

She smiled sadly.

"I appreciate your support and the fact that you're being so understanding, given how I sprung everything on you today."

"A true friend is not going to judge you for how you feel," she said. "All the way through the wedding planning, I've sensed that something wasn't right. Now it finally makes sense. The fact that you'd been thinking of him right before he showed up proves you two have some kind of soul connection. It was almost like you could sense him."

I nodded and looked over at the kids playing. Was I delusional to think Dorian would meet me with open arms? He had a girlfriend now. I looked at the time and stood. "I'd better get going. I have to start getting ready."

"Where does Casey's mother think you're going?"

"She thinks I'm going out there to meet up with old college friends. Sort of like a mental-health break. Casey hasn't told her the truth, and neither have I. But as long as I'm being up front with Casey, I won't worry so much about holding things back from anyone else."

"Totally. And hey, it's not a complete lie. You were in college when you met Dorian. So he could be considered a college friend."

"Nice try." I chuckled.

• • •

A couple of days later, the moment I'd been dreading finally arrived. I was dropping Rosie off at preschool, knowing I wouldn't be here to get her this afternoon.

"Grandma will pick you up after school, okay?"

"You're gonna be on the plane?"

"I'll be headed to the airport at that time to get ready to board the plane. But remember, I'll be back in seven days, okay?"

When Rosie started to cry, my eyes filled with tears. I held her tightly. "I love you so much, baby. Please don't be sad."

"I don't want you to go."

"I know. But I'll call you every day. I promise." *Mother of the Year.*

She sniffled. "Okay."

"Be a good girl for Grandma and Daddy. I promise to bring you back something, okay?"

"A toy?"

"Maybe. Is that what you want?"

A smile spread across her face as she nodded.

"Then I'll find you a cool toy that has something to do with California."

I wanted the toy to be the last thing she remembered, so she'd be left with a happy thought. I gave her a quick kiss before waving her off, praying I wasn't making a mistake.

CHAPTER 30
Primrose

The flight to California was bumpy—probably foreshadowing the week that lay ahead of me. The plane had been delayed, getting me here in the evening instead of the afternoon. Not telling Dorian I was coming had seemed like a good idea until I landed. Now my nerves had really started to kick in.

The airport was crowded, but somehow I felt alone, lost in the world at the moment. In some ways, I didn't recognize the person I was anymore. It felt like I was on the outside, watching myself and wanting to warn the woman to be careful. The only thing keeping me from booking another flight and running straight back to Ohio was the memory of Dorian's eyes as he'd told me he loved me the last time we were together.

After I got into the car waiting for me and confirmed my destination with the driver, he looked at me in the rearview mirror and asked, "What do you have going on in Orion Coast?"

"Oh, you know..." I took a breath. "Just a little getaway." If only it were that simple.

"That's a pretty fancy area. Where are you staying?"

I stupidly hadn't booked a hotel, figuring I'd sort all of that out after seeing Dorian's reaction. Maybe Benjamin would be kind enough to let me stay in the guest house if Dorian didn't feel comfortable with me sleeping at the mansion.

I cleared my throat. "With a friend."

I couldn't get my legs to stop bouncing. The only other time I could remember being this nervous was the other night when I'd told the best man I'd ever known that I wasn't going to marry him.

As the car drove along the Pacific Coast Highway, I tried to calm myself, gazing out the window at the gorgeous California landscape—dangerous cliffs that reminded me of this very situation. *Please be easy on me, California.*

When the driver finally pulled up at the mansion, my heart pounded in my ears.

"Fancy place," he noted.

"Yes. It's nice, isn't it?" I said, gazing up at the house.

He got out and retrieved my suitcase from the trunk. "Well, have a good visit."

"Thank you," I said. "I appreciate you getting me here safely."

As the car drove away, I took a deep breath. The mansion looked exactly the same from the outside. But something told me the inside might be unrecognizable.

I couldn't tell you how long I stood outside before I finally garnered the courage to approach the front entrance. Time stood still as I pondered whether to knock.

Then I heard it: music coming from the pool area.

Rather than wait at the door, I walked around to the bushes that surrounded the patio. While you couldn't access it, you could see what was going on if you looked through a certain spot. The music was indeed coming from here. I recognized the song as an old one: Frank Sinatra's "The Summer Wind." Remington had loved Sinatra. I finally garnered the courage to peek through.

Dorian and a woman who looked like the person from the photos on Candace's Instagram were slow dancing. The beautiful glow from the lights of the pool cast a rainbow over them. My insides twisted as I stood there, taking it all in. Every doubt I'd ever felt bombarded me at warp speed. I should've turned around immediately, but instead I quietly observed the living aftermath of my decisions. I could see the man I loved falling in love with someone else before my eyes in real time. This moment set to music was a nightmare come true.

Was it fair to disrupt his life when *I'd* sent him away? Just because I had reservations about marrying Casey, just because I still loved Dorian—did that give me the right to interrupt what might have been the only stability he'd had in years? I felt like a fool for ever thinking I could insert myself back into his life. When Dorian turned, his hand at the small of her back, I could see his eyes were closed. He looked at peace as they swayed.

You can't do this.
You have to leave.

I turned and walked back toward the driveway. Suddenly a light flashed on.

Security light. Oh no!

Picking up my pace, I ran right into someone as I fled the house. "I'm sorry. I was just—"

"Primrose?"

I looked up at his face. His old, familiar face.

My voice trembled. "Benjamin..."

"What are you—"

Panicked, I whispered, "I can't let him see me."

"Come into the guest house." I followed him, and he ushered me inside.

After the door closed behind us, I took a deep breath.

Benjamin's phone chimed. "Hang on," he said. "Dorian's texting me."

Fuck.

"What does it say?" I asked frantically.

"He said he noticed the light go on outside. But I'm typing back that I checked it out and it was probably a false alarm caused by an animal."

My chest rose and fell. "He won't come here?"

"He rarely does. You're safe."

Benjamin waited for a moment. "All good. He bought it."

I sat down on his couch, my back sinking into the pillows, and closed my eyes. "I just need to calm down for a moment, okay?"

"Take your time. Can I get you anything? A glass of water?"

"That would be great."

Benjamin went to the kitchen and poured me some water before joining me on the couch.

After taking a long gulp, I said, "I nearly had a heart attack when those lights came on."

He nodded and let me decompress in silence for a minute. Then he said, "I think now is a fair time for me to ask what's going on and why you'd be here if you didn't want to be seen."

I finished the last of my water. "I made a horrible mistake in thinking I could come here, Benjamin. I suspected Dorian had moved on, but I didn't realize how bad it would be."

"I need you to back up a bit, okay?"

"Sorry." I shook my head. "I'm getting ahead of myself."

"Take your time, Primrose. I'm not going anywhere."

"Thank you." I rubbed my palms on my pants. "I called off my wedding to Casey."

He took a breath in. "I see."

"Marrying him wasn't what I wanted in my heart of hearts. It took me a while to reach that conclusion, but it was inevitable. I'd felt that way even before Dorian came to town. I was still in love with him and never got over the heartbreak. It affected my ability to fully give myself to Casey, despite what a wonderful man he is."

"You're leaving Casey altogether?"

I nodded. "He's determined to save our relationship somehow. But he knows about Dorian."

"He knows you're here?"

"He *told* me to come here and sort out my feelings. He broke up with me to give me that freedom. I'm here for a week."

"You came here to get Dorian back, then..."

I shook my head. "I don't know what I expected, Benjamin. I needed to see Dorian while I had nothing holding me back and to apologize for not being brave enough to accept my feelings for what they were when he was in Ohio."

"What made you run like that from the main house tonight? Second thoughts?"

Looking down, I played with some lint on the sofa. "I saw him with her."

"Ah." He closed his eyes. "I feared it was something like that."

"They're serious?" My stomach tensed.

After a brief hesitation, Benjamin nodded. "It's new, but things seem to be moving fast. I believe she's helping him get over you. I also believe he's happier than he was before he met her. But if you were gonna come here, I think you might've arrived just in the nick of time."

Beads of sweat formed on my forehead. "What if I'm too late?"

"I can't answer that for you, sweetheart."

I chewed on my lip. "Maybe I should go home."

"Don't you think he deserves to know you're here? You came all this way."

"I think maybe what he really deserves is peace. My being here will only disrupt that."

"I think Dorian finding out that you came here and left without seeing him would provide him anything but peace."

"Well, he doesn't need to know."

"Primrose..." Benjamin frowned and quite frankly looked a little sorry for me.

"I wanted to believe that love conquers all, but haven't I done enough, Benjamin? And who's to say he doesn't love her now? This is my fault for not being true to my feelings when he gave me the opportunity to choose him again. I was a coward."

"None of this is your fault," Benjamin assured me. "It's no one's fault. It's just the way things happened. Not to mention, you had a *very* good reason for not jumping back into Dorian's arms."

"Does she live with him now?" I asked.

"She's not officially moved in."

I stared off. "They were slow dancing," I said softly. "It looked so romantic."

"I'm sorry you had to see that. But you need to remember, he thinks he lost you. Anything he's doing is based on that."

Benjamin refilled my water before returning to his spot on the sofa. "How about this?" he said. "You relax tonight. You're very worked up, which is completely understandable. I'll make us something to eat. Then you try to get some sleep. Tomorrow, when you have a fresh mind, we'll decide what your next step should be. But I don't think it's wise to leave just yet. You've made plans to be here for a week. You should take advantage of what I'm sure is a much-needed break, if nothing else."

I took a moment to think. I'd prepared my daughter for my absence. Coming home now would only confuse her. This time away was a rare gift, and I *did* need to take advantage of it, even if just to clear my head in private.

"You're right," I said. "I don't think I can go back without at least letting him know I came here. I'd regret it forever."

He nodded. "So now we have a plan. You'll sort your head out tonight and face him tomorrow."

Adrenaline pumped through me. "What if she's still here?"

"I'll figure something out, even if I have to ask to speak with him privately to get him over here alone."

"That makes sense." I inhaled a calming breath and let it go. "Thank you so much for your help."

"Liv is a nice girl, Primrose. But make no mistake, I'm on *your* side. I will always be rooting for you."

I felt tears behind my eyes. "The fact that you're here with me right now is a blessing."

"Very well, then." He stood. "Now that you're properly hydrated, what *else* can I get you to drink?"

"Something strong." I chuckled.

"I've got just the thing. Coming right up."

He bustled in the kitchen and brought me over a shot glass of what smelled like tequila. I downed it.

Benjamin laughed. "How about another?"

"No." I held out my palms. "This should do it. I just needed something to help me relax a bit."

"I've ordered us some takeout—the fried chicken you used to like from the restaurant on the boardwalk."

My stomach growled. "Thank you so much. I haven't eaten since this morning."

He brought over a glass of wine for himself and kicked his feet up. "How's that beautiful little girl of yours?"

"She's truly wonderful. This is the first time I've left her."

"I think it's good for kids to learn how to adapt to different situations. It will be helpful for her in the long term to experience time away from you."

"Thank you for trying to make me feel better, Benjamin."

He smiled. "You and I have a long history. We've been through some difficult circumstances together. Just as I look at Dorian like a son, I care for you like I would my own daughter."

This time, when I felt the urge to cry, I let go and my tears spilled over. "As someone who has no living parents, that means a lot."

He smiled and stood. "While we're waiting for the food to arrive, I'm going to go set up the guest room for you."

"Thank you again, Benjamin."

Alone in the living room, I thought about how different this moment felt from what I'd imagined it could be. Instead of running into Dorian's open arms, I'd seen another woman in his arms instead. Instead of sleeping next to him in the mansion, I'd be tossing and turning all night in the guest house as I pondered whether staying was a colossal mistake.

• • •

The following morning, Benjamin offered to go out and get coffee for me. He didn't stock any here at the guest house since he only drank tea. Given the headache I was currently experiencing, I wasn't going to argue with him. No way could I handle facing Dorian today without my morning caffeine. So Benjamin left, and I used the opportunity to call home and check on my daughter.

Casey's mother answered. "Hi, Primrose. You have someone here very anxious to talk to you."

"Thanks, Karen. Put her on."

"It's Mommy," I could hear her tell Rosie.

Then came her little voice, "Hi, Mommy."

"Hi, baby. How are you?"

"Good."

"Good! I'm so happy to hear that."

"When are you coming home?"

"Seven days. You know that. I marked it on your calendar."

"I know."

"What are you doing today?"

"Grandma is taking me to the park."

"Very nice. I'm happy you're getting out. Please be good and don't go too far from her, okay?"

"Okay."

"I love you, Rosie."

"Love you, Mommy."

"Can you give the phone back to Grandma?"

After a few seconds, Karen came on the line. "Hey..."

"Thanks for taking her out today."

"Well, the weather is going to be decent."

"Great."

"Are you having a good trip so far?"

"Yes," I lied.

"Very nice. Okay. I won't keep you."

Before she could hang up, I said, "Karen?"

"Yes?"

"How's Casey?" I gulped.

"You haven't spoken to him?"

"No. Not since I arrived."

"I haven't seen him. He left for work before we got up."

"Okay." I paused. "I'll call him later."

I couldn't imagine what was going on in Casey's mind right now.

I'd just hung up the phone when the door opened. I rose to my feet to greet Benjamin, but then I almost immediately fell back on the couch.

Because it wasn't Benjamin standing there.

It was Dorian.

CHAPTER 31

Dorian

It felt like the wind had been knocked out of me.

I'd walked over to Benjamin's to find out if he had any eggs, and now I was face to face with Primrose.

Primrose.

What the hell?

"What...what are you doing here, Primrose?"

She was wearing a crop top. Not once had she worn one back in Cincinnati. If I didn't know better, I would've thought I'd been transported back in time. Either that, or I was hallucinating.

When she didn't answer me, I asked again. "Primrose, talk to me. What's going on? Why are you here?"

Her eyes glistened.

Is she about to cry? "Are you okay? Did something happen in Ohio?"

She shook her head. "No. Nothing bad happened. I'm sorry to have scared you. My daughter's fine. Everyone is fine. But you weren't supposed to find me here. I'm just in shock right now."

Now I was *really* confused. "Why would you be here if not for me to find you?"

Before she could open her mouth, the door opened again and I turned to find Benjamin, holding an iced tea in one hand and a coffee in the other.

His face reddened. "Shit," he muttered.

Just as he opened his mouth again, I cut him off. "What the hell is going on here?"

"I haven't had a chance to explain it," she said to Benjamin. "He just walked in and found me."

I looked between them. *What the fuck are they doing behind my back?*

"We were going to call you today to let you know she came into town last night," Benjamin explained.

My head whipped toward her. "You've been here since last night?"

Her breath shook. "Benjamin, would you mind leaving Dorian and me alone for a bit?"

"Of course." He set the coffee on the end table. "I'll be out back drinking my tea." Benjamin placed a supportive hand on her shoulder as he passed.

"When did you get in?" I asked her once he'd closed the door.

"I flew in yesterday and came straight to the mansion last night. Before I could ring the doorbell, though, I heard music coming from the pool area. I peeked through the bushes and saw you with your girlfriend."

I closed my eyes for a moment. The security lights. That explained it.

She exhaled. "It didn't feel right to interrupt, so I ran off. The motion set off some lights, and Benjamin ran into me while checking things out. I really wanted to leave, and I was ready to head back to the airport, but Benjamin insisted I stay the night and think things through before going home."

"Why would you have gone home without saying anything if you came all the way here?"

"Because clearly it was a mistake, Dorian."

"What were you hoping to tell me last night?"

She looked down at her feet. "I called off the wedding."

Holy shit.

She went on. "I couldn't go through with it. It wasn't the right decision for me even before you showed up. But after? I was never able to get you out of my mind. And it culminated in a panic attack at my final wedding dress fitting." Primrose stood and began to pace. "The night I decided to tell Casey everything, he said your name before I had the chance."

My eyes widened. "What?"

She sighed. "Apparently he'd been looking at my search history and had seen how often I'd googled your name in recent weeks." She looked away. "I missed you and kept wanting to stay connected. I didn't feel like it was okay to contact you once I'd told you I was moving forward with the wedding." She shook her head. "I made a mistake in thinking I could lie to myself." Primrose took a step toward me. "But you've moved on with your life, and I have no right to disrupt things just because I came to the right conclusion at the wrong time. I'm in way over my head here because I waited too long. That's on me."

I scrubbed a hand over my face. "I don't know what to say."

She nodded. "Much like you needed to see me to tell your truth, I needed to see you to tell you mine. If all I get to do is tell you I made a mistake, I'm still glad I came."

She stood before me, her eyes filled with vulnerability.

"How long were you planning to stay if I'd been alone last night?"

"A week. My return ticket is in seven days. My daughter is sad that I'm gone. It's the first time I've ever left her. But I needed to do this. I knew you were dating someone, but I guess seeing you with her last night made me realize how serious it is."

Wait. My eyes went wide. "How did you know I was dating someone?"

She hesitated. "I saw photos on Candace's social media."

I took a deep breath in and let it out. "Her name is Liv. She's at the house right now," I said. I needed to remind myself of my girlfriend's existence, considering how consumed I was by Primrose at the moment. "I came over here to see if Benjamin had eggs because I was going to make breakfast. I need to get back before she comes looking for me."

Primrose fidgeted. "Of course. I'm gonna change my ticket and head back."

I shook my head. "You can't do that—not until we've had a chance to talk this through."

She nodded, and I was relieved. I needed to hear more of what was going on in her head, just not right at this moment.

I walked over to the refrigerator and removed the carton of eggs. "I'll be back as soon as I can. Wait for me, okay?"

She hugged her arms and nodded again. I squelched the urge to embrace her. I couldn't do that, nor could I assure her of anything right now, since it felt like my head wasn't attached to my body.

As I left the guest house, the sky almost seemed to sway. To think this had started out like any other morning. I'd gotten up early and watched the sunrise, grateful for the life I was starting to reclaim. Little did I know about the storm brewing just across my driveway.

My chest felt raw. I felt terrible for Primrose, coming all the way here only to find Liv and me in an intimate moment. And I felt even worse for Liv because if there was one thing I knew: I was done telling lies to protect people. I'd learned that the hard way with Primrose.

The only question was *when* I would tell Liv what the hell was going on. Would I carry on and make breakfast as if my entire world hadn't just been turned upside down, or would I come clean the second I looked into her eyes?

When I walked in the house, I still didn't have the answer. The smell of freshly ground coffee, which was normally a pleasant aroma, turned my stomach. When I entered the kitchen, Liv was pouring what she'd just brewed. With her hair tied up in a messy bun and wearing my T-shirt, she was oblivious to what I was about to hit her with. I'd gone for eggs and come back with a hell of a lot more than that.

Liv turned, and the moment she smiled, I felt my heart break. It was a wonder the damn eggs didn't slip out of my hands and crash to the ground. I was barely conscious of anything besides the fact that I was about to break the heart of the woman who'd been mending mine. The last thing I wanted was to hurt her. But there was no way around this.

Her smile faded. "What happened, Dorian? You took so long. Is something wrong with Benjamin?"

I shook my head and stepped toward her.

Liv tilted her head. "What is it?"

There was no easy way to say it. "Primrose is here."

Liv's face went white. One of the first things I'd done when she and I met was unload the past five years onto her. She knew *everything*, including how broken I'd been when she'd met me, which wasn't long after Primrose had announced she was moving forward with the wedding. Things with Liv had been platonic before they'd morphed into more. It was the first time I'd allowed that to happen since Primrose, but I'd finally been moving on from her—or *trying* to. And now everything I'd known had turned on its axis yet again. How many times could I survive my life being upended?

Liv's voice was shaky, panicked. "*Why* is she here?"

"She flew in last night. She spent the night in the guest house, planning to talk to me today."

Liv crossed her arms. "Talk to you about *what* exactly?"

She had every right to be upset. I swallowed. "She ended her engagement."

Liv stepped back in shock. "So...she thinks she can just waltz back into your life because things have changed for her?"

"I don't know," I muttered.

She examined my face. "Please tell me you're not going to run right back to her."

If only I felt I had a *choice* in the matter. And it certainly wouldn't be running—more like a cautious walk. The way my heart reacted to Primrose wasn't something my mind had control of. I couldn't stand here, though, look Liv in the eyes, and assure her that she and I were safe. My wounds when it came to Primrose had never healed. And now they'd been broken open all over again.

My relationship with Liv had been like a giant Band-Aid, one I had hoped would turn into a cure for my broken heart. Liv was the closest thing I'd ever have to a second chance. Yet I didn't know if what we'd built was enough to withstand what might transpire with Primrose. Because that Band-Aid? It had just been ripped off.

I cleared my throat. "I've promised myself I would be honest with those I care about. Too many have been hurt because of decisions I made in the name of protecting people. I need you to understand that you mean so much to me. But I can't let her go back to Ohio without seeing this through, whether that means ending things with her once and for all or..." I hesitated.

Liv raised her voice. "Are you telling me you're going to just forget about everything we've built and run back into her arms? A woman who was supposed to be marrying someone else?"

"I'm far from running back to her, Liv. I have no idea whether I can trust her feelings. For all I know, she'll leave and go back to him the second she lands in Ohio. But what I *do* know is that it's not fair for me to stay with you while I'm figuring things out."

Her eyes widened. "You're breaking up with me?"

"I wouldn't blame you if you never speak to me again. But I can't continue to date you and have an emotional affair with someone else. Please believe me when I say I never saw this coming, and I would never have led you on if I'd suspected it. I believed she was getting married. I feel like a terrible person, but I'd feel worse if I wasn't honest with you."

Liv bent her head back, staring up at the ceiling. "I can't believe this," she whispered.

"You deserve better," I said.

"You're damn right I do."

I felt numb. I hated myself at the moment, but there was no way to avoid needing this space.

Tears glistened in her eyes. "The sad part? If you come to me after this, I'll probably consider taking you back, and I'm angry at myself for being weak." She wiped her eyes. "As fucked up as it is, I agree that you need to get your shit together and figure things out with her once and for all. I'd rather this happen now than later, when I've invested even more time in our relationship." She sniffled. "Because I *was* falling in love with you."

"You're amazing for understanding," I said, unsure how else to respond to her admission. "I don't think I'd handle it the same if the situation were reversed."

"Just remember who was here for you when she threw you away," Liv spewed. She dumped her coffee in the sink and turned to go.

"You don't have to leave—"

"You just told me we're breaking up. You think I'm gonna stay and have eggs?"

I hung my head. "I'm so fucking sorry, Liv."

"Call me when she leaves. But don't expect anything from me, because I'll probably never trust you again." She turned around one last time. "I hope you get what you want, whatever that is."

This time, I let her walk away. You'd think I would've felt some relief. But my nerves kicked into overdrive. Primrose had given me no reason to believe she wouldn't use this trip to put the final nail in our coffin. She'd gotten closer to her wedding date and panicked after seeing photos of me and Liv. Some kind of fucked-up FOMO. If reality set in, and she decided once again that the best thing was to keep her family intact, there was now a very good chance I'd end up alone.

CHAPTER 32

Primrose

Since the moment Dorian left, I'd done nothing but pace. The coffee Benjamin had brought me was ice cold by the time I took my first sip. Despite nuking it several times, I still hadn't managed to finish it. Nothing seemed to settle in my stomach.

At least an hour had passed, and Dorian hadn't come back. He might've been thinking better of further engaging with me. Why come back and deal with me and my baggage when he had a beautiful, blonde girlfriend waiting at the mansion? I imagined them enjoying their eggs while he thought about how to let me down easy. *Over easy*. Probably like their eggs.

Then again, that wasn't the Dorian I knew. He'd seemed pained to see me.

I was still pacing when the door opened, and Dorian again stood before me. He looked incredibly handsome in gray track pants and a fitted T-shirt. His hair was wet from the shower, and the sight of him, along with his familiar smell, caused my nipples to stiffen.

"You came back..."

"Did you really doubt that I would?"

"I wouldn't blame you if you didn't."

Dorian stepped toward me. "I need to set the record straight."

My stomach sank. His demeanor wasn't exactly warm. *Oh no*. Pushing my shoulders back, I gulped and prepared for the worst. "Okay..."

"Obviously I wasn't expecting this. So bear with me if I'm still processing." He exhaled. "I made a decision that might seem rash, but I feel it's for the best right now."

Every muscle in my body tightened as I closed my eyes. In my head, I was already on my way home.

"I broke up with Liv."

My eyes flashed open. "What?"

"The moment you walked back into my life today, all the things I felt when I last saw you came flooding back. I need the space to work through this while you're here."

"That was the last thing I expected you to say," I admitted, letting out a relieved breath.

"This doesn't mean I have confidence, Primrose. I don't feel I can trust that you won't go back to him and continue on with your life once you leave."

I smiled sadly, opting not to try to convince him. It would be actions, not words, that made a difference.

"Something changed in me when after everything, you chose him," Dorian said. "And even though I understand, it took away a level of trust I had in us that I'm not sure I can get back."

That was hard to hear, but it made sense. I was relieved, though, that he wasn't telling me to leave. He'd chosen me, even if I hadn't earned the right to be chosen. He'd chosen me—for now.

"All that being said..." He opened his arms as his mouth curved into a smile. "Please come here so I can hug you."

The breaths I'd been holding finally escaped as I rushed forward and leaped into his arms. I let my body melt into his, feeling both comfort and fear. This was it. The next seven days were our last chance. These seven days would make or break us forever. Still, despite the turmoil in my mind, it felt so very good to be held by him again.

When he pulled back, I looked him in the eyes. "I promise I'm not here to hurt you. And I agree, we need this time to figure it out. But I can assure you I followed my heart here. It was the first time I've done that since I left my heart in this very place more than five years ago."

He patted my back. "Get your bags. Let's go to the house."

"Are you sure? I can stay here while—"

"Of course I'm sure. I'm not gonna let you stay with Benjamin—unless you want to be bored out of your wits."

I laughed, still feeling jittery as I headed to the room where I'd put all my stuff.

Dorian waited as I gathered my belongings, and I texted Benjamin to let him know I was moving to the mansion.

Benjamin responded with a smiley-face emoji.

As I followed Dorian up the walkway to the main house, nostalgia washed over me. Living here felt like forever ago and just yesterday all at once. How was that possible? He opened the door, and I looked around. The mansion looked much the same, except the furniture in the living room had changed. Some of the same artwork hung on the walls.

I dropped my bag and walked over to the old grandfather clock, which I was pleased to see still ticking. "Hey, old man," I murmured.

Then it hit me. *The dogs.*

"What happened to Tallulah and Tess?"

"When Benjamin and I left for Turkey, they were rehomed." He smiled. "With Chandler and Candace. They're still there."

"No way!" I sighed. "Candace didn't mention that."

After I said it, my eyes widened.

"You've been in touch with Candace?" he asked.

I nodded. "Long story short, after I stalked her page online, I accidentally liked one of her photos, which prompted her to reach out to me. We talked once on the phone to catch up. That was it."

"Well, that doesn't surprise me. You two always got along. She loved you."

He looked into my eyes. I wanted him to hold me again, to reiterate that *he'd* always loved me, too. But I knew that validation was something I'd have to earn. He'd poured his heart out to me in Ohio, and I'd thrown it away the moment I chose to move forward with the wedding.

"Can I ask you a favor?" I said.

"Okay…"

"I know we have a lot to talk about. But can we put off the heavy stuff until tomorrow and chill for the rest of the day? Maybe enjoy some of the things we used to? I miss it. I miss *her*—the old me. Even if I can't ever be her again, I want to live in that world again for one day."

"We can do that." He smiled, gesturing toward the stairs. "Can I show you to your room?"

"Yes. Please."

To my shock, he led me to my old room, the main bedroom.

I turned to him in surprise. "You haven't taken over this space?"

"Well, it's kind of haunted." He shrugged. "First because of Dad. Then because of you."

Unlike the living room, this suite hadn't changed a bit. Even the linens were the same. Dorian followed me around the room, his hands in his pockets, his body language just as guarded as his attitude had been back at Benjamin's.

I walked into the empty closet that had once been my art room.

"Was she living here with you?"

"No. But she stayed over quite a bit."

"I'm sorry my being here caused you to break up. I'm sure she was devastated."

He arched a brow. "I thought we weren't gonna talk about the tough stuff today."

"There's something about this closet that makes me want to purge my thoughts."

"We did have some deep conversations in here, didn't we?" Dorian cracked a smile.

"It all feels like just a moment ago."

"Time is probably an illusion anyway." He sighed. "It does seem like yesterday. And yet so much has changed. You've created a beautiful little human. You're a mom. And I managed to drive my father's business into the ground."

"That's a good place for it, considering it nearly got you killed."

"That's not all it did, right? You paid a price, too, even if you didn't know it at the time."

"For whatever reason, the universe planned it this way." I smiled sadly.

"All of that, and we end up right here right now in the place it all started. I woke up this morning to get eggs and somehow by the afternoon I'm in the closet with Primrose. It's like a dream." After a long moment of silence, he said, "I need you to clarify something."

"Okay."

"You said you ended the engagement. Does *he* understand that you and he aren't together right now?"

"Yes," I answered emphatically. "He wanted to give me the freedom to make sure I was making the right decision."

Dorian let out a breath, seeming relieved. "And little Rosie? Where does she think you are this week?"

"Visiting old friends."

"Friends in quotation marks?" He winked.

"Massive quotation marks and a question mark."

He nodded. "It had to be hard for you to leave her."

"It would've been harder not to come to you when my heart felt ready to explode. I'm finally figuring out that I'm no good to my daughter if I'm not happy."

"In case I wasn't clear in my absolute shock this morning, I'm glad you came, Rosebud." He nodded. "So glad."

His use of my old nickname sent a warm feeling through my body. Yearning to touch him, I reached out and ran my fingers through his hair, watching as he closed his eyes, letting out a low groan. But instead of returning the touch, he placed his hand on my arm, prompting me to pull away.

"I'll let you decompress for a bit," he said. "Come down when you're ready, okay?"

Feeling a bit dejected, I cleared my throat. "Okay."

After he left, I sat on the closet floor for a few minutes before forcing myself to go put my clothes in the drawers. I freshened up before heading downstairs.

Dorian was standing at the window, looking out pensively when I found him in the living room.

"Hey."

He turned. "Hi."

"What's the plan?" I asked, feeling a bit tense.

"I want to show you something," he said, leading me out back.

Dorian brought me over to a beautiful rose garden.

"Your mom's garden is back."

"Yep. I'd love to say I did it myself, but I hired a gardener to put it in." He chuckled. "But I do maintain it. This is where I come now to think, meditate…to feel gratitude."

"That's beautiful."

"*You're* beautiful," he murmured. "Never thought you'd get to see this."

"Is this where the rose you sent me came from?"

"Yes."

"I'd thought that package was pretty formal until I reached inside and pulled out that rose."

"I wanted you to know I was still thinking of you."

"I knew that." I grinned. "Also, it was kind of you to send me Christina's ring. I wasn't expecting that."

"No one but you should have it." Dorian fell silent. "Can you tell I'm still in shock that you're here?"

"Yes, but I don't blame you."

"Are you hungry?"

"Only if you're not cooking." I winked.

"Wiseass." He chuckled. "I was thinking we could go down to the boardwalk."

"That sounds good." Maybe a change of scenery would lighten things up a little.

That evening, Dorian took me to one of my favorite restaurants in Orion Coast: Judy's Oceanside. During dinner, the mood gradually softened as we reminisced about the old days living together at the mansion. He told me about the consulting work he was now doing, and I bragged a bit about my daughter, how smart she was for her age and her interest in art. Every minute it felt more like old times.

"I'm glad to see you've relaxed," I said.

He nodded. "I think getting away from the mansion was a good idea."

Then my phone rang, and I looked down to find it was Casey.

Shit.

CHAPTER 33

Dorian

The look on Primrose's face told me who was on the other line.

"Hello?" She paused. "Is everything okay?" Then after a few seconds, she looked over at me briefly. "Put her on."

I crossed my arms and watched as she spoke to her daughter.

"Hi, sweetie. You can't sleep?"

I smiled sympathetically from across the table, feeling like a complete jackass for being the obstacle that kept this woman away from her baby right now.

"I'm sorry. I know it's hard," she said. "But I'll be home in less than a week." After a few seconds, she frowned. "No, honey. I can't." She paused. "I know. Try to sleep and be a good girl for Daddy."

After a long pause, she said, "Of course. Anytime she needs to hear my voice, don't hesitate."

I noticed her chewing her lip, a clear sign she was anxious. Looking downright sad, she wrapped up the conversation. We'd made a good effort to stick our heads in the sand tonight. But this call had forced reality back to the forefront.

"What did he say that made your face change like that?" I asked when she hung up.

She moved some food around the plate with her fork. "He said she wasn't the only one who needed to hear my voice."

Stiffening, I nodded. "He's not going to give up easily, is he? This is going to be messy. If you decide you want a life with me, are you prepared for what that's going to look like? Will he try to use your daughter as a pawn?" It was a harsh question, but it needed to be asked.

"You mean like custody?"

I nodded. "I don't know that he wouldn't do something like that."

She stared off in thought. "Casey would never do anything that might hurt Rosie. He's a good person, and he loves her more than anything. Taking her away from me would be detrimental to her, and he knows that."

"Okay." I downed the last of my drink, feeling very uneasy. I looked away from her as my mind began to race.

Any reminder of her life in Ohio was a reminder that I stood to lose Primrose yet again. And I wouldn't withstand it another time. The next time would be the last.

"I wouldn't be here with you if I didn't want to be, Dorian," she said after a moment, interrupting my worry. "You know I didn't make this decision overnight. Even if the unknowns scare me, I'm all in."

She had a point. It wasn't like she'd gotten on a plane with me the first time I'd tried to steal her away. Primrose had given it careful consideration, and I had to give her credit for that. Ultimately it was *my* fear getting in the way right now. I wanted to protect myself, but there was no way to get her back without risk. It did help to hear that she was all in.

After I paid the bill, we rode in silence back to the mansion.

When we arrived, she stood across from me in the foyer. At least for now, I had her all to myself. I'd dreamed of Primrose returning to this house so many times, and now here she was. I needed to get out of my own way long enough to enjoy it before her time here was up.

I had no idea how we were supposed to spend the rest of this night without crossing a line I'd promised myself I wouldn't cross. Despite the complexities of this situation, suddenly all I could think about was sex. I wanted her, yet I'd stopped myself from even touching her.

"There's no place I'd rather be today than here with you, Dorian," she said. "I've been dead inside without you. And as complicated as it is, I wouldn't change a thing right now."

With that, I finally felt myself exhale. In this moment, it was just me and my beautiful Rosebud. No years between us. Nothing standing in our way. We still had lots to work out, but the entire freaking world could change tomorrow. We were only ever guaranteed today.

All we had was this moment. And I had no fucks left to give. I needed this woman more than my next breath.

I reached over, took her face in my hands, and practically swallowed her whole as I began devouring her mouth. Primrose moaned. She tasted just as sweet as I'd always remembered, but even sweeter given how many years I'd longed for this.

She sighed into my mouth, as if she'd been starving for it. I wasn't going to stop unless she told me to. She walked backward as I led her toward the couch. I didn't even have the patience to take her upstairs. I needed her right here, right now.

When she fell back onto the sofa, I sat down next to her and guided her body on top of mine. As she straddled me, her long hair covered my face. I was drowning in her: her taste, her scent, and the warmth of her pussy through our clothes.

Tugging at her hair, I groaned as I pulled her toward me to bite her neck. "Fuck, I missed you, baby."

Nothing had ever felt like this. Other women were just filler for what I'd been missing: my beautiful Rosebud. I was determined to make her forget every remaining shred of doubt she might have about us.

Lifting her shirt over her head, I unclasped her bra and buried my face between her beautiful tits, my breaths coming faster with each second.

"Do you know how many times I've dreamed of this?"

"Me, too," she whispered.

I felt her hands fumbling at my waist.

Fuck. As much as I wanted more, I wasn't a hundred-percent sure she was ready. I'd half expected her to stop me when I tried to take things further. But the way she reached for my belt, struggling to take it off...that made her desires clear.

"Let me help you," I rasped, whipping my belt off. It landed with a loud clank on the floor.

Primrose moved off of me. I worried she had changed her mind, but then she slipped out of her skirt before sliding her panties down her gorgeous legs. She stood before me totally naked, her beautiful bare pussy taunting me. I marveled at her beauty. She'd been through so much, both emotionally and physically, having given birth to a human in the time we'd been apart. She was curvier in all the right places, and I'd never been more attracted to her—never more attracted to anyone in my life.

A primal need erupted within me as I slid my pants to my ankles. Her eyes fell to my crotch as I lowered my briefs. My dick bobbed out, so hard it was painful, precum oozing from the tip as I ached to be inside of her.

"Come here," I said gruffly.

She returned to sit on top of me, sliding her clit along my shaft. I didn't know which one of us was wetter. She lowered her mouth to mine as I struggled to stop myself from exploding before I even had a chance to be inside of her.

I positioned my cock at her opening and pushed inside in one hard thrust. I nearly came, tightening my abs to stop the need for release.

"Shit. How are you so fucking tight?" I muttered.

She thrust her hips as I rested my head on the back of the couch. I was as deep inside her as I could possibly be, yet it wasn't enough. "I've missed fucking you. There's nothing like it."

"You feel so good, Dorian." She moved over me faster. "I've dreamed of having you inside of me for so long."

My hands on her back, I pushed her down, bucking my hips to meet her movements. The feel of her hot, wet pussy wrapped around my cock threatened to undo me.

"You're mine, baby, aren't you? I can feel it."

"Yes." She panted, swaying her hips faster.

Her breathing quickened, and I felt her tighten around my cock. Primrose bent her head back and shrieked, her voice echoing through the living room. I let out an unintelligible sound that was even louder as I let myself go, coming hard as my orgasm filled her.

"You're so in trouble," I murmured.

I could feel her smile against me as she slumped over my shoulder, her body limp. We'd just given each other everything we had.

I had no idea whether she was on the pill, but I didn't care. I hadn't had sex without a condom with anyone else—never trusted anyone like I did Primrose. And anyway, I wanted my own baby with this beautiful woman someday.

She finally moved back so I could look into her eyes.

"Are you okay?" I asked.

"Yeah." She smiled. "More than okay. You have no idea how much I've needed that."

"I hadn't intended for this to happen tonight."

She rubbed her finger over my lips. "Did we really have a choice?"

"Sure as hell didn't feel like it." I rested my forehead against hers.

"I don't ever want to leave," she whispered.

I felt the pain of her words in my chest. *She doesn't want to leave.* But she had to, and she knew it. Still, I wasn't willing to go there yet, wasn't willing to taint this moment with worries about the future. Because to talk about logistics would mean ending the euphoria of this night. We deserved to have this last a bit longer.

"Don't think about that now, okay? Just be with me," I said.

We stayed there in that spot, connected by our bodies for the longest time. I didn't want to pull out or even move at all. If this moment could've lasted forever—if I could've died right here and now inside this woman—that would've been just fine by me.

CHAPTER 34

Primrose

The week flew by. Once Dorian and I made love that first night, we were inseparable, but we still hadn't discussed what was supposed to happen after I left.

It was my last afternoon in Orion Coast, and we were having Chandler and Candace and their kids over for a barbecue. That could be a little awkward, I worried, since Liv was one of Candace's acquaintances. But since I didn't know the next time I'd be back in California, I wanted to take advantage of every minute here.

When the doorbell rang, I got goose bumps.

The moment Dorian opened the door, Candace opened her arms.

"Primrose!"

"Oh my gosh." I hugged her. "It's so good to see you."

Chandler was holding their son. I rubbed the little boy's arm. "Hey, buddy. It's good to finally meet you."

Their daughter clung to her mother's leg. It made me miss Rosie so much.

Candace looked down at her. "This is Maya." She looked over at the boy lovingly. "And that's Mitchell."

I felt my eyes watering. I'd never forget the time Candace had shared her fear of some other woman getting to live out her dream. It brought me so much relief to know she'd gotten her own beautiful family instead.

"How has the trip been?" she asked as they entered the house.

"It started out a bit rocky, but we've found our way," I told her.

As Dorian and Chandler went out back with Mitchell, I turned to Candace.

"So, I want to say something..." I paused. "I know Liv is your friend. I'm sure she was pretty hurt when—"

"Primrose." Candace shook her head. "You don't need to explain. I knew Dorian was still in love with you when he started dating her. I would've been rooting for their relationship, if it weren't for that. But Liv was going to get hurt anyway. I knew in my heart of hearts that Dorian was using her to get over you. My goal when we talked was to get you to understand that there was still a chance to stop it, if for any reason you wanted to. You have nothing to apologize for, so long as you and Dorian are happy."

"You're amazing." I let out a breath. "Thank you for caring enough to reach out to me."

"So...what's next for you guys?"

"I don't know," I answered. "I wish I could tell you. We've been just trying to enjoy each other, so we haven't had that difficult talk. I assume we will tonight, since my flight leaves in the morning. Obviously, his life is here. My life is there."

"How has your daughter handled you being away this week?"

"Not well, honestly. That's been the toughest part."

"And her father?"

My stomach sank at the thought of Casey.

"I feel like he's expecting me to come out here and realize it was a mistake. But he doesn't realize the depth of my feelings for Dorian. I wish I could somehow love Dorian without hurting Casey, but that's not possible." I exhaled. "Going home is not gonna be easy."

She put her hand on my arm. "I don't know him, but I'm sorry this is happening. He seems like a good guy."

"He's an amazing dad. And he was an amazing partner. He doesn't deserve to be hurt. But even before I knew the truth about Dorian, I'd been hesitant to fully give myself to him, to promise him forever."

"I guess your soul knew things weren't finished with Dorian."

"Maybe." I sighed. "I just wish I could enjoy reconnecting with Dorian without the looming dread of hurting the two people who've kept me together these past five years."

"Go easy on yourself, Primrose. If it's any consolation, I think you're doing the right thing. If I were in your shoes, I'd follow my heart, too. Casey will find someone someday who loves him as much as you love Dorian."

"I hope so." And I meant it. I waited for jealousy, but felt none. I wanted Casey to find someone right for him. And that further validated my decision.

Dorian appeared in the doorway. "Can I butt in?"

"Sure," Candace said.

"I have a surprise for you, Rosebud."

I turned to find that two more had joined our gathering, Benjamin—and Patsy.

"Oh my God." I ran to her.

She opened her arms to hug me. "Primrose..."

"It's so good to see you. Oh my gosh, this is the best surprise."

She squeezed me. "I'm happy to see you, too."

"I'm so sorry we lost touch."

"Benjamin filled me in on everything," she said. "I'm glad I could be here today."

"How have you been?" I asked.

"I'm married now. Doing very well."

"That's amazing."

"I heard you have a beautiful little girl," she said.

"I do." I reached for my phone and pulled up a photo of Rosie.

Patsy looked down at it. "She's precious. She looks just like you."

"She does." I smiled, looking forward to seeing my daughter soon—the only good thing about leaving.

As the others went out to the patio, Patsy pulled me aside, lowering her voice. "I want to apologize to you about something."

My eyes widened. "For what?"

"Years ago, I tried to discourage you from trusting Dorian. I assumed that because he was Remington's son, he couldn't be honorable. Now that I understand things better, I believe that was an irresponsible assumption on my part. I'm sorry if I planted seeds of doubt."

I shook my head. "Thank you for your apology. I never let your opinion deter me, though. Your warning did occur to me when I thought Dorian had ended things for no good reason. But of course, that was never the truth."

"I know. I'm very sorry for what you both had to go through, but I'm happy you've found your way back to each other."

"Thank you, Patsy. I was thinking about looking you up, but since I was only here for a short time, I was a bit overwhelmed. I'm so glad Benjamin brought you to me."

"Me, too." She grinned.

Having everyone over turned out to be a wonderful distraction from my anxiety about leaving. We spent a lovely afternoon together, but eventually I began to worry about not getting enough one-on-one time with Dorian now that the clock was ticking.

After everyone left, he and I cleaned up, a tense silence replacing the jovial mood from earlier. And later, we sat together out by the pool, welcomed by the old familiar lights I'd painted in Ohio the day Dorian had given me my inspiration back. I rested against his chest as we looked up at the starry sky.

Dorian spoke in a low voice. "When you saw me dancing with Liv out here the night you arrived, I'm sure that looked very intimate. It *was* an intimate moment, I suppose. But there was never a time I heard beautiful music or looked up at the sky like this when you didn't come to mind. I carried you with me. No one else even came close to the connection I have with you, Primrose. If there's any doubt, because I know I haven't said it since you've been here, I love you." He paused. "I love you with all of my heart and soul."

I turned to face him. "I love you, too."

"I'd been waiting for the right moment to say it. I've felt it so strongly this entire time. I just didn't want to throw those words out at the wrong moment...like during sex." He shrugged. "And we've had a lot of that."

I grinned and caressed his cheek. "I'm gonna miss that *so* much."

"Why will you miss it?"

I blinked, unsure what wasn't clear about that statement. "Because we won't be together tomorrow."

His eyes sparkled. "We will if I come with you."

CHAPTER 35

Dorian

The look of pure shock on her face told me she hadn't even considered that I'd be willing to leave everything behind here. But the thought of staying was much harder than that.

"Rosebud, do you really think this is going to work if we're across the country from each other?"

She shook her head. "I hadn't allowed myself to think about the logistics for fear it wouldn't make sense. I would never ask you to—"

"I know. But the thing is, you don't *have* to ask me. I don't want to live apart from you. Your hands are tied because of your daughter. There's only one solution, and that's for me to move."

"What about the mansion? You just got it back."

"You think this lump of concrete means anything to me? The only thing meaningful about it are the memories *we* have together here. My heart is where you are. And I need to follow my heart, just like you did when you risked everything to come here."

"I may not be able to move out of the house I share with Casey right away."

"It doesn't matter, as long as we can see each other. I'll rent a house for now, and we'll take things slowly. You'll live with your daughter as you always have. And when you're ready, I'd love to meet her. But not until you feel it's right. I know you have things to take care of. That'll require patience on my part, but I've waited five years. I can wait longer. Like I've said before, this is going to be messy. But at least I'll be there when things get tough. I can't do that from here." I looked into her eyes. "But before I make assumptions, I need you to tell me whether *you* want me in Ohio."

Her eyes watered. "Yes, of course I want you there."

"Then it's settled."

"Who's gonna take care of the mansion?"

"I've already asked Benjamin to move into the main house. And I'm rehiring Patsy. Maybe someday I'll sell this place again. But for now, I'll keep it. In any case, it's served its purpose."

"What do you mean?"

"I needed to be here long enough for you to come back to me."

• • •

The moment we stepped out of the airport in Ohio, things felt different.

The California sun had been replaced by clouds and an ominous undertone in the air. I knew this was a risk. I still worried Primrose could be guilted into believing she was better off keeping her family together. If that happened, I'd have to face it. But at least I'd *be here*. At least I'd know I'd tried everything. And I felt more confident than ever about us, despite my fear. As I looked around, though, there was nothing about this place besides Primrose that made me want to live here. It would take some getting used to.

We picked up a rental car, and Primrose was tense the entire way home. I parked the car down the street from her house so Casey wouldn't see us together.

Primrose hadn't had a chance to talk to him about anything yet, let alone tell him she'd brought more back from California than just a toy for Rosie.

I rubbed her shoulders. "You okay?"

Her breath trembled. "Yeah. I'll be fine. This is gonna be hard, but at least I get to see my baby girl." She took my hand in hers. "Be patient with me, okay?"

"There's no rush, as long as you come back to me. I'll be here."

After a goodbye kiss that was wrought with pain, Primrose rolled her suitcase down the street toward her house.

As luck would have it, the rental house I'd occupied last time Benjamin and I were here was still available. I'd been in touch with the owner before I left California and would be able to stay there on a month-by-month basis.

Walking into the big, empty house, especially without Benjamin, was bittersweet. I knew Primrose was likely having a very difficult talk with Casey right now and wished I could be there with her. I felt almost guilty to be granted the peace of this quiet place when she had to face the turmoil of ending her relationship.

I turned the heat on and lit a fire.

Later that evening, I realized I hadn't eaten anything all day. There was no food in the house. I figured I'd go shopping tomorrow, but for tonight I'd sift through the menus in the kitchen and order takeout.

I settled on orange chicken from the Chinese restaurant and called it in for delivery.

Ten minutes later, there was a knock at the door.

But it wasn't the takeout.

Instead, it was someone I was sure wanted to take *me* out.

Casey.

CHAPTER 36

Dorian

"That didn't take you long," I said when I opened the door.

"She doesn't know I'm here. She never gave me the address." He moved past me into the house without permission.

The door was still open when I turned to him. "How did you know where I lived if she didn't give you the address?"

"Before she left for California, she told me where you'd been staying when you first came out here. Tonight she mentioned you'd booked the same place. I never forgot the address. Told her I needed some air. Ended up driving here instead."

I closed the door. "I don't blame you for wanting to confront me. Not sure I'd be able to wait either, in your situation."

He squinted. "You know, I thought I'd never seen your face. But now I realize I have. You're the guy from the supermarket."

"I'm surprised you recognize me."

"Well, you're a good-looking bastard, unfortunately for me. Not the kind of face you forget."

"Thanks. I think?" I watched as he began to pace. "Anyway, that supermarket run-in wasn't planned. My friend and I just happened to be there, and I wasn't sure how to react."

He stopped and stood looking at me.

"Should I grab a bat for you or something?" I asked.

He looked around the space. "I'm not here to fuck you up, even if I should."

"Well, like I said, I wasn't expecting this confrontation so soon."

"Yeah." He ran a hand through his hair. "Neither was I. I thought I'd have more time with her when she got back, more time to convince her that keeping our family together was the right choice. The moment she told me she'd brought you here with her, though? I knew it was over. I knew staying with her *wasn't* the right choice anymore, as hard as that is to admit to myself. There's no point in prolonging the agony. I probably knew it was over when she never called while she was away, other than to check on Rosie. I'd told her I wasn't going to give up easily. But if it's really right, you shouldn't have to fight to convince someone of that. It should just *feel* right for both parties. Being with me never felt right for her. I've sensed it, even if I didn't want to believe it. So, even as much as I love her, I have to accept this." His eyes met mine. "But here's what I *won't* accept…"

I braced myself. "I'm listening."

"I won't accept you breaking up my family for nothing, pulling a fast one on her again. I don't care if you seem to think you had a legitimate reason for it. If you hurt her ever again, you'll have to answer to me. I *will* use a bat for that one."

I had to respect this guy. I nodded. "Understood."

"And even if that were to happen, she and I are done. I won't take her back. She doesn't love me the way you need to love someone. I know that now. So if you fuck up her life, she's gonna be alone. Or at least not with me."

"I don't intend to fuck up anything, Casey."

"I don't want you meeting our daughter yet, either. It's too soon. She needs to get used to me not living at home first."

"That makes perfect sense."

Casey began to pace again. "You got anything to drink?"

Okay, this bizarre night just got a *whole lot* more bizarre.

"Well, I just moved in, so I haven't had a chance to stock the place, but let me see if there's anything in the liquor cabinet."

As luck would have it, Benjamin's bottle of whiskey was still there.

I lifted it. "Do you drink whiskey?"

Casey glared at me. "My fiancée is leaving me for the Prince of California. I'd drink Drano if it fucking made me feel better right now."

"Okay, man." I went to the kitchen to grab a glass. "But I'm not letting you drive drunk. I'll take you home."

"Whatever," he said, staring out the window.

After I poured Casey a drink, he took it over to the couch and sat in front of the fire. I sat across from him. Ironically, he was in the same spot Primrose had been in when she'd secretly come over here to talk.

He shook his head as he looked down into his glass. "Something was never right with her, from the moment we met. She had this...hidden pain in her eyes. When I would ask what happened, she never wanted to talk about it. I should've known I could never get close to someone keeping so much inside. When she finally told me about you, it made a lot of sense." He downed the drink. "She and I probably wouldn't have stayed together if she hadn't gotten pregnant. I've denied that for a very long time. But I did the best I could. And I *did* love her. I always will." He let out a deep sigh. "Someday, way down the line, maybe you and I could be friends." He turned to me. "But not today. Not tomorrow. Know what I mean?"

I nodded. "I get it."

He held out his glass. "I'll have another, please."

"Yeah." I stood and grabbed the bottle, pouring him another and setting the bottle next to him.

He pointed the glass in my direction. "I can forgive you for stealing my once soon-to-be wife. But there's one thing I would never forgive you for."

"What?"

"You have all the money in the world to buy my daughter's love. I can't compete with that. I think you know what I'm saying here..."

The pain in his eyes was palpable, as was his fear. I wished I could convince him I would never try to do that. But only time would show the truth of my good intentions.

"You're Rosie's father. That doesn't change. I can understand why you might worry I'll use my wealth to my advantage there, but I assure you, I don't intend to do that."

"You'd better not, pretty boy. I'm serious." He chugged the whiskey again.

Then we sat in silence for a bit. Casey looked into the fire, an eerie sadness on his face. Even though I was currently his worst nightmare, I felt a kinship with this man. He'd once taken Primrose from me, like I'd just done to him. We'd both experienced the same loss. The difference was, he hadn't done anything to cause it. He didn't deserve what my actions had led to any more than Primrose had.

The very least I owed Casey was to make sure I didn't overshadow him when it came to his daughter. He'd taken care of the woman I loved all those years when I couldn't. And he wasn't standing in the way of my happiness now. That demanded my respect. It demanded that I look out for him, too. That had already started tonight.

He poured another glass. "Don't worry. This is the last one."

"It's all good," I assured him. "Just let me know when you want me to take you home."

CHAPTER 37

Dorian

It was three months before I finally got the go-ahead to formally meet Rosie.

The day was today—a Saturday afternoon. Casey was taking a golf vacation with some friends and had given his blessing for Rosie to meet me. Primrose was bringing Rosie over to my place before we took her to the playground.

The now four-year-old daughter of Primrose and Casey had been through a lot of transition over the past few months, so I hadn't been eager to complicate things even further. While Casey had now moved out of the house he'd shared with Primrose, he still joined them for dinner a lot on weeknights. Primrose and he had both tried to maneuver things so Rosie still felt like everything was semi-normal. The main difference was that Casey didn't sleep there anymore. But he often went over there in the mornings to take Rosie to school.

I'd continued to rent the same house, though I'd been casually looking for a place I could call my own. Consulting work, which I was able to do remotely, kept me busy most afternoons. It was rare that I got to see Primrose on weeknights. But the weekends were different, and I lived for them.

While Casey and Primrose didn't have a formal custody arrangement, many weekend evenings, Casey took Rosie over to his new place overnight. He'd set her up with her own room there. They'd explained as best as they could to a four-year-old that her parents had decided to be friends but live separately. She was probably too young to grasp the full implications of that, but she seemed to be accepting it.

I was nervous as all hell to meet that little girl today, afraid she'd see through my guise of trying to play the part of a casual friend to her mother. Would she somehow sense that I was the reason her parents weren't together? Would she blame me?

When the doorbell rang, my heart rate spiked. *Calm down, homewrecker.*

I put on my best smile before opening the door. "Hey!"

"Hey!" Primrose smiled, holding Rosie's hand.

I looked down to meet Rosie's eyes. "Hi."

"Hi." She held her hand up in a wave, her soft little voice piercing my heart.

"Rosie, this is Mommy's friend, Dorian," Primrose told her.

"Hi, Dorian."

I knelt. "It's really nice to meet you, little lady."

I doubted she remembered our brief encounter at the supermarket, even if it played on repeat in my head whenever I thought about her.

"Can we come in?" Primrose finally asked.

Shaking my head, I waved them inside. "Of course. What am I thinking? Come in. Come in."

Rosie sniffed the air. "What's that smell?"

"It's apple crisp. Have you ever had it?"

"Mommy makes it…"

Arching my brow, I turned to Primrose. "You do?"

She shrugged. "Might've been one of the ways I kept connected to you through the years."

I smiled at Rosie. "Wanna piece?"

She nodded enthusiastically.

I led them to the kitchen where I served Primrose and her daughter each a slice of the dessert I'd baked.

Opening the fridge, I took out a canister of Reddi-wip. "A little bird told me you love whipped cream, Rosie."

She bounced in her seat. "I do!"

I sprayed a huge dollop on top of her apple crisp. I'd give her as much as she wanted, so long as she liked me.

"Thank you," Rosie said.

"You're very welcome, sweetheart."

Primrose and I shared a smile.

"So…" I sat down next to Primrose, across from Rosie. "What's the plan today?"

"Well, Rosie wants to go to the playground. It's supposed to be nice out."

"Sounds perfect. I love the playground."

Primrose laughed. "Have you even been to a playground in the last twenty-five years, Vanderbilt?"

"Don't rat me out," I whispered.

After they finished eating, we got into my car and drove to the park with the giant jungle gym. I'd started to feel a bit calmer.

Once we got out of the car, Primrose stepped back a bit, allowing me time to get to know Rosie. For a few minutes I was officially in charge of her safety while Primrose made conversation with another mother. Couldn't remember a time when I'd been responsible for anything so precious. No way in hell I was gonna let her get injured on my watch. *How do people do this, day in and day out?* I was a nervous wreck each time Rosie climbed anything.

I watched intently as she went up a ladder numerous times, then slid down the long, twisty slide.

"Your turn," she finally said in that sweet little voice.

"My turn?"

"Yeah. Your turn to go down the slide."

"I think I'm too big for that, sweetie."

She giggled, then took me by the hand and led me up the ladder. Guess she wasn't taking no for an answer.

She watched from the top as I entered the tube and barely squeezed myself out before I emerged at the bottom. Rosie then slid down after me.

A few seconds later, she pointed and laughed.

"What are you laughing at?"

"You have gum on your bum-bum."

"Shit. Really?" I cringed. "I'm sorry. I shouldn't have said that."

I patted my behind. She was right. There was a big dollop of fresh pink gum stuck to my ass. Rosie continued to giggle. I'd take one for the team if it meant amusing her.

Primrose was still talking to that other mom. I couldn't tell if she was involved in conversation or specifically giving me alone time with her daughter.

When I took Rosie over to the swings and started pushing her, she smiled big as she swung my way. "My daddy says hi," she announced.

I slowed down. "Your daddy?"

She nodded.

"He told you to say that?"

"Yup."

Hmm... Casey knew I was going to be meeting her for the first time this weekend. Perhaps this was his way of throwing me a bone, indirectly putting in a good word for me, though I was certain that couldn't have been easy for him.

"Tell him I said hi, too, okay?"

"Okay!" she said with glee as I pushed her faster.

This little angel was blissfully oblivious.

Primrose finally sauntered over. "How are you guys doing?"

"Dorian has gum on his butt!"

Primrose looked down at my ass. "Oh wow. I see that." She laughed. "I got you. Happens to us all the time, doesn't it, Rosie? Nothing some ice and vigorous rubbing can't fix."

I wriggled my brows and whispered, "Sounds interesting."

Primrose nudged me with her elbow. "How did that happen anyway?"

"Someone must've thrown it down the slide," I said.

Her eyes widened. "You went down the slide?"

"Yep."

"How did I miss that?"

"Well, you were busy talking and abandoned us."

She winked, and now I was certain she'd left me alone with Rosie intentionally.

Late that afternoon, we took Rosie out for pizza, and then the best thing ever happened afterward. Rosie asked if I could come over to their house and watch a movie with them before bed. That was the easiest "yes" I'd ever uttered.

Back at their house, the three of us sat together on the couch. Rosie had changed into her pajamas and chosen the kids' movie *Sing*. It surprised me how much I enjoyed it.

At one point, Rosie leaned her head against my shoulder. I didn't dare move. A profound appreciation for everything I'd been through from the moment I was born came over me. It was the first time I realized that even though I'd never be this little girl's father, in a strange way, she was here because of me. If I'd done even one thing differently, it would've changed the course of my life, Primrose's life, and the state of Rosie's existence. If I hadn't left Primrose out of fear for her safety, she'd never have met Casey and had Rosie. Indirectly, it meant Rosie was mine, too. *Probably won't bring that up to Casey, though.* Still, that perspective made me feel warm inside.

Rosie broke my trance when I sensed her looking up at me for my reaction during the movie. I could tell the scene was supposed to be funny, so I gave her my heartiest laugh as I looked down to meet her smile. Her beautiful, innocent eyes sparkled in the glow of the television. *Neither blue, nor green. Aquamarine.*

EPILOGUE

Primrose
Two Years Later

Dorian had his arm around me as we strolled through the mansion.

My throat felt tight with emotion. "I can't believe this is the last time we'll ever see the inside of this place."

We'd come out to Orion Coast for the weekend, and tonight was our last night. The new owners had bought the house furnished and would be moving in next week.

"It's time. Don't you think?" Dorian said. "Our life is in Ohio now. As much as I wanted to hold on to this place, it deserves new blood that can appreciate it and give it the care it deserves."

"I agree. It just makes me sad for you to have to say goodbye to it."

He stopped walking. "Why? I'm happier than I've ever been back home with you."

"It's weird to hear you describe Ohio as home."

"Well, it is my home now. Home is where you and Rosie are. For the first time in my life, I actually feel settled. I never felt settled here, as much as the nostalgia sometimes gets to me."

"Speaking of settled, is everything all set with Benjamin?"

"Yup. He's on board to move to Ohio." Dorian smiled. "I also have a bit of a surprise for you."

"What?"

"I've been waiting to tell you... I know you've been worried about Patsy being out of a job with the sale of the mansion. Well, the new owners are taking her on as their housekeeper."

My mouth dropped open. "No way."

"Yep. They asked if I could recommend someone, so it was the perfect solution."

"You're right. That *is* the best surprise. I'd been feeling so guilty."

Dorian led me out back to the patio.

"What are we going to do for our last night in the mansion?" I asked.

"Well, I was thinking we could watch a movie in the theater for old times' sake. Maybe I could burn some dinner, too, or we could get takeout."

"I'll choose the latter, thanks."

"Okay." He rubbed my back. "I miss Rosie."

"Already?"

"Yeah," he said. "I wish we would've brought her. Casey said it was okay. Not sure why you nixed the idea."

"Because it's only a weekend. And I wanted to fully focus on giving this place a proper goodbye."

"You're right." Dorian pouted. "But she'd love the pool."

"Well, we're gonna put one in our new place, right?"

Dorian and I were finally moving out of the house I'd shared with Casey to a new home we planned to make our own. I couldn't have been more excited for the year ahead.

Later that evening, when we went down to watch a movie in the theater, I was met with the most unexpected sight. Sure, it was the theater I'd remembered. But hanging on the walls, replacing the old movie posters, were each and every one of the monkey portraits I'd painted back when I was in college.

"Oh my God." I covered my mouth. "What's happening? Where did you get these?"

Dorian beamed proudly. "I bought them."

"But how? They were all over. Different owners. How did you find them all?"

"I contacted the school and gave them a hefty donation to track down the owners for me. Then I made each one an offer they couldn't refuse."

"But why?"

He smiled as if the answer was obvious. "I wanted them for myself. They're special to me because they remind me of the night we met and the magic of that time in our lives."

I shook my head incredulously. "How long have you had them?"

"I started the search back when I was in Greece and slowly began accumulating them."

I'd never hit it big as an artist, but that particular monkey exhibit had done really well, each painting selling for a decent amount. Back then, the school had split the profits with the artist when a piece was sold. I was sure, though, that Dorian had paid way more than the original prices. "This had to have cost a fortune."

He shrugged.

Of course. Sometimes I forgot who I was talking to. That's how normalized Dorian had become in the past couple of years. It was easy to forget he was still a multi-millionaire—though not the billionaire he used to be. He'd donated a lot of his father's fortune to charity after he gave up his stake in Vanderbilt Technologies. But he was still certainly wealthy enough to purchase all of these paintings and then some without feeling a dent.

Dorian took my hand. "For so long, I thought these would be the only pieces of you I'd have left. They brought me joy and made me feel close to you. They're my prized possessions." He grinned. "And you know, I'm anal about having complete collections of things. I tucked them away in storage until I had them all and could figure out the perfect space for them."

"Wow." I started to cry. "Looking at them all in one room makes me miss how I used to feel when creating them."

"Well, good. Because they're coming with us to the new house in Ohio. Maybe you can get your mojo back once we finish your art room."

Excitement raced through me. "I hope so."

I finally felt like I could breathe. Any remaining guilt over ending things with Casey had dissipated once he began dating a woman he really seemed to love about six months ago. He and Caitlin were getting serious, and by some miracle, Casey and Dorian had become friends. We'd even had Casey and Caitlin over for dinner a couple of times. I knew fostering a true friendship with Casey was the best gift I could give my daughter.

Rosie was now fully aware that Dorian was not only my friend but someone I loved. After he moved in with us six months ago, I had a talk with her and made that clear. I didn't want to have to hide my love from her. Dorian and I'd spent too much time living apart to have to continue to hide. Thankfully, Rosie had grown to love him, too.

This evening, Dorian and I decided to watch—what else?—*Pulp Fiction* on the theater screen. When the movie ended and the credits rolled, Dorian dropped to one knee. I covered my mouth in surprise.

"Rosebud, I couldn't think of a better place to do this—at the end of the movie that first bonded us in the room where I first knew I was falling for you..."

"Oh my God." Now it made sense. The monkey paintings displayed. His insistence on watching *Pulp Fiction*.

"You are the love of my life," he said. "I feel like everything we've been through was so you and I could have this life together with Rosie. I consider her my daughter, too. You know that. And I'm so lucky to have you both." He opened a small box, displaying the most beautiful diamond I'd ever laid eyes on: a sparkling round stone on a pave band. "Presenting this to you is long overdue. But I want to show you the receipt for this ring." He reached into his pocket and handed it to me. "If you look at the date, you'll see that it was actually purchased a couple of weeks before we broke up seven years ago—before I realized what was happening with my father's death investigation. I'd planned to ask you to marry me even then. I lost several years with you, yet my love has only gotten stronger. Back then, I thought I couldn't love you more. I now realize that my love for you knows no bounds. Seeing the amazing mother you've become has only made me love you more."

He paused, his eyes glistening. "And the fact that our son is inside of you right now is the greatest gift I've ever been given. To know my family name won't end with me is something I never imagined."

I was three months pregnant, and we'd taken a special blood test that predicts gender early. We were having a little boy. Dorian and I were beside ourselves with excitement, but we hadn't told anyone until we could tell Rosie first when we got back to Ohio.

He took the ring out. "I know I've done everything in a whacky order. Friend-zoned you. Fell in love with you. Broke up with you. Practically came back from the dead. Stole you away again. Got you pregnant before we had a chance to get married. I'm hoping you won't use all that against me now—because I really need you to say yes. Will you do me the honor of being my wife?"

"Yes!" I wrapped my arms around him as I burst into tears.

We embraced for a long time before Dorian took me over to one of the paintings on the wall. It was the last monkey I'd created.

"Can I ask...when *exactly* did you do this one?" He smirked. "Because it wasn't part of the original twelve."

My cheeks tingled. *I'd hoped you'd love it.* "I painted it for you before things went south and was going to give it to you on your birthday," I explained. "But then we broke up, and I just let the school sell it."

"It's my favorite." He grinned.

"I'm so glad to hear that."

The painting depicted a monkey in the same wool coat Dorian had worn the night I met him. He wore a confident smile and had the most perfect mane of black hair, along with blue eyes the color of oxidized steel.

It was aptly titled, *The Gorillionaire*.

ACKNOWLEDGEMENTS

I always say the acknowledgements are the hardest part of the book to write. There are simply too many people that contribute to the success of a book, and it's impossible to properly thank each and every one.

First and foremost, I need to thank the readers all over the world who continue to support and promote my books. Your support and encouragement are my reasons for continuing this journey. And to all of the book bloggers/bookstagrammers/influencers who work tirelessly to support me book after book, please know how much I appreciate you.

To Vi – You're the best friend and partner in crime I could ask for. Here's to the next ten-plus years of friendship and magical stories.

To Julie – Cheers to a decade of friendship, Rebel cheese, and Fire Island memories.

To Luna –When you read my books for the first time, it's one of the most exciting things for me. Thank you for your love and support every day and for your cherished friendship. See you at Christmas!

To Erika – It will always be an E thing. Thank you for your love, friendship, summer visit, and Great Wolf Lodge bar time—one of my favorite moments of the year.

To Cheri – It's always a good year when I get to see you, my dear friend! Thanks for being part of my tribe and for always looking out and never forgetting a Wednesday.

To Darlene – What can I say? You spoil me. I am very lucky to have you as a friend—and sometimes signing assistant. Thanks for making my life sweeter, both literally and figuratively.

To my Facebook reader group, Penelope's Peeps – I adore you all. You are my home and favorite place to be.

To my agent Kimberly Brower –Thank you for working hard to get my books into the hands of readers around the world.

To my editor Jessica Royer Ocken – It's always a pleasure working with you. I look forward to many more experiences to come.

To Elaine of Allusion Book Formatting and Publishing – Thank you for being the best proofreader, formatter, and friend a girl could ask for.

To Julia Griffis of The Romance Bibliophile – Your eagle eye is amazing. Thank you for being so wonderful to work with.

To my assistant Brooke – Thank you for hard work in handling all of the things Vi and I can't seem to ever get to. We appreciate you so much!

To Kylie and Jo at Give Me Books – You guys are truly the best out there! Thank you for your tireless promotional work. I would be lost without you.

To Letitia Hasser of RBA Designs – My awesome cover designer. Thank you for always working with me until the finished product exactly perfect.

To my husband – Thank you for always taking on so much more than you should have to so that I am able to write. I love you so much.

To the best parents in the world – I'm so lucky to have you! Thank you for everything you have ever done for me and for always being there.

Last but not least, to my daughter and son – Mommy loves you. You are my motivation and inspiration!

OTHER BOOKS FROM PENELOPE WARD

The Rocker's Muse
The Drummer's Heart
The Surrogate
I Could Never
Toe the Line
Moody
The Assignment
The Aristocrat
The Crush
The Anti-Boyfriend
Just One Year
The Day He Came Back
When August Ends
Love Online
Gentleman Nine
Drunk Dial
Mack Daddy
Stepbrother Dearest
Neighbor Dearest
RoomHate
Sins of Sevin
Jake Undone (Jake #1)
My Skylar (Jake #2)
Jake Understood (Jake #3)
Gemini

OTHER BOOKS FROM PENELOPE WARD AND VI KEELAND

Denim & Diamonds
The Rules of Dating
The Rules of Dating My Best Friend's Sister
The Rules of Dating My One-Night Stand
The Rules of Dating a Younger Man
Well Played
Not Pretending Anymore
Happily Letter After
My Favorite Souvenir
Dirty Letters
Hate Notes
Rebel Heir
Rebel Heart
Cocky Bastard
Stuck-Up Suit
Playboy Pilot
Mister Moneybags
British Bedmate
Park Avenue Player

ABOUT THE AUTHOR

PENELOPE WARD is a *New York Times, USA Today* and *#1 Wall Street Journal* bestselling author.

She grew up in Boston with five older brothers and spent most of her twenties as a television news anchor. Penelope resides in Rhode Island with her husband, son and beautiful daughter with autism.

With millions of books sold, she is a 21-time *New York Times* bestseller and the author of over forty novels.

Penelope's books have been translated into over a dozen languages and can be found in bookstores around the world.

Subscribe to Penelope's newsletter here.
http://bit.ly/1X725rj

SOCIAL MEDIA LINKS:

Facebook
https://www.facebook.com/penelopewardauthor

Facebook Private Fan Group
https://www.facebook.com/groups/PenelopesPeeps/

Instagram
@penelopewardauthor

TikTok
https://www.tiktok.com/@penelopewardofficial

Twitter
https://twitter.com/PenelopeAuthor

Made in the USA
Middletown, DE
02 September 2025